DIAMOND IN THE ROUGH

DIAMOND IN THE ROUGH

First edition. December 4, 2022.

Written by Gina LaManna.

To all of my readers - thank you!

Dedication:

This book is dedicated first and foremost to all my readers who have been patient over this last year while I worked to get this book to you. Thank you for your understanding and for sticking around!

Second, this book is dedicated to the people of Ukraine during a difficult holiday season. Slava Ukraini!

Special Thanks:

To Alex and Leo and Max—You boys are my world! я тебя люблю!

To my family—I love you!

To Stacia—Not only my editor but a best friend as well.

BLURB

When Kate Rosetti is called to the scene of a gruesome murder on the morning of Valentine's Day, she's hardly surprised. After all, it seems love just isn't in the cards for her. Fortunately, Detective Rosetti has a new case to throw herself into headfirst. This time it isn't just any dead body. This time it's personal, and Kate stands to lose everything.

However, solving a murder is never as easy as it sounds, and neither is Kate's love life. As Kate dives deeper into the investigation involving a man who played a pivotal role in her family's past, her future is getting all sorts of blurred. A certain billionaire seems intent on keeping her close. A former flame isn't completely out of the picture. So what's a girl to do when the new case she's working suddenly puts the lives of the people she loves in danger?

Chapter 1

I yanked the steering wheel and lifted my foot off the brake to coast over a patch of black ice leading into the precinct's parking lot. I hadn't quite slowed enough as I'd approached, and I felt the telltale winter tires slip and slide as my vehicle careened toward my mother's café.

Adding a few curse words to the morning's tally, I straightened the steering wheel before I plowed through the shop's front window. I hardly noticed Detective Frankie Dunkirk as he gave me a wave while I sailed on by. I did, however, catch his smirk as I skidded past.

Dunkirk held a container of salt in his hands and had obviously drawn the short straw on this nippy Monday morning. He'd been sent out to do the dirty work after the weekend's snowstorm and was tossing more salt down in the parking lot as my car finally, blissfully, landed in a parking space.

I cut the engine, looked longingly at my mother's coffee shop, and made a snap risk-reward analysis in my head regarding the pros and cons of popping in for my caffeine haul. Pros: Good coffee, free coffee, lots of coffee. Cons: My mother's presence.

Normally, the latter wasn't a huge issue, but today I suspected that wouldn't be the case. Seeing as it was Valentine's Day, and I was somewhat newly single, I was pretty certain my mother would have questions for me. Or worse.

"Taking that corner a little fast, eh?" The empty salt canister dangled from Dunkirk's fingers. "I thought you were going to take me out before sliding through your mother's front window."

"I had it under control." I slammed my door shut.

My pros and cons list had shifted slightly with the appearance of Dunkirk. I didn't really feel like walking with him into the precinct and getting teased about my lackluster driving skills on this Monday morning. It was already such an awful holiday, and I felt no desire to pile on the misery.

"I'm going to grab a coffee." I thumbed toward the Seventh Street Café, the little bakery business my mother owned next door to my place of employment. Weakly, I added, "Want something?"

"Sure, thanks."

I rolled my eyes. "What do you want?"

"Surprise me."

"Does this mean you're not going to mention my driving skills to Jimmy?"

Dunkirk gave me another good-natured smirk. "Better make that a large latte."

I headed toward the café, curling in against the bitter cold wind. I hadn't worn a hat or mittens because I was a Minnesotan through and through, which meant I had the illogical notion that just walking a little faster would ensure I didn't get cold. It was a thing. A dumb thing, but a thing.

The second the warm air from my mother's shop embraced me, I let out a long sigh and released the tense muscles of my shoulders. I straightened, stretching after the crisp jaunt across the parking lot. I pretended to look at the menu, as if I really needed to think about what I wanted to order.

"Good morning!" My mother poked her head out from behind a massive bouquet of red roses. "There's my sweet pea. What can I get you today?"

"Don't do that, Mom." I unzipped the top few inches of my jacket and rolled my shoulders, trying to avert the stress before it hit me. Maybe I should've just gone with Dunkirk and taken the heat for my crappy driving this morning.

"Do what?" Her voice rose an octave.

"That voice. I'll take two venti lattes."

"Two?" My mother's eyes widened. "Elizabeth, did you hear that? Two lattes, right away. Who's the other one for?"

"Dunkirk blackmailed me into buying his coffee." I met my mother's gaze head-on. "Romantic, huh?"

"Why do your dates always end in blackmail or murder?" My mom visibly deflated. Her voice returned to its normal register. "So you've got nothing to tell me?"

I sneezed. "I think your flowers are giving me allergies."

"Don't be ridiculous. Nobody's allergic to roses."

"Okay. Tell that to my doctor who told me to take Benadryl after I broke out in hives from that rose scented lotion you gave me for Christmas last year."

My mother ignored me and arranged her bouquet pointedly. "Your father did a wonderful job this year. Twenty-four long-stemmed red roses."

"Guess he's trying to make up for all those Valentine's Days he missed while he was in prison."

"Kate." My mother clucked at me, but she didn't seem bothered. She seemed elated.

"Sorry," I mumbled. "I'm glad. You deserve it."

"Oh, sweetie. So do you. How are you, really?" My mother leaned against the counter, her eyes softening as she looked at me. "It's your first Valentine's Day single. Do you have plans?"

"It's hardly my first Valentine's Day single," I corrected. "And no. No plans. On purpose. I'm not sad about it."

"Thou doth protest too much."

"Those lattes?"

"What about—"

"The lattes."

Elizabeth, my mother's college-aged employee, sought pity on me and handed me two large drinks. She'd put little heart stickers over the lip of the cup as drink stoppers. I gave her a smile.

"I've got to get to work," I said. "Thanks."

"Tell me you don't have a murder today," my mother said. "Nobody should be murdered on Valentine's Day."

I gave my mother a funny look, peeled the heart sticker from my cup, and tossed it in the trash. Then I kicked the door open and made my way back to the precinct—freezing once again because I'd forgotten to re-zip my jacket, and I was too stubborn to stop and correct my error.

I caught a glimpse of my own pink cheeks and a red nose in the window as I made my way into the precinct and cursed myself for never wearing a scarf. Not to mention I'd taken the stupid heart sticker off my drink, so my latte had gone practically frozen. I debated switching it out with Frankie's, but my conscience won out. I handed Dunkirk his coffee as I slid by his desk, waiting for a wisecrack about my slip-and-slide parking job this morning.

Frankie took one look at the heart on his cup and gave me a wink instead. "I knew you loved me, Rosetti. Sorry, I'm not interested."

Jimmy Jones, my longtime partner, barked a laugh from his desk. I narrowed my eyes at him. He shut right up.

I made it to my desk and found a doughnut waiting for me. It was in the shape of a heart. Pink frosting covered it. The whole thing was a little mushed and misshapen. But it was definitely a heart. And a doughnut.

My own heart started racing. It pounded for a good long minute before I looked up and realized Jimmy was staring at me expectantly from his desk. I let out a massive breath of relief.

"Valentine's sweets from your secret admirer," Jimmy said with a twinkle in his eye. "Me. That's me, Rosetti. *I'm* your secret admirer."

"Aw, you shouldn't have," I said with heavy sarcasm. "Won't your wife be jealous?"

"Let's not tell her about this," Jimmy said. "I got the buy-two-get-one-free special at the gas station this morning, and I'm supposed to be off doughnuts for another week on my dumb diet."

"Wow, you got me a squished, freebie doughnut." I sat at my desk. "I love you too."

"You didn't get me a squished, freebie doughnut," Jimmy replied. "I'd appreciate a squished free doughnut sometime. Let's say St. Patrick's Day. Or President's Day—that's much sooner."

"Point taken." I sat, took a bite of my squished, freebie doughnut, and decided it definitely wasn't the worst way to start a Valentine's Day.

I flicked on my computer and washed down the cheap sugar high with a swallow of caffeine. The combination hit my bloodstream about two seconds later.

Before I could check my email, an instant message popped up on my screen. I frowned when I saw it was from Jimmy. I glanced over at him, but he was deftly ignoring me. I clicked into his message to find out what he was up to.

JIMMY JONES: I saw that.

KATE ROSETTI: Saw what?

JIMMY JONES: You panicked when you saw that heart doughnut. Pale as a ghost. Looked like death warmed over.

KATE ROSETTI: You're descriptive this morning. And you're reading too much into it.

JIMMY JONES: Who'd you think the Valentine's gift was from?

KATE ROSETTI: Who'd I think cared enough about me to leave a squished free doughnut on my desk, you mean?

JIMMY JONES: You panicked.

KATE ROSETTI: Chief is calling me.

"Hello?" I leaned back in my seat and answered my phone. "Yes, sir, he's here. Okay, sure. I'll meet you there."

Jimmy looked torn. He still looked somewhat amused from our private chat session, but a look of concern had entered his eye. He knew me better than just about anyone, and I was pretty sure he could see the change in my disposition.

"Saved by the bell, huh?" Jimmy prompted.

"Thank God," I said. "We've got a dead body."

"I'm gonna let you think about the words that just came out of your mouth," Jimmy said, a little twinkle in his eye, "and I'm gonna let you rephrase that before everyone in this room thinks you're a psychopath."

"The chief needs us at a scene. Now. He asked for me and you specifically, and only us. That's all I got."

"The chief's actually at the scene?" Jimmy's eyes lost all signs of amusement. "Live and in person?"

"Sounds like it," I said, feeling the same heavy weight descend on my shoulders as I processed the meaning of it. "Which means we've gotta get going before the press gets wind of whatever's happened."

Chapter 2

The body in question was on the Minneapolis side of the river this morning. I drove through town with Jimmy alongside me. A part of me had expected some lighthearted chatter as we headed through St. Paul toward the crime scene. A little more teasing about Valentine's Day followed by a few innocent enough, but still pointed, questions about my lack of plans for the night.

Instead, I got a lot of silence. Apparently I wasn't the only one uneasy with the chief's summons. Chief Rex Sturgeon, my boss, had the sort of job that required a lot of sitting behind a desk, heading up meetings, and facing the press. Though he was an accomplished detective in his own right, he'd graduated to the political side of the police business. The side of the business I tried to steer far, far away from. Still, I had a lot of respect for the chief, even though we'd been known to butt heads over the years.

The fact that he was at the scene in person, early on a Monday morning, spoke volumes. If I had to guess, the crime was either particularly heinous, extremely dangerous, or involved a prominent person. At the risk of sounding cynical, my money was on the latter.

"Happy Valentine's Day, huh?" Jimmy rubbed at his forehead. He glanced out the window as I merged onto the highway. "Sure to be an extra sweet one for the chief to grace us with his presence. My money's on a big name. You?"

"I'm not going to pony up a wager on that bet."

"Any idea who it might be?"

I shook my head. "I didn't recognize the address. I know the area. It's a nice spot near the river. Houses are pricey there now, but I feel like a good chunk of the people have been living there forever and nabbed them for cheap back in the day."

"I've been over this way a few times. The street name sorta rings a bell. Can't quite put my finger on it. It's been a long time."

More uneasy silence. A few minutes later, we reached the street that Google had directed us to. I flicked on my blinker and took a sideways glance at Jimmy to see if this had jogged his memory.

"I came to a Christmas party here once," Jimmy murmured, as much to himself as to me. "It was a long time ago, a couple of decades."

"Oh, yeah? I'm sure the owners have changed over since then."

"I'm sure."

Despite Jimmy's agreement, I could see worry creasing his eyes as I began to slow. He began to shake his head as I applied the brakes and pulled over to the side of the street. A few houses up, several officers were on the scene, still roping off the area. The chief stood elbow to elbow with a man I recognized as a longtime member of the fire department. I thought I glimpsed a charred vehicle behind him.

I parked and opened the car door. Jimmy cursed under his breath as he exited. The air surrounding the quiet, tree-lined street smelled like a barbecue. An SUV barbecue, to be exact. A thin plume of smoke snaked through the air.

"Arson?" I wondered aloud as Jimmy joined me. I cleared my throat and hesitated. "Do you recognize this place?"

Jimmy cursed again. He didn't seem inclined to expand.

The chief caught sight of me and Jimmy. He waved us over before I could pester my partner about what he knew and wasn't telling me.

"Rosetti, Jones, this is Joe Fritz. You guys have met."

Chief Sturgeon quickly waved between the firefighter and us. We were all vaguely familiar with one another and exchanged brisk nods. Nobody seemed in the mood for small talk. Even the dark humor that usually pervaded crime scenes felt out of reach this morning.

"We got a 911 call about half an hour ago," Chief Sturgeon started. He gestured at the vehicle. "Car fire. One of the neighbors called it in when they smelled smoke."

"Did they see what happened?" I asked. "Did anybody come forward with additional information?"

"Not yet." Chief Sturgeon glanced at Fritz as if looking for approval. Fritz nodded, and Sturgeon continued. "Fritz and a couple of his guys were first on the scene. He happened to recognize the address."

I frowned as I cast a glance at Jimmy, then Fritz. If both of them recognized the address, that didn't bode well. I caught Jimmy and Fritz exchanging yet another look. Fritz had a fully gray head of hair and looked to be similar in age to Jimmy. As if to confirm my theory, Sturgeon nodded at me.

"It's a little before your time, Rosetti." Sturgeon cleared his throat. "But your dad would know the name."

"Sir, I'm not sure how that's relevant to this case," I said briskly. "Can someone tell me what's going on? Who's in that car?"

"We can't say for sure yet—"

"Chief," I said warningly, "you called me for a reason this morning."

"Does the name Jeff Heinrich mean anything to you?"

A worm of dread slithered down my spine. The name sounded familiar, and with it came a sense of foreboding. I couldn't exactly place who he was in relation to me, or why I was supposed to know of him. The confusion must have shown on my face because the chief continued.

"Retired detective of the St. Paul force," Sturgeon said. "A lot of the guys who've been around for a while worked with him."

I looked to Jimmy, who was staring at his feet. Fritz watched me with interest.

"There's more to the story, isn't there?" I met the chief's gaze. "Based on the way y'all are tiptoeing around me here."

"He was a candidate to be chief, once upon a time," Sturgeon said. "I beat him out, but there was no bad blood between us. He didn't want the title. He'd only been in the running because he was a damn fine detective."

Alarm bells rang in my head. I remembered the name; I was sure of it. The link between Jeff Heinrich and me hovered somewhere in my subconscious, and all I could recall was that it wasn't associated with oodles of positivity.

Chief Sturgeon cleared his throat a second time. I'd never seen him so uncertain.

"Kate, he testified against your father."

Ding, ding, ding. The floodgates opened, and suddenly I could put a face with the name. Newspaper articles appeared in my memory—a picture of Jeff Heinrich displayed next to a mug shot of Angelo Rosetti. And I remembered. I remembered all of it.

Jeff Heinrich had been propelled into his candidacy for chief *because* of his testimony in my father's trial. He'd come forward with the piece of evidence that had clinched my father's prison sentence. He'd offered brutal testimony that berated my dad's character, his work ethic, his morals. Then he'd presented the cold hard facts that had locked my father behind bars for most of my developmental years.

"I see." My voice sounded a little hoarse. "How sure are you that he's in that car?"

I took my first real glance behind Sturgeon and tried to soak in the sight of the SUV's corpse. The arson guys were already combing through the car. A photographer was snapping pictures. I felt like I was going through the motions, but I couldn't process anything. I just kept seeing the photos from the newspaper in my head. Jeff Heinrich, the brilliant truth teller. Angelo Rosetti, the awful sinner. As different as two cops could be.

"We can't be one hundred percent sure." Sturgeon gave a nod toward the vehicle. "The body's too burned to get anything definitive just yet. We've called out the best forensic analyst in the state, and she'll be focused on getting us some answers as quickly as possible."

"But?" I prompted.

"But because of the potential media circus around this one, we're going to begin by operating under the assumption that it's him," Sturgeon said. "We'll keep the case as close to our chests as we can for now. That's why you got the personal call, Rosetti, Jones. I don't want anyone else in on it just yet. It's too early."

"But you can't waste time," I said. "You want us to start looking into things before the leads go cold."

"If it is Heinrich, we can't waste time." The lack of doubt in Sturgeon's eyes gave away his conviction that the retired cop was indeed the victim. "He's put away a big list of high-profile criminals in his career. We'll have a lot of work ahead of us if it's him."

I swallowed hard. "Are you sure you want me to be the one to get started?"

The chief's eyes were hard. "I want you on the case."

There was a big *but* that remained unspoken. *But my father was one of the people he put away.* My father had a motive to want this guy dead, a motive named revenge. Not that I believed he had anything to do with this, but I could already imagine the headlines: "Old Rivalries Die Hard."

"We'll get to work," I said. "Is Melinda here?"

"Dr. Brooks is just pulling up." Sturgeon nodded behind me at the expensive ride rolling to a stop. "You were my first call."

We waited for Melinda to join us. She looked especially peppy for a Monday morning. She was wearing a very pale pink business suit, gently reminding everyone that beyond horrific crime scenes and charred vehicles, it was still a day shrouded in love for the rest of the world. She flashed a smile in our direction. Diamonds dangled from her ears. Only Melinda could get away with looking like she'd stepped straight off the *Legally Blonde* set before snapping on a pair of gloves and digging into burnt flesh.

Melinda and Joe Fritz coupled up and made their way toward the charred vehicle. The other techs continued to work while I hung back with Jones and Chief Sturgeon.

"We don't know for sure it's him," I ventured. "The location could be a coincidence."

An echo chamber of silence came from the two men at my shoulders. I glanced around, squinting, analyzing the street. Only one side of the street was populated by residences. The other side of the street was lined heavily by evergreen trees.

Through the bristled branches, I spotted several headstones that signaled a cemetery stretched beyond. An oddly fitting view for a former homicide detective to have from his front window. I briefly imagined myself chomping on my morning bagel and gazing out at gravesites—surrounded by death on the job and off.

"It's a quiet street. Aside from the two immediate neighbors, this spot isn't visible from any of the other houses," I suggested. "A smart criminal could have chosen this spot for the sake of convenience. There was probably very little risk of anyone seeing them early on a Monday morning. And if they did notice, the person responsible probably knew they'd be long gone before the call went through."

"It was planned," Sturgeon agreed. That was where his agreement ended.

None of us believed it was a coincidence. None of us believed it was anyone other than Jeff Heinrich in that car.

"What do we know about Heinrich?" I glanced sideways at the chief.

"He was a hard worker. Good cop," Sturgeon said gruffly. "He was about as polarizing a cop as one can be and still be on the right side of the law."

"What's that supposed to mean?"

Sturgeon looked at me and raised his eyebrows. I understood.

"Look, my father was guilty," I said. "Detective Heinrich had evidence that proved it without a shadow of a doubt. He didn't convict my dad: the jury did. My dad made his own choices. Heinrich did the right thing."

"He did," Sturgeon said mildly.

But it went beyond that, and we all knew it. Heinrich had been brutal in his testimony of my father, almost ruthless. He'd not only presented the evidence, but he'd also torn my father's character apart and painted him as a dangerous monster. From what I could gather, most people had believed he'd gone a little over the top in villainizing my dad.

The newspapers had guessed, somewhat accurately, that there was no coming back after Heinrich got off the stand. The jury had made their decision in forty-five minutes the next day, and I suspected the result wasn't a coincidence.

"Heinrich was responsible for a lot of people getting put behind bars," I said. "That case was one of many."

"That's what I'm banking on." Sturgeon gave me a faint smile that came off as a grimace. "You can start at the bowling alley."

"The bowling alley?"

"Heinrich never married," Sturgeon said. "From what I remember, he wasn't close with any family members. He didn't have a lot of buddies at the precinct. He minded his business and went home."

I nodded. "But the bowling alley?"

"I ran into him a year or so back at Leitner Lanes." Sturgeon made a general wave in the direction of St. Paul. "I guess he's a regular. Took up a new hobby in his retirement. Probably the closest friends he had, if I had to guess."

We fell silent as Melinda straightened, brushing back a wisp of hair with her wrist. Her hands were gloved, and she'd ducked her head into the car to check out the state of the body. Her festive spirit had dulled. Her heels clicked through the light snow toward us as she sighed.

"Well, someone's not celebrating Valentine's Day," she said sadly, as if that were the biggest travesty of this whole thing. "There's someone in there, all right. Male. If I had to loosely guess age, I'd put him between sixty and seventy years old. But Dr. Michaelson will be able to give you better information when she arrives."

Dr. Kelly Michaelson was a forensic anthropologist who sometimes helped out on cases like this one. Cases where identification was difficult for whatever reason. She studied the long-dead bodies. Melinda studied the freshly deceased. They'd formed a loose friendship over the last few years.

"That fits," Sturgeon muttered.

"You're talking about Detective Heinrich?" Melinda nodded knowingly. "Joe filled me in. Seems like the criteria is a fit, but there are plenty of retired guys living in this neighborhood. It doesn't mean it's him."

"Anything else?" I asked. "Care to venture a guess at the cause of death?"

She shook her head. "We won't know until we get him back to the lab. It very well could've been caused by the explosion. The guys are saying there was a bomb inside the car."

"*Inside* the car?" I frowned. "It wasn't triggered when the car was turned on?"

She shook her head. "Preliminary analysis points to the bomb being placed on the front seat next to him."

"But why—"

"The victim was handcuffed to the steering wheel. Both hands," Melinda said. "Even if he had known there was a bomb there, even if he had seen it counting down, I don't think he would have been able to do anything about it."

"Sounds personal." A storm cloud passed over Jimmy's face.

Melinda gave an inconclusive shrug. "That's your territory. I'm going to grab my kit and dig in. I just got off the phone with Dr. Michaelson. She's on her way and will be here in thirty minutes. I have a feeling the longer you can hold the press off, the better off we'll be."

Jimmy cleared his throat. He nudged me gently with his elbow. I chanced a glance behind me and rolled my eyes. Several cars lined the street already. Two people who could only be reporters hovered nearby.

Melinda watched our exchange. "Ah. Too late."

"Kate Rosetti, a question for you!"

One of the reporters, a male, seemed to have mistaken my glance over my shoulder as one of interest. I turned away.

"Trevor Sime of the North Star Press," he called. "Can I get a moment of your time?"

"Hey, Hollywood." Melinda batted her eyelashes teasingly at me. "You've got fans, Kate."

I groaned.

Jimmy grinned. "Rosetti's fans are stalkers and reporters. She's got quite the entourage."

"I'm not jealous," Melinda quipped.

"Enough," Sturgeon said. "I'll handle this. Get out of here, Rosetti. You, too, Jones. You can get together with Dr. Michaelson and Dr. Brooks back at the office."

The way Sturgeon's jaw was set had me realizing that he was—somewhat nicely—kicking me off the crime scene.

"Sir, if you want me to work the case," I said quietly, "I think I should take a look around."

"Five minutes," he barked. "Make it count. You can get everything else you need from the photographs and evidence collected by the forensic team."

I didn't waste another second standing around. I made efficient use of my five minutes—stealthily stretched to seven—until I could feel the chief staring daggers into the back of my head. I retreated to the tune of Trevor Sime calling questions in my direction as I made my way back to the car. Jimmy, good man that he was, stood staunchly between Trevor and me.

"You don't have to be my bodyguard," I told my partner as we slid inside my car, but I offered him a grateful smile that I hoped told him how much I appreciated the gesture anyhow.

"I don't need to do anything, but I want to." Jimmy gave a fond pat to his somewhat round stomach. "What the hell do I eat all those chicken wings for if I can't throw my weight around a bit? I was a linebacker in high school, you know."

"I don't believe you." I turned the car on, buckled in, and ignored the reporters staring in my direction.

"Got the trophy to prove it. I keep the uniform around, too, in the back of the closet somewhere. The missus thinks someday I'll be able to fit into it again."

"Gross."

"I could have had any lady I wanted in high school. If I'd been that sort of dude."

"I don't believe that, either."

"Yeah, that part is a lie," Jimmy agreed good-naturedly. "Figured you'd see through that one, brilliant detective that you are."

I gave a short laugh. Even as I did, I felt a pinch in my stomach, a thread of discomfort just waiting to be tugged. It seemed that each day I worked beside Jimmy brought us closer. He knew when to make me laugh, when to give me space, when to offer a helping hand without a word. And his clock toward retirement was ticking down. Each day with Jimmy made me appreciate him more, but each day was one less that I'd have him by my side.

If Jimmy noticed my brief foray into a nostalgic, bittersweet mood, he didn't say anything about it. Instead, he looked out the window and commented, "That Trevor fool is gone. I guess he was only here to see you after all."

"That's not—" I started reversing and stopped when I felt a little *thunk* behind me.

I cursed under my breath and glanced in the rearview mirror again. I'd been watching where I was reversing, then I'd glanced forward for one second, and—

I cursed again. I threw my door open.

"What are you doing?" I faced the annoying reporter who'd been hollering at me. He was sitting on the trunk of my car. The *thunk* hadn't been me hitting something—it'd been someone hitting *me* as he'd hopped aboard. "Get off my car."

"I just thought we could talk."

"No comment," I said. "Pretty sure the chief covered that already."

"Who's in the car?" Trevor Sime crossed his legs like we were sitting down to a tea party. He looked completely unruffled to be riling up a homicide detective. "The dead guy, I mean. I know Jim Jones is in the car with you. Good guy, that Jones."

"Detective Jones," I corrected, my blood beginning to boil.

I absolutely hated when people I'd never met pretended to know things about me. I also hated feeling one step behind. I immediately and intensely disliked Trevor Sime.

"Funny thing. Turns out this address belongs to a former cop." Trevor nodded at Jeff Heinrich's house. "I read up on him. Old Detective Heinrich. Interesting career. Put some real big baddies behind bars. Do you think this could be a case of revenge?"

As instantly as my blood had boiled, it now plunged in temperature until my fingers were shards of icy glass. He knew my name. He knew Heinrich's name and legacy. He'd have put two and two together, and he seemed adamant to stir the pot. Out of the corner of my eye, I caught a glimpse of Sturgeon approaching.

I moved close to Trevor. Close enough so that only he could hear my words. "I'm going to give you one piece of advice. Stay out of this, or you'll regret it."

"Oh, a threat from a cop." Trevor tapped at the notebook splayed on his lap. "Like father, like daughter."

I felt my fist itching to pop him one in the nose. If I'd had a single moment longer to process what Trevor had said, I wouldn't have been able to hold back. Fortunately, or unfortunately, Jimmy had gotten out of the car. He was at my side in a second, his presence a solid reminder that I was on the clock and needed to maintain my composure.

"Oh, you must have misunderstood me. That conversation wasn't coming from the cop part of me." I gave a thin smile at Trevor. "That part was personal."

Jimmy gently managed to sweet-talk me back into the car by the time Sturgeon arrived. Sturgeon took one look at me, and his eyes flashed with something that could only be anger.

"If you don't get off the damn car, Mr. Sime, I'm going to look the other way when my detective accidentally runs over your foot," Sturgeon said. "Leave my detectives alone. I mean it."

Trevor hopped happily off the trunk of my car. "Good day to you, too, sir. I think I've got everything I need."

Something about the way Trevor spoke, the little twitch of a cunning smile, the way he gave a finger wave in my direction had me feeling more and more uneasy by the second. I knew this wasn't over. I just knew it. And if the feeling in my gut was correct, things would get much, much worse before they got better.

Chapter 3

"Do you think another coffee is really what you need?"

Jimmy stared me down as I pulled into the drive-through lane at Starbucks.

"Are you insinuating I'm overly caffeinated?" I frowned at him. "My blood's eighty percent caffeine. It's almost impossible for me to have too much coffee."

"You're a medical anomaly. But I was referencing the reporter."

"Trevor?" I feigned disinterest. "What about him?"

"He's got your adrenaline going. Just not sure another cup of coffee is what you need. You seem a little on edge."

"We were at the scene of a vicious and likely very personal crime this morning. Why wouldn't I be on edge?" I shrugged and deadpanned a look at Jimmy. "There's a murderer on the loose."

"You're always chasing a murderer. You're more stressed when you're *not* on a case. This one is different."

"It doesn't have to be."

"You and I have worked together long enough for me to know when you're lying."

"I'm not lying. It doesn't have to be different."

"It is for you. Everyone knows it. Look, Kate, you know I want the best for you. You're one of the best partners I've ever had."

"*One* of the best?"

"I'm trying not to get too sappy on you."

I gave him a glimpse of a shadowy smile.

"I'd die for you, but one thing I'm not going to do is lie to you," he continued. "Being a good partner means telling you the truth even when I don't want to."

"You think I shouldn't be on the case."

"I think you should be on the case, but if you keep acting like this, you're going to get kicked off."

"What do you mean?"

"Let's start with the whole threatening to run over the reporter thing."

"I didn't threaten to run over him."

"You're right. You left the threat up to his imagination."

"I wouldn't *do* anything about it." I felt my nostrils flare a little in frustration. "If you know me as well as you think you do, then you should know that too."

"That's exactly my point." Jimmy met my burst of anger with a cool, passive expression. "I know you can handle this case. You've handled far more personal cases. I know you'd lock up your own family members if they broke the law. It's everyone else I'm worried about."

"They're none of your business. As long as the chief says—"

"The governor's up for reelection soon. The chief reports to him. They're not going to want a splashy debacle in the news."

"There won't be a splashy debacle."

"There doesn't have to be. All Trevor Sime needs is an inch. Heck, a millimeter. A guy like that can twist a phrase into something it's not in a heartbeat. You're a good detective, Rosetti, the best. But you're an awful liar, a terrible actress, and a political candidate's worst nightmare."

"Wow, what a list. I should update my résumé to include that sparkling review."

"I'm just telling you to look out. Don't say anything that could come back to bite you in the rear. Straight 'no comments' all the way—you hear me?"

I grumbled an unintelligible response.

"We need you on this case." Jimmy shot me an imploring look. "If it's as complicated as I think it's going to be, then we need the best on it, and that's you."

"And you."

"Someone killed a retired cop. Heinrich, like it or not, was one of us. It's a hit against the department. Not to mention the fact that Heinrich was smart and lasted a long time in an ugly business. He was paranoid. He was careful."

"And someone got to him anyway."

Jimmy tapped his fingers against the passenger's side door in agreement.

I pulled forward to order. A gloomy silence seeped out of the car as I rolled my window down.

"How may I help you?" the barista chirped cheerfully. "Something extra special on this chilly Valentine's Day morning?"

I glanced at Jimmy.

"Cake pop," he mouthed.

"What are you, three?" I asked him.

"The pink one," he replied.

"One birthday cake pop," I said with an eye roll. "And a latte." On second thought, a little bitterly, I added, "Half caf, please."

Jimmy nodded in approval. I inched forward as the woman announced my total. We didn't need to say another word for us both to know I understood the gravity of the situation. A former cop had been killed. He had personal ties to my family, as well as the rest of the police department. Who-ever'd blown him to bits had meant to make a statement, and if I had to guess, there was a big-time motive behind it.

The press would be on this like hounds, looking for any crack, anything that would give them a story, something to run with. A pit had already developed in my stomach over my interaction with Trevor Sime this morning. Even if he'd been overbearing and rude, I shouldn't have caved to my frustration.

"Couldn't go all the way decaf, huh?" Jimmy asked as the barista handed over a bag for Jimmy's cake pop, along with my coffee cup. "Too big of a commitment for you?"

I glanced at him with a tiny smile. "No comment."

***

When we got to Leitner's Lanes, I was still nursing my latte, more for the warmth it provided than the burst of caffeine. My adrenaline was starting to cool off from the morning's events, but I could feel my fingers shaking slightly as I slid out of the car.

"Those cake pops are so small." Jimmy patted his stomach again and quoted *Zoolander*. "It needs to be at least three times that size."

"Dude." I stared at him. "Then you'd just be eating a piece of cake."

"Exactly."

Jimmy grinned at me as we strolled into the bowling alley.

"Bring up bad memories?" Jimmy pulled the door open and waved me through. "You're good at a lot of things, Rosetti. Bowling's not one of them."

"Remind me not to ask you for a letter of recommendation," I said smartly. "You're fantastic at pointing out all my flaws."

"There aren't many. I'll take what I can get."

I gave a short laugh as a clap of warmth embraced us as we stepped deeper into the bowling alley. Someone, probably an underpaid high school kid, had likely been responsible for the cheap decorations that were spread across the bowling alley.

A banner of construction paper hearts hung over the shoe counter. A glowing neon heart was perched next to the cash register. A platter of stale looking, overly sugared cookies sat on a bar table next to a pink punch jar that had no punch in it yet. A stack of napkins with candy heart shapes on them sat next to pink plastic cups.

"Good morning. We're not actually open yet." A young woman popped up from behind the front desk slightly out of breath. She'd been bending over and impossible to see from the door. "I'm just getting ready for the singles' mixer that starts over happy hour."

"Well, look at that." Jimmy gave me a broad grin. "Rosetti's single. Do you have any open slots?"

"Oh, tons." The young woman brushed a red curl behind her ear and gave me a smile. "Are you looking for a date? Can you bowl?"

The fact that they had tons of slots open probably didn't bode well for the event. I gave the young woman, who couldn't be older than twenty-one, a forced smile.

"No," I said shortly.

"No, she can't bowl," Jimmy clarified. "I've seen this woman get a gutter ball with bumpers."

The young woman laughed. "Hey, you're funny. If you're single, mister, you should come. We need more guys in your age range."

"He's taken," I said quickly. "And he left off an important part about why we're here. I'm Detective Kate Rosetti, and he's Detective Jimmy Jones. We're here on police business."

The woman paled slightly. Her freckles popped. "I-I swear I didn't lie on my application. I mean, okay, a little bit. But it's just because I need money for college. I don't drink any alcohol on the job. If I'd told Marshall that I was only nineteen, he would've given the job to that loser Jacob. He was stealing from the register. I just didn't want to snitch on him. I really need this job."

"We're not here for any hiring violations," I said. "We're just hoping you'd be able to help us out with a few questions."

"Sure, anything," she said. "I'm Lori. Lori Palozzi. I work here, like, six nights a week. Honestly, all Marshall does is sign the checks and sit behind the bar. If you need to know something, I'm your gal."

"Do you know this guy?" Jimmy pulled up a photo of Heinrich on his phone.

Asha had already sent through some preliminary information on Heinrich—photograph, age, history.

"Oh, sure, Mr. Heinrich," Lori confirmed with a nod of her bouncing red ponytail. Her thin lips twitched into a little smile. "He tips well. Quiet guy, doesn't cause trouble. The good kind of customer."

"Could you tell us more about him?" I asked. "Just the general stuff. When he comes in here, who he plays with, that sort of thing."

"Sure. He's probably the most regular client we have. He comes in like clockwork. He has a standing reservation for Monday and Wednesday nights at 7 p.m. That's just him at those times. He buys out the whole lane and practices for an hour straight."

I pulled out a small notebook and jotted down a few notes.

"He's in here on Thursdays, too, but that's for his game. He bowls with a couple of other guys."

"Always the same crew?"

Lori nodded. "I can get you a list. I don't remember all their names offhand, but I could pick them out of a lineup." She froze. "Wait a minute. I don't need to pick anyone out of a lineup, do I?"

"No, Lori—"

"Oh my gosh." The weight of having the police standing before her seemed to sink in with a resounding *thunk*. She cursed under her breath. "Something happened to him, didn't it? And you think one of his bowling buddies killed him? Over a strike or something? I know Mr. Heinrich takes his games seriously, but for someone to..." She gulped, unable to finish the sentence.

"That list?" I asked.

"Yeah, yeah, sure. Just let me check the logs from last time he was here. It would've been Thursday night."

"Were you working?"

"Yep. Always am." She gave a heavy sigh, seeming to forget the gravity of the situation in lieu of her personal burdens. "I remember the lane was full. I think all the regulars were here."

We waited a moment while she flipped through an ancient looking book. I studied the lanes for a moment, the dimly lit space smelling faintly of fried food and mildewy shoes.

I turned my attention back to Lori. She was pretty, smiley, optimistic. But she also seemed to have a heavy weight on her shoulders. I had the raw, unexplained feeling that she was trustworthy.

"Okay, here you go." She scratched a few names onto a sheet of paper. "These are the guys he bowls with. I don't know much about them, but if you have specific questions, you can ask me and I'll do my best to answer."

"Did Heinrich seem to get along with everyone?" I asked. "Had he had any disagreements lately?"

"Over bowling?"

"Over anything." I shrugged. "Whatever comes to mind."

"Honestly, I don't think so." She returned my shrug. "Like I said, he was quiet and serious. Not much of a sense of humor. He always ordered a Coke Zero and tater tots. That's it. Never any alcohol. I don't know if I ever really saw him smile. He never once asked how my day was going or referenced me by name, despite the fact that I've been working here for almost two years and check him in three times a week."

"Huh."

"But it wasn't, like, in a bad way, you know?" Lori gave me a pointed look. "You get a lot of guys hitting on you in a place like this. Mr. Heinrich rarely made eye contact. He tipped well, seemed respectful—in a way, it was a relief."

"I understand," I said. "Thanks. What about these guys? Any of them give you weird vibes?"

She looked at the list. "I probably shouldn't say."

"You can tell us," I said. "We're not going to make any rash decisions based on what you say. We'll investigate everything thoroughly."

"But it's just a gut feeling, you know? Nothing concrete."

"That's fine," I said. "Sometimes a hunch is the only thing we have to go on. Trust me, the more information you can give us, the safer everyone will be. This is a murder investigation."

She paled further. "You think a murderer might be bowling here?"

"Not necessarily. We're just trying to learn as much as we can about Mr. Heinrich. Anything you can tell us about the company he kept would be helpful."

"I've never liked Will Comice." Lori spit out the words and pointed at the paper, as if she couldn't control her outburst. "He just gives me skeevy vibes. He's slipped me his number, like, three times. He was drunk for at least two of those times, and I doubt he remembers doing it. But still." She gave a little shudder. "Sometimes I take my bathroom break when he comes in just so Marshall's gotta sign him in."

I nodded toward the book. "Why do you sign people in, anyway?"

"It's just for the league." She flipped through a few pages. "We track scores. We give awards at the end of the season, things like that."

"How's the competition?"

"I know it sounds ridiculous, but it's pretty intense." She blinked. "You don't really think Heinrich was murdered over bowling scores, do you? I mean, he was good. But honestly, it's just a couple of guys hurtling a ball down a lane at some pins. It's not worth killing over."

"That's what most people think," Jimmy muttered. "Though I'd be lying if I said I hadn't seen someone kill over less."

"Was Heinrich often near the top of his league?" I asked. "Did he have any regular opponents?"

"Mr. Heinrich won the last four out of five years. He takes it very seriously." Lori raised a hand to shield her mouth and lowered her voice, as if afraid of being overheard in the otherwise empty building. "I think he's the male equivalent of an old cat lady."

"What's that supposed to mean?" Jimmy asked. "I like cats. I'm old."

"I just mean that this is his *thing*." Lori gestured between Jimmy and me. "You two have your careers. It sounds like you have a relationship," she said to Jimmy. "You have other things in your life to keep you occupied. From what I gather, Mr. Heinrich didn't have a lot else going on in his life, so he directed his passion here."

"I thought he didn't talk much," I said, "so how would you know any of that?"

"I'm just going on a hunch, like you asked me to do." She sounded a little defensive. "That, and the fact that he has the ability to be here on such a consistent basis. If he had, say, grandkid ball games to go to or whatever, don't you think he'd miss now and again? The only time he missed a bowling league game was when he was in the hospital. And he called in from the hospital to explain he couldn't make it because they were operating on him."

"I see."

"Is there any chance I could get Will Comice's information?" I asked. "We might swing by to chat with him."

"I don't think I should give that out." She looked unsure, but her voice gained confidence the more she spoke. "It's private information. I think you need a warrant."

I let a beat of silence pass.

"I know you're doing me a favor and all," she said weakly, "but I really can't get fired from this job. If Will complains to Marshall, I'll totally get fired. I can't afford to look for another job now."

Jimmy gave an easy wave of his hand. "Don't worry about it. We can have our people get that information easily enough."

Lori still looked panicked. "But he'll know the tip came from me. Unless—" She looked up, her eyes brightening as she swiveled her gaze toward me. "I'll do you one better. You're single, right?"

I glanced sideways at Jimmy and said icily, "Not sure why that's being brought up. *Again.*"

"Come to the mixer tonight." Lori gestured to the currently empty punch jar along with the plate of stale cookies that would be left out to get increasingly stale for another few hours. "I'll put your name down as a guest. Will Comice will be there. You can meet him yourself, and then maybe I won't get drawn into the mess at all."

"It's not a bad idea." Jimmy waggled his eyebrows at me. "You never know who you might find at an event like this."

I groaned.

"Some of Mr. Heinrich's other buddies might be here," Lori added. "Since I'm working tonight, I can discreetly point them out to you. You can get a feel for them in their natural habitat."

"I'm upgrading my previous statement to say that I think this is a great idea." Jimmy could barely contain his glee. "It's not like Detective Rosetti has any plans for the evening anyway."

"Right. Thanks, *Detective*." I huffed at Jimmy.

Lori gave a quick smile between us. I could see in her eyes that she already knew she'd won the battle. The two did have a point. It would be nice to meet everyone in person, and it would be even better to see them all interacting. I'd be able to watch them behaving organically before blowing my cover as a cop.

"She'll be there." Jimmy clapped me on the shoulder, obviously coming to the same conclusion I had. "That'll be Kate Rosetti for your invite list, one *s* and two *t*'s."

"Great!" Lori jotted something in her trusted logbook. She glanced up with a critical eye in my direction. "You're going to change, though, right?"

"What do you mean?" I glanced down at my uniform of black slacks, a tank, and a well-loved blazer.

"Change your clothes. I mean," Lori added unhelpfully, "you look like a cop."

"I don't—"

"We'll get it taken care of," Jimmy said. "I'll make sure she looks presentable for the occasion."

"Pleasure doing business with you, Detective." Lori winked at Jimmy. Then she pointed her felt-tip pen in my direction. "And I'll see you tonight, Lady Detective."

Chapter 4

My mood had significantly tanked by the time we returned to the precinct. Considering I'd threatened to run over a reporter earlier this morning, that was an impressive feat.

"It's not so bad," Jimmy told me as he pulled the doors to the precinct open. "It beats sitting at home and lamenting being single."

"I wouldn't be lamenting being single."

"What would you be doing? Eating a pint of ice cream and watching *The Holiday*?"

"Is that what you think women do when they're alone on Valentine's Day?"

Jimmy gave a shrug, but his face had taken on an unsure look. Smart man that he was, he knew when he was treading on thin ice, even with a friendly partner like me.

"I'm not a female," he added when I remained silent. "It was an educated guess."

"I'm happiest when I'm single," I retorted. "It's far easier to worry about one person—*me*—than it is to worry about someone else."

"Okay then."

I eyed Jimmy, ready for him to pick a fight, but he pressed a button on the elevator and began humming a little ditty under his breath that told me he was trying to keep the peace. I gave in for the sake of the case.

Melinda and her new pal, Dr. Kelly Michaelson, were just returning to the lab when Jimmy and I arrived downstairs. The body hadn't yet been transported back to the facility.

Melinda waved us into her office. "Dr. Michaelson, do you remember Detectives Rosetti and Jones? I think you've all worked together before."

We did a round of handshakes and friendly nods. We weren't more than acquaintances, ships passing in the night, on previous cases. I'd read her reports and she'd read mine. I was pretty certain that we all respected one another's work.

"So what do you think?" I asked Dr. Michaelson, once we'd all taken seats around a small table in the corner of Melinda's oversized office. "Any additional information to share?"

"It's very early in the case," Dr. Michaelson said. "Until we can get started, I really can't give you a whole lot of definitive detail."

I glanced at Melinda. "Yeah, I've heard that before. How about theories?"

"I also can't—"

"We won't repeat anything you say here," I assured her. "But Jimmy and I are looking to get a head start on the case in the instance it really is Heinrich in there. The media's already on us like crazy. We can't afford to wait."

Dr. Michaelson gave a frustrated sigh and glanced at Melinda. Melinda returned her look of frustration, then she gave a nod and a smile in my direction that told Dr. Michaelson to go ahead and speak freely.

Dr. Michaelson glanced down at a sheaf of papers before her. "I'd have to agree with Dr. Brooks's preliminary findings. The profile of the victim fits the man who goes by the name

Jeffrey Heinrich. I think it's fairly safe, given all of the details, to make an educated guess that it is him." She raised a hand and spoke sternly. "That is not to be repeated until my official report comes out."

"Understood." I gave an agreeable nod. "Cause of death? Did the bomb kill him?"

"Also not confirmed, but yes, if I had to make a guess, I would say he was likely alive at the time the bomb detonated."

"Fireman Joe's guys confirmed the bomb was sitting in the front seat next to him," Melinda said. "They're looking into what sort of container held the bomb."

"You mean, like a suitcase?"

Melinda nodded. "Exactly, though they haven't given us any guesses yet. They did state that at this time they don't believe it was a professional-caliber bomb."

"You mean whoever killed him was an amateur and Googled how to make an incendiary device?"

"That's what it's looking like, so far."

I frowned and glanced at Jimmy. "It might be worth pulling a list of guys that Heinrich put behind bars who had priors with explosive devices. It might be a long shot, but it's a place to start. There must be a few of them."

"It's a good idea." Jimmy jotted a note onto his pad of paper. "It might not be as long of a shot as you think. Bombs aren't the most common way to kill someone, especially if the person has to figure out how to build it themselves. It's much easier to stab someone, or shoot someone, or poison someone, or—"

"We get the idea," I said. "And I think you're right. For someone to go through the effort of creating the bomb, we have learned a few things. First, that there's a chance someone has prior knowledge of bombs—hence their choice of weapon."

"There's more?" Dr. Michaelson asked, looking at me.

"It was personal and meant to make a statement," I said. "As Jimmy pointed out, a bomb isn't subtle. It's splashy."

"I suppose that's true," Dr. Michaelson said. "That's why I leave the theories up to you all."

"Speaking of theories, Kate's already got a lead." Jimmy smirked and hid behind his notepad when I glared at him. "A potential lead," he corrected.

"What?" Melinda swiveled to face me.

"It's nothing," I said. "I'm just going to an event at the bowling alley where Heinrich spent a lot of his spare time."

"You think this could be..." Dr. Michaelson cleared her throat and tried not to look amused. "You think this murder could be related to strikes and gutter balls?"

"We've seen stranger things," Jimmy said. "Plus, it's a double whammy. It gives Kate a way to celebrate Valentine's Day."

All eyes were on me again.

It was my turn to clear my throat and shoot some more eye darts at Jimmy. "Technically, it's a singles' event."

Melinda sniffed, unable to hide a smile. Dr. Michaelson continued to look amused.

"It's work," I said, standing. "On that note, if nobody has anything else to add to the case, I'll be taking off. I should start reading through some of Heinrich's old files before tonight."

"While you do that, I'll pester Asha for a list of Heinrich's old criminal buddies who might've been involved with arson and the like," Jimmy said. "We can swap notes later."

Jimmy and I headed toward the door of Melinda's office, thanking the two doctors on the way. But before I could leave, Melinda called me back.

"Kate, may I have a word alone, please?"

I turned and paused. Dr. Michaelson smoothly slid out of the room. Jimmy followed her. The latch clicked shut behind them.

"A singles' event, huh?" Melinda's manicured nails tapped on her desk. "Interesting."

I crossed my arms. "It's for work, like I said."

"I fully understand that." Melinda gave me a faint smile. "I'm wondering why you were available in the first place."

"It's just any other night to me. I've never celebrated Valentine's Day."

"It's difficult to celebrate when you don't have anyone to celebrate with."

"Not really," I said. "I do pretty good celebrating with a box of chocolates all by my lonesome. I don't even have to share."

"Have you heard from Jack?"

"Why would I have talked to Russo?" I evaded her eye contact. "We've been broken up for a month and a half."

"You've seen him recently."

"Yeah," I agreed.

"You visited him in the hospital after he was shot."

"He saved my life. The least I could do was thank him."

"You haven't checked on him since?"

"He texted me when he was out of the hospital to let me know he was heading home and had a clean bill of health. I replied, and that's been the end of it."

"Uh-huh. And Gem?"

"We haven't talked much," I said. "He left on a two-week business trip to Tokyo."

"So I should read between the lines to understand that in reality, Gem texted you, and you forgot to respond?"

"Something like that." I wrinkled my nose. "But he knows where I stand. I'm not ready for anything. He's giving me my space. He's busy with his business. He's working on something big. He hasn't shared it with me, but he's been crazy busy."

I didn't bother to add that I'd kept up on his travels a little bit, but only because one of my best friends, Erin Lassiter—the popular blogger known as Lassie—made sure her blog posts about the billionaire went directly to my inbox. Somehow she'd made it impossible for me to unsubscribe.

I'd seen Gem in photos boarding private jets, speaking in front of rich-looking investors, out for fancy dinners. I ignored the ones where he was surrounded by beautiful women because, as I'd told Melinda, I'd mostly rejected his advances to be anything more than friends.

Melinda didn't need me to say any of that. She was watching my face. Judging by the knowing look she flashed my way, she understood well enough.

"If you need to come out for drinks after your mixer tonight, I'll set something up with the girls," she offered. "I think most of us are single at the moment, so we could use a big pitcher from Bellini's."

"Why don't you just let me know if there's something I need to know from the lab tonight, eh?"

Melinda stifled a smile. "Aye, aye, Captain."

I gave her a salute and returned to the door. Once again, on the way out, she called my name to stop. I faced her, one foot in the hallway, the other in her office.

"Good luck at the event tonight." She gave a little claw motion with her hands. "Knock 'em dead, tiger."

I couldn't help my laugh. "Too late for that. The victim's already dead."

Melinda looked disappointed, then waved me off. "I'll call you once we confirm his identity. Happy Love Day to you, too, sunshine."

***

I stopped by Asha's desk when I returned upstairs. As I greeted the tech genius, her long, coffin-shaped, black nails never once stopped *tip-tip-tapping* at the computer. Asha's braids swished audibly as she flicked them over her shoulder.

"Hello to you too," she grumbled. "What do you need from me today? Just a note: I'm only working for chocolates. What sort of person dumps a girl two days before Valentine's Day?"

"I'm sorry," I said. "I didn't know you were seeing anyone."

Asha gave an exaggerated sigh. "We'd only been out on three dates, but I was going to offer to cook tonight. I don't even cook. Then I get a text two days ago saying some mumbo jumbo about how I work too much. Do I work too much?"

Asha stared me down. I suspected there was a correct answer to this question.

"You realize I'm probably the wrong person to ask," I said.

"I'm not stupid." She huffed back. "But you were *supposed* to be sympathetic. You really need to work on your bedside manner, Rosetti."

"That sucks?" I offered. "Dude. I'm going to a singles' mixer at a bowling alley tonight. My love life isn't exactly the stuff dreams are made of."

Asha considered my update. Her lips, tinted orange with makeup, turned up in a small smile. "You're right. That makes me feel better. Your love life is a dumpster fire."

"Hey, thanks."

"I'm the one wallowing today," Asha retorted. "I have dibs on wallowing."

"Sorry."

"Give me something to do today, Rosetti. Lots. I want to work until midnight."

"Melinda said she'd meet you guys out at Bellini's."

"Okay, give me work to keep me busy until I can dive into a large margarita headfirst with goggles on."

I filled Asha in on the developments we'd made on the case. She nodded along, promising to get me reports on as many of Heinrich's bowling buddies as she could.

"Has Jimmy talked to you yet?" I asked. "He said he was on his way up here."

"He came up here and walked right by me." Asha rolled her eyes. "Someone brought in some cinnamon rolls. Good detective that he is, he followed the scent right past my desk and into the conference room. Nothing gets by that slugger."

"My nose is ringing," Jimmy said, sidling up behind us. He smelled like a Cinnabon shop. "My ears are ringing? What the hell's the saying?"

"I don't know, but you've got cinnamon on your nose," I said. "I was just filling Asha in on Heinrich."

"Right." Jimmy cleared his throat and tried to look dignified as he brushed a patch of frosting off his upper lip. "We're going to need some details on the guys Heinrich put in prison. Especially those with arson backgrounds."

"Yeah, I'm gonna be able to take you a little more seriously once you don't have powdered sugar on your shirt," Asha grumbled.

Jimmy harrumphed.

"She's sore," I whispered loudly. "She just got dumped."

"Bedside manner," Asha snipped.

"Right. I'm going to pore over some files before I have to shove myself into"—I looked down at my outfit—"apparently something that isn't *this* for tonight."

"Need help?" Asha asked hopefully. "I can pick out something really scandalous for you."

"Nope."

Before Jimmy could team up with Asha in an attempt to strong-arm me into wearing something ridiculous, I took my leave of the tech whiz's desk and marched back to my own. I plopped behind my computer, slipped on some headphones, and sank into the nitty-gritty details of Heinrich's life.

I came out of my self-induced research coma a couple of hours later when Jimmy dropped a sandwich on my desk.

"Happy Valentine's Day," he said. "Eat something so you don't faint."

"Love you too," I said, taking a big bite of the meatball hoagie before slipping my headphones back onto my ears and focusing my attention on Heinrich's long, interesting, and quite controversial career.

I stopped only to read a report that came in from Asha. She'd been able to blitz through her research on Heinrich's bowling buddies. As it turned out, most of his buddies had iron-clad alibis, as they'd all been celebrating at a birthday party together. There were photos with timestamps from social media.

On the other hand, Will Comice was on probation. Her notes made it easy to see that the focus of the evening should land squarely on Comice. According to Asha, he had a real mean streak and had been in and out of trouble with the law his entire life. Seemed one of his ex-girlfriends had gone so far as to file a restraining order on him.

"You know, it's starting to get dark." Jimmy wheeled his chair over next to me. "Also, I've been keeping tabs on the number of times you stepped away from your computer today, and let me just say this: The amount of coffee you drink does not seem to match up with the number of restroom breaks you take. Like, the math confuses my brain."

"Has Asha gotten back to us on the list of guys Heinrich's put away?"

Jimmy shook his head. "She's been focused on the bowling alley guys. I'm assuming you saw her report come through. Speaking of, you do know you're going to have to get going soon so you can make it in time, right?"

"What time is it?" I glanced at the clock. "Crap. I forgot I was going to look at bridesmaid dresses with my sister this evening."

I glanced down at my phone. There was one missed call. If I really flew, I could make it to the dress shop only nine minutes late for our appointment.

"What about the singles' mixer?"

I shot Jimmy a quizzical look. "I've got over an hour before I have to be there. How long does it take to pick out a bridesmaid dress?"

"It seems like you're seriously asking me that question, and I've got to say, Rosetti, I've never worn a bridesmaid dress. I have no clue."

I grabbed my purse and pointed back to my computer as I headed toward the exit. "Tell Asha to look into Charles Randolph."

"Randolph?" Jimmy sat back in his chair. It squeaked under the weight of the extra cinnamon rolls. "Why does that name sound familiar?"

I paused, pulling out my phone to text my sister before answering Jimmy. "He was Heinrich's guy. The one that got away."

"Got away? Where's he now?"

"Heinrich arrested him twice during his career. Randolph was supposed to be serving a long sentence for armed robbery."

"But?"

"He got out of prison early."

"On good behavior?"

"Something that involved an explosion in the prison's kitchen and an escape."

Jimmy's eyebrows shot up. "Promising."

"He got picked up by Heinrich a second time a year or so later. For speeding."

"Ouch. A creative guy like Charles Randolph probably didn't appreciate being picked up for something as bland as having a lead foot."

"Long story short, Randolph got thrown back in prison and served his time. These days he's out on parole."

"When was he released?"

"That's where it gets interesting," I said. "Just a couple of months ago."

"I'll get the bloodhounds on the trail."

"Have Asha send me anything she finds."

"Will do. Send me a selfie from the bowling alley tonight or it didn't happen."

I walked away from Jimmy without a response. The deep roll of his laugh followed me out of the room.

Chapter 5

I parked semi-illegally in front of the dress shop, thinking it would be okay, considering I wasn't planning on staying all that long. The place was a small joint in a little strip mall somewhere near Maplewood Mall. The front of the store was all large glass windows and looping pink text.

Hurrying inside, I caught a whiff of an overpoweringly floral scent along with the rush of warm air. Tulle exploded from hangers on all sides of me. Fake diamonds glittered from tiaras in display cases. I'd normally never be caught dead in one of these shops. The one exception being a favor to my sister.

"Kate." Jane shot a glare in my direction. She dropped her voice to a hiss. "You promised you wouldn't be late."

Both sales ladies on the floor pretended not to hear. I gave an apologetic shrug back at my sister.

"Sorry. Dead guy."

Jane's cheeks bloomed pink. She gave a side-eyed glance at the sales ladies and mumbled something about my career choices. Louder, she said, "My sister's a cop. A really good detective, actually."

Both sales ladies made noises in their throat that sounded somewhat optimistic, as if that was the most enthusiasm they could muster for talk of dead guys in a bridal shop.

"Right. Then let's get this show on the road." Jane clapped her hands and smiled around. "Gloria, this is my sister, Kate, as you might have gathered. She's my maid of honor. We're looking for a dress for her today."

The older of the two women, the one presumably named Gloria, offered a more welcoming smile in my direction. "Wonderful. It's lovely to meet you."

"I'm sorry to cut this thing short," I said, glancing at my watch, "but I've got about forty-five minutes before I have to be out of here."

Jane's eyebrows pulled together. "Excuse me?!"

"Something came up."

"Something related to work?" Jane's fingers began trembling.

"Um..." I suspected with every wrong answer I gave, something else on Jane would start trembling until she exploded with anger. "Actually, it's sort of a Valentine's Day thing."

"Huh?" The silk fabric dripping from between Jane's fingertips floated to the floor.

"Valentine's Day," I repeated. "You know, the dumb holiday with Cupid and hearts."

"Right. I'm well aware," Jane said. "I wasn't sure you knew the definition."

"I've got plans."

"You do?"

"You sound shocked."

"Forgive me," Jane drawled, "but I'm absolutely speechless."

"There's this singles' mixer that I got roped into attending."

Understanding dawned on Jane's face. "It's something to do with the case, isn't it?"

"Jane—"

"Forget it. You don't have to try on dresses today."

"No, Jane, I really want to," I said. "I wanted to be here for you. Look, I can skip the singles' mixer tonight. We can stay as long as you want."

"No. You know what, I'll just do like you said and pick a dress I like. I know your size, probably better than you do. I'll just have it shipped to your house."

"Wait—"

"That was what you'd suggested in the first place, wasn't it? That way, 'I'd get what I wanted'? Well, newsflash, Kate: the only reason I wanted to come looking with you was because I thought it'd be a fun sisterly bonding activity. I mean, you only get married once, right?" She looked down. "Have a good time tonight. Maybe you'll meet someone. Like a murderer."

Then Jane stormed out of the shop. I cleared my throat in her absence. Gloria went back to arranging cathedral veils.

"I'll apologize to her later," I said, not quite sure why I felt obligated to share these details with a couple of strangers. "It really is important that I go to this mixer."

"More important than your sister's wedding?" Gloria didn't look at me. "It does only happen once, if you're lucky."

"I'm sorry I was late." I felt uncomfortable but also couldn't bring myself to walk away from the situation. "But I think she overreacted a little bit. My job is incredibly important."

"More important than your sister's wedding?"

"I get it. That's important too. Family first. I get it," I reiterated. "But somebody blew up a cop today, and that person is still walking around on the streets."

Gloria froze, and for a second, I thought I had her in my sights. Then she just turned and shot me a disappointed look.

"I'm sure there are plenty of murderers walking the streets this very second," she said reasonably, as if discussing the weather. "This one can't wait for an hour or two while your sister selects a dress for you?"

I swallowed hard. It wasn't the answer I'd been expecting. Not only did it throw me for a bit of a loop, but it had me second-guessing everything. Then again, the pit in my stomach had already tipped me off that I owed my sister an apology. A big one.

"I wouldn't chase after her now," Gloria said, watching me glance toward the door of my car as if for an escape. "She told me she has plans with her fiancé for Valentine's Day. I'd let her enjoy her evening. Or at least salvage what's left of it."

"You really do a number with your guilt trips," I said, annoyed she knew more about my sister's plans than I did.

She gave me a knowing little grin. "Why do you think I do so well on commission?"

I couldn't help but laugh at her sly little expression. "In that case, Gloria, I've got a challenge for you. I need something reasonably un-embarrassing for a singles' mixer that I'm due at soon. Got anything on your clearance racks?"

She pulled out lipstick and applied it like she was preparing for battle. "You're in good hands, sweet cheeks."

***

There were about seven more ruffles than I would've liked on the dress that Gloria insisted I purchase. I was pretty certain the saleswoman was giving me a little karma by putting me in something she knew I'd hate. But at the end of the day, she'd gotten a sale on an ugly dress, and I'd gotten a cheap outfit that prevented me from having to drive all the way home before heading to the bowling alley.

I made it to Leitner's Lanes just as the mixer was getting underway. The turnout was slightly better than abysmal. There were about twelve people already in attendance, including Lori, who was bustling about the refreshments table shuffling around the same cookies I was pretty sure had been there since this morning.

"So, you're single, huh?" A guy sidled up to me. "Are you an angel?"

I glared at him. "No, I didn't fall from heaven. But I can make you see stars if you'd like."

"Is that a pickup line?" He looked confused. The sticker on his shirt declared his name to be BIG HANK.

I twisted my lips into a smirk. "More like a threat."

"This party blows." Big Hank took off, brushing past me and leaving through the front doors.

"I really can't have you scaring away my guests." Lori scurried up to me and blinked through long, false lashes that had been applied just a little bit lopsided. "There aren't that many to scare away in the first place."

"I didn't—"

"I know I said you should wear something different, but..." Lori studied my ruffles. "Never mind. At least you're here. There's something I wanted to tell you, something I remembered after your visit this morning. I've been thinking about Mr. Heinrich all day. It just sort of popped into my head."

"Okay," I said. "What is it?"

"Come to the front desk," she said. "Pretend you're signing in. It will look less suspicious."

As I jotted my signature down in the book, a completely illegible one, Lori whispered across the desk, "Do you remember how I told you that Heinrich has only missed league night, like, one time ever?"

"Sure. And that was the year someone else won?"

"Yes. The important part of the story, the part I didn't think about until later, was who won that year. A guy by the name of Billy Burton."

I jotted the name down in the notepad app on my phone. "What made you think about Burton?"

"The reason that Heinrich was in the hospital was because he needed surgery on his leg. He got hit by a car, leaving his house, on the way to the bowling alley."

"Ouch."

"Broke it in three places. He was bowling on crutches for months."

"Um, well, it's no wonder he lost."

"Right?"

"Are you suggesting that Billy Burton might have been responsible for the accident?"

"It's not me saying that; it's the rumors." Lori fluttered her wonky eyelashes. "The whole incident was before my time here, which is why I didn't remember right away. I just heard the stories about it. But word on the street was that there might've been some foul play involved."

"Let me guess, Billy Burton was the subject of these rumors?"

Lori glanced over her tray of appetizers to the rest of the lanes. "I'm just relaying what I heard. The guys here get pretty competitive. Seeing as he swooped in and won that year, it's suspicious."

"Burton?"

She nodded. "He hasn't been back to Leitner's Lanes since he collected his prize that year. I've never actually met him. He's just got his picture on the wall."

Lori walked me around the front desk and took me to a billiard room where photographs of all the previous league winners lined the wall. A man I presumed was Billy Burton was sandwiched in a sea of Heinrich photographs.

"Mr. Heinrich had the same photograph used every time he won the league," Lori said, gesturing at four of the exact same pictures of Heinrich on the wall. "We offer a free portrait session of the winner with their trophy to go on the wall. He always refused. Finally, Marshall just pulled an old image from the newspaper to use because Mr. Heinrich wasn't cooperating. Mr. Heinrich hated this display."

"I'm getting the vibe he liked to keep a low profile."

"I guess you could say that," she said. "But speaking of low profiles, I don't believe your dress fits the criteria. Maybe I could just, like, snip off a few of those ruffles?"

I held my arms up. "Go wild."

A few less ruffles and a few more jagged edges later, I returned to the scene of the singles' party. Lori had pointed out some of Heinrich's regular bowling buddies. Will Comice, the reportedly skeezy bowler on probation, was busy single-handedly draining the spiked punch bowl.

"A pretty lady like you must want some punch." Without waiting for me to confirm or deny his hypothesis, Will filled a plastic cup of punch. A little liquid sloshed over the edge as he handed it to me. "Tell me how a pretty gal like you ended up single on Valentine's Day."

I gave him a flimsy smile. "I'm getting over a breakup."

Will looked significantly more enticed. "You must be really torn up. I'm a great listener. I offer exceptional comfort—emotional and otherwise."

It was all I could do not to roll my eyes until they got stuck in the back of my head. Lori was hovering nearby, stacking and unstacking the same cookies. They had to have her fingerprints all over them by now. It really was fortunate that nobody was eating any of them.

"It's okay. I have a license to carry," I said, unable to resist. "My firearm offers me as much comfort as I need."

Lori froze. I could tell she was getting nervous I'd expose myself too early. I took a cue from Lori's wonky lashes and fluttered my own, hopefully less wonky, eyelashes in Will's direction.

"I'm just kidding. I mean, I do like to take to the range every now and again, single woman that I am. But it's nice to have the protection of a man too."

I felt a little sick to my stomach. Lori eased, and I was pretty sure I'd said the right thing. Will was looking at me like I was a Thanksgiving feast. Everything about this event was gross, from the cookies to my battered dress to Will's smile.

"I hear you're quite the bowler," I said, swiftly handing my punch glass to Lori when Will wasn't looking. I felt the splash as she tossed it surreptitiously into the nearest trash can. "How long until your picture's on the wall of fame in there?"

I nodded to the billiard room. Will winked at me and puffed his chest out like a sort of drunk penguin.

"Not long now, baby. This is my year. I can feel it."

"Oh really?"

"Yeah, though competition is stiff this year."

"Stiff like rigor mortis?" I mumbled, then louder I said, "That's what I hear. Looks like that one guy—what's his face—has his name on the wall a couple of times in a row."

"Let's just say I don't think he's going to be a problem this year."

"Is that right?"

Will looked a little uncertain. "I mean, I just think he's not as good as he's cracked up to be."

"Because he's dead?" I muttered again, unable to help myself.

"What's that?"

"I said the competition's dead in the water with you playing, I'm sure." I waved a hand at him. "Just look at you. I don't know how anyone can compete when you have such a...bowler's physique."

Will preened, catching a glimpse of himself in the dirty mirror behind the front desk. "Yeah, all those years at the bowling alley really add up."

All the beers and tater tots, I thought, feeling pretty proud I'd managed to actually keep my mouth shut this time.

"Who's the fellow who won, anyway?" I glanced around at the other guys in the lane. "Is he here tonight?"

Obviously feeling the sting of competition, Will's eyes blazed an inferno. "Of course not. The idiot's only here on game night. And his practice nights, but whatever."

"Is he single?"

"What the hell does it matter? He's an idiot anyway. He's married to his bowling balls."

"I guess that's why he's the reigning champ." I was pick, pick, picking away at Will's breaking point. The alcohol in his system had lowered the bar significantly. I could tell he was getting close to bursting. "Plus, he's sort of handsome. Must be humble, too, not wanting a new picture taken with all the different times he's won."

"He's freaking old," Will said. "What's Heinrich got, like, thirty years on you?"

"I'm just saying—"

"The dude's not going to be an issue this year. I've got it in the bag. I made sure of it."

"How sure?" I asked. "Like, did you put him in a body bag?"

Will hesitated, the expression on his face a little maniacal. He seemed to bring himself back down to earth, fighting against the fuzziness from the punch, attempting to keep a straight face.

"What'd you say your name was anyway? You're sick," he said. "What sort of joke is that?"

"Not really a joke," I said. "And you didn't ask my name. Though I'm pretty sure you could tell me my bra size with how much you've been staring at my chest."

Will had to yank his gaze up. He flushed.

"The name's Kate Rosetti, but you can call me Detective Rosetti."

"Huh?" Will grunted, staring in confusion at me. "Why would I call you..."

"I'll be here waiting while you connect the dots." I pulled my badge out of my bra. I tapped it against my hand until I saw the understanding dawn in his eyes. "That's right. Detective Rosetti with the TC Task Force. I investigate homicides in your neck of the woods."

"But nobody's dead yet."

I blinked. "Excuse me?"

"I said..." Will realized what he'd said. It was obvious alarms were blaring full force inside his head. "I said nobody's dead. So why would a homicide detective be crashing this stupid party?"

"Uh-huh."

"Hey, Lori, this chick says she's a detective," Will called over my shoulder to Lori who'd gone still and pale as she perched over the sign-in log. "I think she's a fake entry into your singles' party. Does anyone know if this chick is actually even single?"

"Because that's definitely the biggest issue here," I said, "whether or not I'm single."

"Well?" Will bugged his eyes at me. "Are you?"

I flashed my badge at Lori. "He's right," I said to her. "I am a detective. I'm sorry for crashing your party."

"What?" Lori blinked again. One of her eyelashes fell off. It really played up the effect of her being startled. She squeaked, "Why, I had no idea you were law enforcement!"

"I was undercover," I added, watching Lori relax at the same rate Will seemed to be growing angrier. "I'm investigating the murder of Detective Heinrich. We know he liked to hang out here." I turned back to Will. "We know you bowled in the same league as him. Now, I'd like you to come with me down to the station to answer a few questions."

"Aw, man, it's Valentine's Day," Will groaned. "The party was just picking up steam. Sally Monrovia was supposed to come by later."

"Sally's going to have to wait," I said. "You've got a date with me at the precinct."

"But—"

"Unless you want me to arrest you, I suggest you come willingly so we can have a nice discussion over cut-out heart cookies."

Will looked longingly at the bowling lanes. Then he looked at me. "So are you actually single or not?"

Chapter 6

I called for a squad car to come and collect Will Comice from the bowling alley. When it arrived, I staunchly ignored the officers' smirks as they caught a glimpse of me in my dumb dress. Once I was sure Will was tucked into the cruiser, I dialed Jimmy on my cell.

"Don't worry," Jimmy answered, "you don't owe me a selfie."

"Huh?"

"Officer Pete Winkler texted me a picture of you in the dress. It's too good to be a fake. I believe you were there."

I grunted at him, swearing I'd get revenge on Pete Winkler, a cop that'd been helping us out while we were stretched thin with cases, at the next opportunity. Then I gave Jimmy the lowdown on my evening with the bowlers—everything from my conversation with Will Comice to the rumors floating around about Billy Burton.

"I'm going to head to the precinct to question Will tonight," I said. "I don't have any plans anyway. Don't feel obligated to come down."

"Are you sure?"

"I know you and the wife have plans. I'd hate to get on her naughty list by interrupting."

"You know I'd come down if you needed me, but she got me this amazing gift. It's a bouquet of flowers made out of meat. Can you believe it? Little salamis wrapped into roses on beef jerky stems."

"You enjoy," I said. "I don't honestly think Will's our guy."

"Do you think he knew something?"

"I think it's possible, and that's what I intend to find out. I just don't see him as the mastermind behind a bomb. He's got plenty of red flags, but I don't think arson is one of them."

"You really do have sweet stuff on the mind today."

"I practically got thrown out of my own bridesmaid dress shopping date. I got hit on by a jerk. Freaking Pete Winkler documented my dumb dress, and I'm sure everyone and the chief's mother is going to have my picture as their screensaver by morning. I'm not in the best frame of mind right now."

"Call me if you need an assist with Comice."

"I'll let you know how the interview goes."

I cruised back to my place. My little house in the West Seventh neighborhood of St. Paul was mere minutes from the precinct on a good day. On a bad day, it was twelve minutes. I parked on the street since I hadn't shoveled my driveway in—well, most of the winter—and crossed my fingers that the snowplows wouldn't come by in the next few minutes and block me in.

Hopping out, I made my way to my front door, shivering in my short dress and winter jacket. I had my key in the lock when I froze. I had my gun out in three seconds flat. I stepped back against the side of the door and waited, holding my breath, as the door opened without my having to do a thing.

"Stop," I hollered. "Hands up. I've got a gun and—"

"Dang it, Kate!" Jane's shrill voice pierced the air.

A liquid slopped at my feet, stinging my cold legs with splashes of something hot. I had my gun dropped by my side in a heartbeat, though my pulse was still racing.

"Jane, what in the ever-loving world are you doing at my house?" I asked. "How'd you get in?"

"The key," she said, holding it in my face. "The key you gave me, for crying out loud. You said I could come and go as I pleased."

"Right. But you don't live here anymore. You have to admit it was a little bit of a surprise to see you coming out of my house."

"Dude. You have issues. Most people don't walk up to their house armed. How many murderers do you have stalking you, anyway?"

"I thought you had plans with Wes," I said. "Gloria told me—"

"Oh, you and Gloria had a nice chat at the bridal shop without me, did you?" Jane gave me a once-over. "Is that your maid-of-honor dress? I hope you didn't have them alter that because those cuts are horribly uneven, and I'm rethinking having them work on my wedding dress."

"You're not explaining anything," I said. "Why are you here? What happened with Wes?"

"Nothing happened with Wes," she said crossly. "I had this time blocked off to shop for your dress, remember? He didn't expect me for another hour or two at the earliest."

"And you just decided to swing by my house for a..." I hesitated, glancing at the travel mug in her hand. "For a cup of coffee?"

"Aren't you supposed to be chasing some killer dude?"

"I'm on my way to the precinct to interview a suspect. You'll understand why I have to change." I gestured to myself. "Awful alterations and all."

Jane finally gave me a flicker of a smile. "I just stopped by for a second, okay?"

"Why?"

"Stop ruining everything! Cripes!" She stomped down the front steps. "Bye."

I waited as she stalked off to her new car. I wasn't used to seeing the shiny Range Rover around. Wes had bought it for my sister shortly after their engagement. It made me happy that my sister was finally with a man who was dedicated to making her life better.

Jane got into her car, then waited for another vehicle to cruise by. She gave the other driver a wave and then curved into the street without a backward glance in my direction.

"Well, that was..." I stared into the silent, snowy night. "That was weird. Right?"

I looked around, pretty sure I was officially going a little bit nuts as I conversed with my lonesome.

"Okay," I said, turning to my front door. "Well then."

I pushed open the door, which hadn't yet gotten locked, and set my purse on the front table. I kept my gun with me. Just in case.

Something smelled off about my house. I paused, took a sniff. It wasn't coffee, which had been my first thought after Jane had splashed java on my leg. I took another sniff and relaxed. It was a little bit floral, and I realized it was likely the perfume from the dress shop clinging to my mutilated bridesmaid outfit. After the day I'd had, I was getting a little jumpy. I relaxed my gun arm again.

I took another step into the living room, surprised it was so dark. "Come on, Jane," I muttered. "Isn't it the first rule of single-womanhood to leave a light on when you're not home?"

"That would be my fault."

A deep, rumbling voice just about sent me skyrocketing into space. My gun was raised a second later as I ducked off to the side of the room.

Then a man cleared his throat. Half a second later, the living room blazed into an angelic, yellow hued glow as the person standing before me pressed a button on a remote control.

"You have got to stop pointing that thing at me." Alastair Gem gave me a cocky little smile.

"You have got to stop asking for it." I placed my gun in the locked drawer at the entryway. "What is all this, anyway?"

"It's Valentine's Day."

Gem left it at that, giving me a moment to let my racing heart recover and resume its thudding at a more manageable rate. I took a few deep breaths and realized that the floral scent I'd gotten a whiff of upon entry into my house wasn't, in fact, leftover perfume from the dress shop. Any perfume on my person was now masked by the dozens of roses that had been stuffed into my living room.

The yellow glow came from hundreds of teeny-tiny fairy lights that had been strung across the ceiling, down the walls, around my fireplace. In lieu of overhead ceiling lights, Gem and I stood encased in a halo of magical glow surrounded by the overpowering scent of a garden full of roses.

"What is this, Gem?" I echoed, my voice a mere whisper. "I thought—"

I swallowed. I was going to say I thought we'd agreed to keep things as friends, to move slowly. Instead, I changed course mid-sentence.

"I thought you were in Tokyo."

Gem looked slightly disappointed. "I just got in. I was going to call you when my plane landed, but then..." He let his hands limply gesture to the room around him. He looked the slightest bit uncertain.

"But then you thought you'd flood my house with flowers and fairy lights?"

Gem reached over and lifted up an ornately decorated box. "And chocolates?"

I tried not to smile. "I thought you were trying to be normal."

"It's Valentine's Day. Flowers and chocolates *are* normal."

"Yeah. Like, one flower. Or a bouquet—singular. A box of crappy chocolates picked up at CVS on the way home from work."

Gem sniffed with amusement. "Yeah, same sort of thing."

He waited a beat. I waited a beat. I wasn't sure where we were supposed to go from here. Did he expect me to fly into his arms, crumpling into a mushy mess because of his lavish display? If he did, then he didn't know me very well.

"Come on Kate, relax." Gem tossed the chocolates back on the table. "The chocolates are a pilot we're running with Gem Industries. We're entering into a new line of business."

"Candy?"

"Fine chocolates and sweets."

"Huh," I said, glancing down at the box and realizing it did, indeed, have Gem Industry's signature logo embossed on the front in an elegant silver design. "So this is technically market research, then. Strictly business. You'd like my opinion because of my very advanced palate for fine chocolates."

"You drink coffee from a police precinct," Gem deadpanned. "That's where taste buds go to die. I do worry about your palate, but I've never doubted your love of chocolate."

He ran a hand through his hair, which was shorter than it'd been the last time I'd seen him. He looked sharp in his designer suit. I reminded myself he hadn't dressed up for me. He'd just flown into the country on a private jet after having meetings with other billionaires.

His eyes were the same gorgeous blue, his lips twitching into the same mischievous smile that I suspected he'd worn as a little boy. That was the thing about Gem—his personality burned with an inextinguishable fire. Reluctantly, if I were to admit the truth, I'd have to say his amusement at simply being alive was growing on me.

Gem raised his hand, reinforcing his command to encourage me to relax.

"I didn't buy you flowers so you'd melt into a weepy puddle in my embrace." He paused, crooked an eyebrow, and waited with an impish grin. "Though, if you'd like to surprise me, feel free."

I burst out in a laugh. The adrenaline, the murder, the crappy day I'd had...it had all added up. I wiped my eyes, unable to stop laughing.

"I know you're going to say I went above and beyond, that I'm using my money to impress you, blah, blah, blah." Gem made a talking motion with his hand. "That's not it. Look, Kate, every woman deserves some flowers and chocolate on Valentine's Day."

"But—"

"*Every* woman," he reiterated. "I don't care if the woman gets them from her best friend, her sister, her lover. I don't care if she buys the damn chocolates herself, but every woman deserves a little something to mark the occasion."

"How noble of you."

"I knew you wouldn't buy yourself chocolates, so I just did my civic duty to help you out." He paused, feigning concern. "Do you think I could add it to my tax write-off, seeing as you're an upstanding police officer and all?"

"Thank you for the chocolates, and congratulations on your new business venture. The flowers are beautiful. The lights... Well, the lights are a lot."

"It said they were a shade of flickering romance on the box."

"You're a sucker for some good marketing."

"Don't tell me you're one of those people who thinks Valentine's Day is a Hallmark holiday."

"No comment."

We stared at each other for another moment.

"Welcome back, Gem."

"I missed you, Kate."

I cleared my throat. "Would you like a chocolate?"

"One of my own chocolates?" He grinned. "Is that an invitation to stay?"

"For the road."

"And here I thought you dressed up just for me." Gem's eyes roved over my bridesmaid dress.

"This getup is actually for a suspect," I admitted. "A suspect I need to interview at the precinct tonight."

"Ah."

"The case just came in today. It's sort of a high-priority murder."

"They always are. Anyone I might know?"

"What makes you ask that?"

Gem shrugged. "This is what small talk with a homicide detective looks like."

"I can't comment on an active investigation."

Gem gave a nod. He shoved his hands into his pockets and looked around the love-bedazzled room. "Then I should be going home. I've got some jet lag to get rid of anyway."

A part of me, a large part of me, wanted to stop him from leaving. To offer him a hot chocolate or a drink of water or, God forbid, an actual glass of wine. But in the back of my brain, I saw an interview room down at the precinct.

I'd already strong-armed Will Comice into joining me voluntarily at the precinct on shaky grounds at best. We still didn't have a positive ID on the body I presumed to be Heinrich. I had to get to Will and find out what I could before we lost him. Before his Valentine's Day punch-induced fuzziness cleared and left him asking for a lawyer.

"I'm sorry."

"Don't apologize," Gem said. "This wasn't meant to be anything big."

"And yet..." I gestured to the roses around me.

"If anyone deserves something a little grandiose, without it being grandiose or romantic," he added quickly, "it's you. Doing your duty to save the world one ugly murder at a time. Seems an extra shame to hear about a death on Valentine's Day."

"Everyone is saying that. It's just another day."

"If you say so." Gem headed toward the door.

I followed him, lingering as he pulled it open and stood halfway between the glowing warmth of my house and the chilly darkness beyond.

"Good night, then, Detective."

Gem faced me, the sweet twinkle in his eye just inches from me. He smelled fresh and lovely, and not at all like he'd just gotten off a very long international flight. I swallowed hard.

"Hey, Gem," I called as he took a step down the stairs.

He paused, an eyebrow raised as he turned back, a hopeful smile twitching his lips upward.

"Thanks," I murmured, feeling just the tiniest bit heartbroken at the fact that I couldn't offer him more. That I couldn't ask him to stay, that I couldn't reach out and brush a kiss against his cheek or give his hand a squeeze. "For this. I mean it."

His faced settled into a perfectly contented expression. "Anytime."

Then he was gone, hopping into a car that was driven by someone else. I wasn't even sure the wheels had come to a full stop before Gem was inside, the door slamming shut behind him, the driver pressing the gas pedal and whisking him away in the night.

I turned back to my house and surveyed the damage. The beautiful, complicated, messy damage. I didn't want to think about how many dollars were currently wilting in my living room. I did, however, rip open the box of chocolates and help myself to a couple of nut clusters. It was a major step up from the offerings at the singles' mixer, and I was delayed in realizing that I'd missed any semblance of dinner.

Then I cursed under my breath and jogged upstairs. I pulled on jeans, a sweater, and more sensible boots. I jogged back downstairs and wrapped myself in a winter jacket. My gun, badge, and the partially emptied box of chocolates were added to my collection before I headed outside and locked the door behind me.

***

The second I entered the interview room, I could tell the fuzziness from the spiked punch at Leitner's Lanes was wearing off on Comice. If I had to guess, it was leaving Will with a sugar-induced headache. A headache worsened by the fact that he was sitting across a table from me in a concrete box instead of lounging in bed with Sally Monrovia between soft sheets.

"Is that a box of chocolates?"

I hadn't even sat down before Will's eyes narrowed in on the box I'd tucked under my arm. I'd been in such a hurry to get to him that I hadn't even stopped by my desk to drop my stuff off. I unzipped my jacket and took my time responding.

"I was promised cookies," Will said grumpily. "Cut-out cookies."

"These are mine."

"You promised. Not to mention, you ruined my Valentine's Day. And I'm here voluntarily. Unless you want me to call my lawyer..."

I slid the box of chocolates across the desk to him. "Leave the ones with the coconut for me. They're my favorite."

Will leaned over and delicately picked out all the chocolates with coconut in them. Then he slid the box back to me.

I picked out another nut cluster, sat back in my chair, and waited for him to chomp down on his selection. Then I grinned. "Thanks. I've always hated coconut."

Will looked even more annoyed, but before he could threaten again with the lawyer talk, I continued in a more amiable tone.

"I really am sorry for interrupting your night. I recognize you're here of your own good will—"

Will glared, popping a chocolate into his mouth. "You sorta threatened me."

"I made a suggestion, and you took it. I appreciate it," I said. "I just want to get an idea about how you knew that Heinrich was dead."

Of course, even I didn't know for a fact that Heinrich was dead, but he didn't need to know that. If Will Comice wanted to fess up to the crime beforehand, I wasn't going to hold him back.

"He's really dead?"

I just smiled and let him fill in the blanks of my silence however he wanted.

"Holy moly." Will rubbed his head. "I didn't think he'd really do it."

"Who?"

"Billy Burton."

I blinked. "Billy Burton told you he was going to kill Heinrich?"

"Not in so many words." He shifted uncomfortably. "Am I going to get in trouble for knowing about it? I didn't do anything. I told him no."

"You're cooperating with the police," I said, again being as noncommittal as possible. "That's a very good look for you. Trust me, you're going to want to have me on your side when this case gets to court. Detective Heinrich was a former local cop. There are going to be people watching this case closely. Tell me about Burton. I thought he didn't bowl with you guys anymore."

"Nah. He likes to win too much. He joined the old-farts' league up in Roseville because he knows he can win it. Fact of the matter is nobody can beat Heinrich."

"Except the year he got into an accident. Do you happen to know anything about that accident?"

"I see you know a little bit about our bowling league." Will's eyes sharpened. He glanced at my box of chocolates again. I slid him over a wrapped caramel which seemed to satisfy him. "You've done your homework."

As Will chomped, I glanced down at an incoming call on my phone. I hadn't seen the name pop up in quite some time. I got a chill as I silenced Russo's name and turned back to Will, trying to keep my thoughts in order.

"It's my job. Tell me about the rumors that suggest Heinrich's accident wasn't really an accident."

"I had nothing to do with that, but I did hear the rumors."

"Any chance Billy—or someone close to him—confirmed the rumors to be true?"

Comice shook his head. "It was on the hush-hush, but I wouldn't be surprised. Billy was on his way to losing the league, and he hates losing. Bet he figured a little love tap to Heinrich's leg would give him the advantage he needed to pull ahead."

"A love tap with a car?"

"It's Valentine's Day. I'm playing into the theme. Speaking of, when am I going to get out of here? I'm still hoping to meet with Sally tonight."

"Depends on how quickly you're going to tell me the truth. How'd you know about Heinrich's death before anyone else?"

He leaned forward and dropped his voice. "Billy was mentioning something about how it'd be nice if Heinrich just disappeared. So when it actually happened, I realized he might've actually been serious."

I frowned. "Heinrich didn't disappear."

"I mean, he's dead. I thought you were a cop. Making someone disappear means... Well, you know what it means."

"Still, he didn't technically disappear. He was blown to smithereens, but there's enough left of him to make an ID on the body."

"Then I guess whoever did the deed wasn't very good at their job, were they?" Will paled at my description. "Someone really nailed him with a bomb, huh?"

"Where were you last night?"

Will studied me carefully. The alcohol was definitely leaving his system. A shrewdness was beginning to take over. "Do you have a specific time?"

"Sunday night," I repeated. "Did you have plans?"

"I was at home," he said. "Alone. I had big plans for tonight. Then again, I guess I ended up alone with a pretty woman and the threat of handcuffs. Just would've been a lot more fun if it'd happened in the bedroom."

"We're done here." I stood. "I wouldn't get any ideas about leaving town. You're not off the hook just yet."

He winked at me. "I knew you'd be back for seconds. Don't worry, honey, I'll be around, but you'll have to get in line."

I stalked out of the interview room, leaving Will smirking behind me. My stomach was swirling with a gross mixture of sugar and disgust.

"Hey, are those chocolates?" Officer Pete Winkler glanced at the box under my arm. "Do you think—"

I glared at him and then shoved the box of chocolates into his outstretched hands. "Enjoy. Comice had his paws all over them."

I huffed past Winkler and headed to my desk. I plopped down, typed up a quick report on my findings for the day, and dashed it off to the chief and Asha. I suspected they'd both be rolling their eyes at my sending emails this late on Valentine's Day night, but I had nothing better to do.

Despite the beautiful display in my living room, I was hesitant to go home. Ironically, seeing the lavish gift would only make me think more about everything I was missing.

I'd also been deftly ignoring the blinking light on my phone that designated the fact I had a message waiting for me. Russo calling on Valentine's Day meant only one thing: complications. I wouldn't even presume to know what he was calling about. A part of me hoped it was regarding work. A part of me suspected it wasn't.

On an impulse, I hit dial to listen to my voicemail. Jack's voice slid across my receiver in the way I remembered. Low, confident, a little bit husky.

"Hey, Kate. I'm sorry to call so late on a day... Well, today of all days. I just had something I wanted to discuss with you when you have a minute. Call me back when you can. Thanks."

The vagueness piqued my curiosity. Between Gem's surprise visit and now Jack's intriguing voicemail, I felt jittery and off-balanced. I was pretty sure the lack of dinner and infusion of chocolate wasn't helping.

"I'm going home," I called to Winkler. "Do you have everything under control here?"

"Got it," he called back. "Happy Valentine's Day, Rosetti."

I hopped in my car, tucking my jacket behind me. I glanced at my dashboard and saw I needed gas. Following another impulse, I headed into the gas station and perused their disturbingly limited selection of weird hot dogs and fake cheese. Then I helped myself to two cheesy gas station hot dogs.

I brought both to the register. The woman working, an older woman with a name tag that said Doris, gave me a sad smile.

"You know what goes really well with that?" she asked gently. "A big box of red wine. We've got one in the back. Really cheap stuff. Guaranteed to burn off any bacteria you're getting from the hot dogs."

"As appetizing as that is, I'm okay, thanks."

I gathered my things and returned to the car. Doris gave me a sad little wave as I scooted away. I tried to ignore her while simultaneously taking a bite of my surprisingly tasty hot dog. I guess four pounds of grease and a small volcano of nacho cheese was enough to mask any other flavors pulling through.

I had polished off both hot dogs by the time I got home, hoping the calories would help settle my nerves and calm the anxiety coursing through my bloodstream. It helped mildly, mostly by way of distraction. It was hard to focus on my anxiety with a stomach growling like a rabid animal.

Heading upstairs, I took a shower to scrub off the hot dog grease and the Will Comice germs, then threw on some freshly laundered pajamas and climbed into bed. I could smell the roses downstairs. I wasn't sure if it was the scent of the roses or the aftereffects of the hot dogs making me feel a little nauseous. Or the fact that I was inexplicably tense about what Russo wanted to discuss.

I reached for my phone and dialed. It was late but not so late that I'd imagine Russo to be in bed. I waited, holding my breath, as the phone rang through to voicemail. A perfect symbol of our relationship. Important things to discuss, never having the time to discuss them.

"Hey, Jack, it's me," I said. "Just returning your call. I guess... Try me again sometime. Okay. Well, good night. Or Happy Valentine's Day. Or whatever. Okay, bye."

I hung up, put my phone on silence, and tried to force myself into sleep before Jack had the chance to call me back.

Chapter 7

I needn't have worried. The next morning I woke up to a phone free of cryptic voicemails. The only notifications I had were from my colleagues who had things to discuss about the case. A welcome relief.

Before I made it into the office, there was one uncomfortable thing I needed to address first. That would be my sister.

I quickly texted Wes and asked if my sister was home with him. I wasn't entirely certain Jane would respond to my messages, and I didn't want to alert her to my apology ambush. Wes responded that she was home but wouldn't be awake for another half hour at least. I told him I'd be stopping by but not to alert her about my visit. He gave me the thumbs-up emoji. Simple, direct, easy to work with. I liked Wes more and more.

Despite having showered the night before, I headed to the bathroom for a quick rinse to start the day on the right foot. I toweled off, dismayed at the reflection that stared back at me in the mirror. My eyes were beyond red, and the skin beneath was swollen and strange looking. I looked like I had demon eyes.

I sighed, grateful I'd done my interview with Will Comice the night before. Nobody would take me seriously looking like this. I prayed that popping a couple of Benadryl would take things down a notch before I made it to the precinct or, God forbid, had to head out on another interview.

After rooting around in my medicine cabinet for a while, I realized that the Benadryl would unfortunately have to wait. Ever since Jane had moved out of my house, things were starting to go out of stock more and more. I hadn't realized that Jane had been replenishing things like hand soap and toilet paper. Things had just magically started refilling while she'd been living here, and it was just one extra reason I missed having her in the house. Aside from her company, of course.

As I headed to my car, I tried to take stock of everything I'd been exposed to the night before. Could it have been the gas station hot dogs sending me into allergy mode? The shampoo Jane had left behind in the shower that had a hibiscus flower on the outside? Maybe one of the chocolates I'd eaten? Perhaps the perfume on my awful dress had triggered some sort of reaction from my body—as if my body was revolting against having to wear such an atrocious item.

I popped into CVS and grabbed two packs of Benadryl to be safe. And a pack of doughnuts. I already had demon eyes, so drugstore doughnuts had nothing on me this morning. As I checked out, the lady gave me a sympathetic look.

"Rough Valentine's?" she asked.

"Something like that."

I grabbed my stuff, made it to my car, and washed down half a doughnut and a Benadryl with a swig of flat Diet Coke. Before heading into the office, I made a detour as promised toward the place Wes now shared with my sister. I passed a Caribou Coffee on the way and grabbed two large lattes, seeing as I couldn't show up at my sister's door empty handed. And it spared me from the office sludge and my mother's questions. Wins all around.

I knocked on the door a couple of times before it was pulled open by my sister. She looked grumpy. Pulling a pink robe tighter around her yellow pajamas, the sunny pajamas I never thought I'd miss seeing around my place, I offered her the latte without a word.

"Well, I'm out of here." Wes squeezed around his fiancée, giving Jane a sweet little kiss on the forehead. He took one glance at me, did a double take, and just about tripped on his way down the front steps. "You okay, Kate?"

"Just another day in paradise." I gave him a tight smile.

"Right." He gave a little salute and couldn't stop staring at my bloodshot eyes. "Well, okay then. Have a good day." Almost as an afterthought, he paused, then asked, "You're not contagious, are you?"

"Nope," I said, gently pressing the inflamed skin around my eyes. "Pretty sure it's an allergic reaction."

"Sure is," Jane drawled, reaching forward to pluck the latte out of my hand. "She's allergic to love."

"On that note, I'm out. Have a great day, ladies. Jane, I'm making dinner tonight, don't forget. Seven o'clock."

"If you mean you're bringing home takeout and secretly dumping it onto our fine china, I'm here for it." Jane raised her cup. "How about sushi from that new place by your office?"

Wes winked. "You got it, babe."

I made a little noise of approval in my throat as Wes headed off to the office. Whatever his office was for the day. I couldn't keep up. I knew he worked for Gem in many capacities, but I was never sure what he was managing on any given day.

"Aw. You guys are adorable."

"Yep." Jane sipped her latte.

"I'm here to apologize."

"K," she said, making it a letter instead of a word.

"I'm really sorry about the timing issue with the dress shopping last night."

"The timing issue?" Jane's voice was turning screechy. "*That's* how you're going to frame this?"

"Isn't that why you were upset with me?"

"Just forget it, Kate. I'll have a dress delivered to your door. And I'll find someone to alter it because your dress last night looked like a zombie gobbled it up for breakfast."

"You're very creative this morning."

Jane stared me down.

"Am I missing something?" I asked. "I apologized for messing up the dress shopping last night."

"Uh-huh. The timing mishap. I heard."

"Help me out."

"It's no wonder you have no luck in relationships." Jane took a step back and made to shut the door.

I stuck a hand out. "Please, Jane, I'm trying. Name it. I'll do it. I realize I messed up. I'm really sorry for how I must have made you feel."

"That's a little better, but I can tell you're just throwing spaghetti at the wall to see what sticks." She heaved a huge sigh, then left the door open.

I took that as my cue to follow her inside. "Thank you for hearing me out." I hesitated, racking my brain for what exactly she wanted to hear. "I'm trying to be genuine."

"I know. That's what's sad." Jane eased into a chair at a long, beautiful wooden table in an open dining room.

I hadn't seen Wes's home before Jane had moved in, but even I could tell that Jane had already made herself known around here. Little details that I knew from experience she brought into a place to make a house a home. A bouquet of tulips on an end table. The scent of a hyacinth blooming from somewhere else in the kitchen. An obscenely fuzzy blanket draped over the back of a chair, a furry coat in the entryway, an overturned high heel not exactly where it belonged.

The whole thing made me smile.

"What's so funny?" she asked, guarded.

"I like your place," I said. "It's very you."

"We're going to buy something together after the wedding." Jane studied the area around her. "This will do for now. Wes doesn't mind me making a mark in his place. It's nice."

"I didn't mind it either." When Jane looked closer at me, I amended, "I got used to having you around. And now that you're not there..."

"You miss me." Jane gave a little smile. "How are you so clueless about some things, Kate?"

"Ouch?"

She sighed again. "It's just always about work with you. You are the *only* person in my bridal party. The one person, do you understand? So when you don't show up at the dress appointment that is literally made for you, then I look like an idiot."

"You weren't the idiot. I was. It wasn't your fault. The salespeople knew that too." A careful survey of Jane's face told me this wasn't the correct answer. "But that's not the point."

She nodded along, encouraging me. "I just really hoped you'd care a little more about my special day. I'm not asking you to throw a bachelorette party. You don't have to make any cute table toppers. You literally don't have to do anything except get a dress. Even that was too hard."

"I'm really sorry." The pit in my stomach was still there. "There was this case that..." I raised my hands. "You know what? That's *still* not even the point. Even if the case was super important, I should have prioritized you over the rest of it. I'm sorry. What can I do to make it up to you? Table toppers? Cake tastings? Uh, licking invitations?"

She gave me a small smile. "I'd prefer you lick the envelopes as opposed to the invitations. Anyway, what the hell happened to you last night?"

"I don't know," I admitted, raising a hand to my eyes. "Maybe it was something I ate."

It was a little embarrassing to actually list all of the food I'd eaten the night before, so I refrained.

"I bet it was all those flowers," Jane said. "Wouldn't that suck if you were allergic to roses? How unromantic."

"Sort of fitting for me. I *did* have an allergic reaction to that rose scented lotion."

"Look, don't beat yourself up so much about yesterday," she said. "I know you've got a lot on your plate."

"I ruined your dress shopping thing," I said. "Whether or not I'm expressing it correctly, I do feel bad about it. I wish I could go back in time and fix it."

"We can reschedule. I appreciate your apology."

"You're only being so kind because I look like a disaster."

"It does give you a few pathetic points."

"Gee, thanks." I paused a beat. "So Gem got you to help him out with his plan to demolish my living room, huh?"

"I just had to let him in your house. I did that before the dress appointment. Then when I had time after, I figured I'd take a peek at what he'd set up for you because I'm nosy, and I definitely earned it after the stunt you pulled."

"Fair."

"He also brought you two boxes of chocolates, I have to admit." Jane stood, disappeared to the kitchen, and returned, holding a similar but different box of sweets than the one I'd been given in my living room the previous evening. "I told Gem what happened and that I was stealing your chocolates. He didn't seem inclined to stop me. Want one?"

A little shell-shocked, I processed everything Jane said. "All that seems fair. And yes, I'll take one of those nut clusters. I ended up losing most of my share last night to Pete Winkler. Don't ask."

"I won't," Jane said, "but don't think I'm going to donate my sweets to you because you look like a blowfish."

"I wouldn't dream of it."

We both shared a smile, then a couple of chocolates, and a few sips of our lattes. By the time the sugar and caffeine had combined in our systems, we were both in noticeably better moods.

"So tell me what happened after I left." She blinked her eyes in my direction, feigning näiveté. "You and the illustrious Mr. Gem. Quite a dedication of his admiration for you, I'd say. Wes just got me a card and some earrings I sent him a link to on Etsy because they match my honeymoon bathing suit. It was nice and all, but it was no house full of roses."

"Honestly, nothing happened last night. We chatted a few minutes, then I had to head down to the precinct."

"Ah. And Jack?"

"How'd you know about Jack?"

"I didn't." Jane gave me a winning smile. "But you guys recently broke up. It was Valentine's Day. I figured if there was a chance he was going to reach out, it might've been yesterday."

"He left me a voicemail to call him back. I tried but we missed each other."

"Story of your lives, huh?"

"I had the same thought. I have no clue what he wants. It's probably work related."

"He shouldn't be stringing you along," Jane said. "You don't owe him anything, you know."

"What are you getting at?"

"I'm just looking out for you." Jane shrugged. "You and Jack broke up. He called things off."

"It wasn't like it was his fault, though. It was sort of mutual, really."

"Right, but he ended things. If he really, really, really wanted to be with you, he'd move here or something."

"But his job is there."

"Right." She stared at me. "And you're here. That's the whole issue."

"I'm not sure what you're getting at. It's not like we're discussing getting back together."

"No, but he's still lingering in your life. He was in town for a case a couple of weeks ago. Now he's calling you. It's just a lot to have your ex hanging around when you're trying to move on." Jane sat back in her chair. "Jack's a great guy, but the two of you decided not to work things out."

"Hence the reason we broke up."

"I'm on the other side of things. I see you here, alone and hurting after the breakup. Kate, you deserve someone who will do everything for you. Someone who will move across the planet for you. Someone who will be your other half, your partner. Someone who will support you and your stubborn, independent, gun-and-badge-toting ways."

I nodded, seeing where she was heading with this. "Someone who will fill up my living room with flowers."

"He's trying really hard. You're not making it easy." Jane's fingers picked away at the lid on her beverage. "Gem is patient. He's not pushing you."

"Let me repeat; he filled up my living room with flowers. That's a big gesture."

"And then didn't give a rat's behind when you pushed him out the door without so much as a kiss—am I right, or am I right?"

I just blinked.

"Gem is showing you that he's there. He's reminding you, every now and again, that he's interested. Otherwise, be honest, you'd let him fall by the wayside because you're too busy, because he's not making an effort, because it just wasn't working out. I'd take a long, hard look at what Gem's offering you before you dismiss it. I don't know how long he's going to wait around."

"Has he said something to you?"

"No, nothing. That's the point. He's just a good guy, and I'm not saying that because I'm engaged to his best friend. He's a good guy who has his sights set on you, but even the most patient of guys will run out of steam if they're getting nothing in return. Nobody likes to feel like their affection isn't being returned, over and over again."

"Jane—"

"Don't reprimand me. I'm not going to say any more on the subject. Not for a while," she added with a little blink. "But you're my sister, and I love you, and I want the best for you. Don't let the ghost of your last relationship sabotage what could be a beautiful fresh start for you."

I touched my face. "I'm not sure about beautiful..."

Jane laughed. "Maybe wait for your medicine to kick in before you consider my idea to go and thank Gem for the roses."

"You think I should thank Gem for the roses? Again?"

Jane stood. "I'm glad you're catching on. Now get out of here, sis, and catch your criminal so we can find you a new dress next Wednesday at 5 p.m."

I gave Jane a little hug. "I wouldn't miss it for the world."

"By the way," she said as she walked me to the door, "can I steal a couple of your bouquets if you're allergic to them? I mean, you're not going to use them, right? I wouldn't mind bathing in a bed of roses once in my life. What girl wouldn't?"

I caught a glimpse of my puffer-fish face in the hallway mirror. Jane cleared her throat.

"Right," she said. "I'll just help myself."

Chapter 8

On the way to the precinct, I swung by the same Caribou for another order of coffees. I grabbed four—a half caf for me, a latte for Jimmy, and two flat whites for Drs. Brooks and Michaelson. I cruised to the precinct and slunk a little lower in my seat as I caught a glimpse of my mother through the windows of her café.

There was no way she'd be able to see me from her vantage point behind the counter, but one could never be too safe. Then again, I was pretty sure word would get back to her via my sister. But for now, I wanted to avoid questions about my little situation with Gem in my living room.

I swung by Jimmy's desk and dropped off his latte. Without stopping, I nodded for him to follow me to the elevator. We rode down to the lab without speaking. Jimmy looked at my face approximately seven times in the short interval it took for the elevator doors to reopen.

"You're just not gonna say anything, then, huh?" he said gruffly. "Not a word about why your face looks like that?"

"Thanks, Jimmy. This is the only face I got."

He gave a smirk. "Melinda will get the details out of you. I'll get the details out of Melinda."

"You're confident."

Another laugh. He pushed open the door to Melinda's office. Both doctors were already in. Dr. Michaelson was standing before Melinda's desk, and both women were poring over a report. They looked up at the same time.

Melinda put a delicate hand to her mouth as she caught a glimpse of me.

Dr. Michaelson was noticeably more forward. "What happened to your eyes?"

I smiled. "I brought coffee."

I handed out both drinks. Melinda looked like she wanted to snap on a surgical glove before she took the beverage, in the event I was contagious and spreading my cooties around. Jimmy watched the exchange and grinned.

"I'm not contagious," I spat. "Turns out I'm allergic to some flowers."

"Oh, that's a shame." Dr. Michaelson turned back to the desk. "I like flowers. When they're not dead."

Melinda smiled over the other doctor's head, but it was an echo of her real smile. I could tell underneath she was wondering how on earth I'd come in contact with flowers, seeing as I wasn't exactly Betty Homemaker, who kept a fresh bouquet stocked on her kitchen table every day of the week.

At that inopportune moment, my phone rang. I glanced down at the screen and saw Jack's name on it. Melinda was instantly up on her tiptoes, balancing on a pair of heels as she tried to glance at my screen.

I rejected the call, not feeling like dealing with a personal situation at the moment. I tucked my phone deliberately into my pocket and mouthed at Melinda, "Nosy." Jimmy grunted happily as he watched the situation play out.

"What do you have for me?" Since Melinda was still giving me curious eyes, I added, "About the case, I mean."

"Lucky for you, this guy was easy to ID." Dr. Michaelson straightened, completely oblivious to the batting of eyelashes and silent conversation happening around her. "I noted on my initial report that the victim had undergone surgery on his knee approximately five years ago. He had a specific screw put in that we were able to match with hospital records."

"Heinrich was in an accident that required surgery on his leg some four-ish years ago," I said, feeling my blood chill. "It's him, isn't it?"

Melinda nodded. "Without a doubt. I just notified the chief about half an hour ago. We couldn't get in touch with the hospital until early this morning."

"That's what the chief's doing in his office." Jimmy glanced my way. "He came in early today. Locked himself in there. I bet he's preparing a statement for the press."

"If what I'm hearing is true," Melinda said, "there's going to be a small press conference at ten o'clock."

I glanced at my watch and saw that was just over an hour away. It didn't leave us a lot of time to chase down leads before this case got blown wide open.

"Then we need to get busy," I said. "Anything else we should know before we head out?"

"Not yet," Melinda said. "We're still trying to identify the type of handcuffs used. We're looking through the rest of the debris at the crash site and will let you know if anything turns up important."

Jimmy and I left the two doctors behind.

"You know Melinda didn't touch her coffee, right?" Jimmy asked. "I'm pretty sure she thinks you're going to give her the bubonic plague."

"Nah," I said. "She'll just sanitize it when she thinks nobody's looking and snap on a set of pretty blue gloves and go for it. There's no way she's passing up her favorite drink."

"You're pretty confident." Jimmy repeated my earlier phrase back to me.

I glanced back through the windows into Melinda's office and smiled as I saw her scrubbing the lid with an alcohol wipe.

"Okay, Sherlock," Jimmy muttered. "I see why the chief hired you."

As we made our way upstairs, I felt concerned at the thought of the chief giving a press conference. The journalists would be like vultures, gobbling up every word he said, and I had no doubt that Trevor would be waiting with pen in hand. Maybe he'd even been saving his hard-hitting piece to come out today, just to one-up the rest of the reporters. I didn't have a good feeling about it, any of it.

Officer Pete Winkler stopped me in the hallway. "Good morning, Detective. Are you okay?"

"What are you talking about?" I looked up at Winkler.

He cleared his throat and looked at Jimmy. "Nobody told her about her face?"

I rolled my puffy, bloodshot eyes. "I'm fine. Allergic reaction."

"To the chocolates?" Winkler patted his stomach. "I did spend an inordinate amount of time in the restroom this morning. Then again, I did polish off the box. Those were delicious. The missus actually wants to know where you got them from. I haven't seen them in the stores."

"Nope, I don't think it was the chocolates." I didn't elaborate.

Winkler got the picture. He glanced down at the clipboard he was holding, then looked back up. "Well, I was just coming to let you know that we had a guy follow Will Comice last night after we cut him loose. Just in case he ran off to squeal to someone about getting picked up."

"And?"

"He didn't go home. He went to a someone's private residence. We checked it out. It's a house that belongs to a woman named Sally Monrovia."

"I think she's some sort of girlfriend."

"Some sort of girlfriend?"

"A woman he's seeing," I said. "Will mentioned her name yesterday. I guess she was supposed to be at the singles' event with him. They must have met up after."

"I had that thought, so I went to ask Asha to poke around his phone records just in case. Will Comice didn't use his phone once while he was at the precinct or on the way over. So how did he alert this woman to his change of plans?"

"Good thinking."

"The stranger thing is that Asha couldn't find anything." Officer Winkler shifted his weight from one foot to another. "We dropped him back off at the bowling alley once he'd sobered up enough to drive. Then I had a tail on him who followed him straight to Sally's house. It appears Comice is still there, but we don't have anyone staking him out to be sure. From what we can tell, he didn't use his phone a single time."

"Maybe he showed up unannounced?" I suggested. "I'm sure there's an explanation."

"I thought the same thing, but I asked the guy tailing him, and it turns out that Sally opened the door before Will ever knocked."

"As if she was expecting him."

Winkler nodded. "I don't know if it means anything, but it's what we've got. I think something's off with the guy. I just don't know how involved he is." He handed over the clipboard. "Here's the paper copy of everything I just told you."

"Not so fast." Asha strolled around the corner, waving a sheaf of papers. "I've got something to add."

We waited until Asha had come to a complete stop and tossed her long braids behind her shoulder. She waited a beat longer, just making sure she had our full attention. Then she smiled.

"I don't like when things 'aren't quite right.'" She narrowed her eyes. "And something about this guy isn't quite right. So I did some more digging."

"You're really drawing out the suspense," I said. "What'd you find?"

"He's got another phone." Asha winked. "But I'm guessing you saw where that was going, group of outstanding detectives that you are. It's not all that surprising, considering all the trouble he's been in with the law over the last couple decades of his life. It's not only him either. The woman he's seeing—Sally Monrovia—has been picked up thrice for solicitation."

Asha held up her fingers to let that sink in.

"The most legit job I can find for this Comice is when he worked as a dishwasher after his high school days at a restaurant, and he even got fired from that gig. The guy hasn't paid more than a hundred dollars in taxes in his entire life."

"Sounds like he runs with a shady crowd," Winkler said. "Not surprised after what I saw from him yesterday."

"He's got a regular cell phone under his name, super simple plan. Barely uses it from what I can tell. It seems this guy rotates through pay-as-you-go phones like they're going out of style. I cracked into the latest one he was using because I found the receipt where he purchased it and—" She looked at the blank stares on our faces. "Right, I'll spare you the details. We'll just say I'm a genius, and I got into it."

"He texted Sally from it?" I asked. "That's how she knew?"

"Sure did," he said. "Then he texted another number. Turns out this number goes to a phone number tied to a guy named—drumroll please—Billy Burton."

"Interesting," I said. "So they might run in closer circles than Will was letting on."

"I should think so." Asha flipped her papers around so I could see a record of text messages printed out on it. "Here's what he said."

I studied the message from the unknown number that belonged to Will.

WILL: Might want to pack your bags and head on vacation. Big news dropping tomorrow.

"Ouch." Jimmy spoke first. "What are the chances Billy Burton's already on his way to Mexico?"

"There was no reply to this message?" I flipped the page over and glanced at Asha.

"Nothing. The phone wasn't used for the rest of the night and into the morning. I'm monitoring it," Asha said, "but if I had to guess, this is the part where even an idiot like Comice knows he's got to ditch the phone. There's an incriminating text on it, so he'll toss it first thing if he hasn't already."

"At least you've got this much on record," Jimmy pointed out.

"What I obtain to give you two a preliminary lead and what I feel comfortable presenting in court are sometimes..." Asha twirled one of her braids. "Let's say they're two different things."

"On the off chance that Burton hasn't fled, we need to get to his place. ASAP," I said to Jimmy. "Let's put out a BOLO on him and get his name and image circulating at the airports, just in case. If he gets on a flight, that's it."

"I can do that," Winkler volunteered. "You guys take off."

"Great," I said. "We're going to swing by Burton's place first, and then we'll hit up Sally Monrovia's house afterward. Winkler, can you get someone over to Sally's place to keep an eye on things? I want to know if Will's on the move."

"Not a problem," Winkler said. "Though, at this rate, I'd say you're pretty safe on that front. Comice seems dumb and confident."

Jimmy gave a broad grin. "My favorite kind of criminal."

The four of us parted ways. Asha promised to scour Burton's accounts to see if there were any sudden cash withdrawals or flight purchases or anything that might tip us off as to his next move.

"Oh, and Kate," Asha called after me, "if you need some bartering power, remind Comice about those outstanding parking tickets. Throw in a few acronyms. IRS would be a good one. FBI would help. He'll tell you what you want to know."

I gave her a salute.

"By the way," she said. "You look like you could use someone to deflate your face. Have you heard of Benadryl?"

I left her and Jimmy cackling behind me as I made my way to my desk. I stopped cold in my tracks when the chief's office door swung open. He looked like a man on a mission, and I got a sinking feeling in my stomach when he set his sights on me.

He did a double take, then sighed. "Really, Rosetti?"

I glanced around. "Sir? Did I do something?"

"Your face. Do you have to have devil eyes on the day I break the news of Detective Heinrich's death to the press?" He closed his eyes and rubbed his temples. "The press are going to have a field day getting your picture in the paper looking like one of Frankenstein's creations."

"Um..." I swallowed. "I'm sorry about my face, sir."

He sighed. "Come into the office. We need to talk."

I gave Jimmy a look that silently pleaded for help, then I followed the chief into his office and shut the door behind me. I caught a glimpse of my face in the mirror, and to the chief's point, I looked worse than I had earlier this morning. One of my eyes was looking a little black and blue, and the other was oddly swollen.

"What the hell happened to you?"

I folded my hands before my body. "Flowers, sir."

"I already regret asking."

"Me too." I waited a beat, then set out to plead my case. "I know what you're going to say."

"You do?"

"You have to keep me on this case," I said, launching into my argument. "I've already got a head start. With the ID of Heinrich's body, it's only going to set things in motion faster than they're already going. We're following up on Will Comice and Billy Burton the second I leave this room, and I just can't pass it off to someone else right now. Please don't make me hand over this case to Pete Winkler."

The chief gave a thin smile. "Officer Winkler is a well-respected cop who I asked to help out for a couple of weeks. Our team is growing, Kate. We need manpower."

"Sure, he might be a great cop," I agreed. "But I need to be on this one personally. With all due respect, I'm the one for the job. I'm sure of it."

"I know."

"I'll prove it to you—"

"I called you in here to warn you about the press release. I want you to read it before it goes out to the public."

I sighed, sure that he was going to announce to the whole world that I'd been taken off the case because of Heinrich's connection to my father. I wouldn't blame him. Well, I would a little bit, but I'd understand why he'd done it even if I didn't agree. I looked down, scanned the press release, and I was in the middle of handing it over before I yanked it back and read it a second time.

"Really?" I looked up. "You're keeping me on the case? And you're announcing it to the press? You know you're going to be inviting the sharks to attack."

Sturgeon took the paper from my hand and returned to his desk. "I'm not ashamed of you. I'm not worried about the repercussions."

"Thank you, Chief."

"Don't screw the pooch on this one, Rosetti. Got it?"

I cleared my throat. "Of course, sir."

"What have you done about your father?" Sturgeon asked. "What's he got to say about it?"

My heart raced. "I haven't asked yet. We didn't have a confirmed identity until this morning."

The chief stared me down. I got the gist of it.

"But I'm going to buzz over there just as soon as I check out Billy Burton who, technically, is still our strongest lead in the case."

The chief looked back at the papers on his desk, and I got the impression my time with him had come to an end. As I was heading out of the room, he spoke after me.

"I'd recommend recording everything. Especially when it comes to your father." Sturgeon's eyes were steely as he looked at me. "When this gets to court, and it will, people will be watching."

By the time I made it out of the chief's office, I could feel my fingers trembling. I had been so certain I was going to be kicked off the case that I'd been preemptively angry about it. Then the chief had flipped my assumptions upside down, and the pressure of performing up to his expectations was sinking in. He was putting his neck on the line for me, and I couldn't let him down.

Jimmy looked up from behind his desk as I entered the room. Lines of trepidation wrinkled his forehead.

I didn't bother to stop as I passed his desk. "Ready to go run down Burton?"

Jimmy gave a broad smile. "'Atta girl, Rosetti."

Chapter 9

Billy Burton lived in a small community outside of the Cities called Sunfish Lake. The minimum price for a home in his neck of the woods went for close to a million, and the fancier houses went for much more. It was a place where local stars, athletes, and the like often chose to purchase property because of its close proximity to the city yet incredibly private properties. Most of the homes here came with several acres, some of them lakefront. Not a single house was visible from the road.

"It's hard to believe a guy this wealthy might be willing to lose it all over a game of bowling," Jimmy mused as I turned down the road that wound through the community. "If I had this much cash, I'm pretty sure I'd just bathe in dollar bills, get massages every day, and hire a chef."

"Interesting line of priorities."

"I guess money does funny things to a person," Jimmy mused. "Where'd he get his money from, anyway?"

"According to Asha, Burton is in software development. He worked for a couple of companies when they IPO'd and made out big."

"Little bit of smarts, lot a bit of luck."

"Pretty good summary of it," I agreed. "He's been here for the last few years. Asha has the details in her report. Do you think we'll catch him at home today?"

"Nah," Jimmy said. "If he's got ears and eyes across the city, he'll be gone already. And he obviously does, seeing as the first thing your guy Will did when he was released last night was squeal to him."

I thought Jimmy was probably right, but as we pulled off the dirt road into an oversized, roundabout brick driveway, I began to think differently. A Jaguar was parked out front. A three-car garage sat off to one side, and from what I could tell through the windows, all slots were filled with expensive vehicles.

The lights at the front of the house were on. One window on the second floor glowed from inside. It gave every impression of a house that was currently occupied.

"Could be a housekeeper," Jimmy said, his eyes following mine to the second-floor window. "A guy this rich probably has a couple of people helping him out."

"Only one way to find out."

Jimmy followed me closely as we reached the front door. I could sense his movements becoming stiffer, more tense. I knocked and waited.

"Coming," a female voice called from inside. A moment later, the door was thrown open, and a smiling woman with dirty-blonde hair stood before us in a velvet robe. "Good morning. Can I help you?"

"Is this the residence of Billy Burton?" I asked.

"Sure. I'm Kendra." She looked between us. "His girl-friend. Why?"

"I'm Detective Kate Rosetti, and this is my partner, De-tective Jimmy Jones. Is Billy home?"

"He's in the shower. He's not the earliest riser." Her smile faltered for a little bit. "Are you going to come back later, or..."

I showed her my badge. Jimmy flashed his as well. "We'd really like to come inside and speak to him."

"Like I said, he's—"

"We'll wait," I said, rocking back onto my heels so she knew I meant to stay right where I was. "Thanks."

"I guess if you're going to wait, you can come in. I just made coffee." Kendra stepped back. She seemed a little flustered. "What's this about? Why do you need to talk to Bill? He didn't say he was expecting you."

"He's not," I said.

"I guess I'll just pop upstairs and let him know you're here," she said, easing backward toward a grand, spiral staircase with ornately carved wooden banisters lining it.

"We'd prefer you don't," Jimmy said. "It's probably best if you wait with us."

"Bill's not known for his fast showers," Kendra argued. "It would probably—"

"Do you bake?" Jimmy asked. "Smells good."

"I just took a quiche out," Kendra said. "Would you like a slice?"

"Nah," Jimmy said. "I already ate. How long have you dated Mr. Burton?"

Kendra looked a little whiplashed at the change of tone in the conversation. "Um, two years."

We all heard the stream of water audibly shut off. She looked a little sheepish.

"I guess he's done, then," Jimmy said. "Good timing."

"Do you live here?" I asked. "I mean, permanently?"

"I have my own place, but I stay here often. Bill works remotely most of the time, so his schedule is very flexible. I come over when I have time between my shifts."

"What do you do?" I asked.

"I'm a nurse," she said. "Labor and delivery. I work long hours. My apartment is near the hospital, so sometimes if I'm working a couple of days in a row, I'll stay there. Then I'll have a few days off and will stay here."

"How'd you meet Billy?"

A little smile crept onto her face as she remembered the moment. "I was dragged out for my friend Lauren's birthday. I didn't really want to go. They were getting dinner and drinks and going bowling. I hate bowling."

I saw where this was going but let her continue uninterrupted.

"We went up to some place in Roseville I'd never been to before, and I was having a pretty miserable time until Bill came up to me. We started talking, and eventually he challenged me to a bowling game. I guess the rest is history. We knew early on that we were a good fit."

The sound of footsteps on the staircase seemed to pull Kendra out of her reverie. She glanced toward the top of the magnificent stairs and smiled at her boyfriend. Billy Burton smiled down at her, a guarded smile, as he took in his two surprise guests.

"I didn't know we were hosting brunch," Billy said, toweling off his hair as he jogged down the steps. He tossed the towel over the banister as he reached the landing. "Who's the happy couple?"

I got the idea that Burton knew exactly who we were and was purposefully playing dumb. Burton didn't look like I'd have expected him to look. He didn't look like a bowler. He looked like a rich computer programmer.

Despite the chilly temps outside, Billy was wearing workout shorts and a fitted V-neck shirt. Both black. His dark hair stood up on end, still a bit damp. The smell of his aftershave was spicy and strong.

"Kendra, why don't you head upstairs for a bit?" Billy suggested, depositing a quick kiss on his girlfriend's cheek. "Draw yourself a relaxing morning bath. Finish up that bubbly from last night."

Kendra looked between me, Jimmy, and Billy. "Maybe I could help—"

"I think it's best if you let me handle this." There was no arguing with Billy's tone.

Kendra obviously got the picture because she gave a shaky nod and stepped away from Billy. She jogged up the stairs, pausing at the top. "The quiche is ready. Help yourselves."

Billy waited, his head cocked to one side. I sensed he was waiting for something specific. I glanced at Jimmy, but he seemed just as confused as me.

A moment later, the sound of running water filtered through the pipes. Billy relaxed and looked at us.

"Shall we?" he suggested, gesturing toward the kitchen. "Kendra makes a fantastic quiche. Egg whites and crustless."

Jimmy looked like he'd been stabbed. "She left out the best parts."

"It's much healthier." Billy gave a pointed look at Jimmy. "I try to keep myself at the top of my game."

"I see," Jimmy said. "Bowling is a pretty physical sport, after all."

It seemed Jimmy's subtle jab at Billy didn't go unnoticed. The computer programmer laughed as he led us into a large gourmet kitchen with pale blue walls and sparkling marble countertops. A single pie dish full of quiche sat on the counter, the smell very appetizing indeed.

Billy grabbed a plate, then glanced our way. When we both shook our heads no, he dished himself up a sizeable portion. Then he headed over to the pot of coffee and poured himself a cup.

"Shady of you to corner Kendra like that." Billy slid onto a barstool at one end of the kitchen island. "Have a seat."

Jimmy and I sat on barstools on the other side of the island.

"Corner Kendra?" I repeated. "We showed up and asked for you. She let us in."

"She doesn't know anything."

"About?"

"About anything." Billy didn't seem perturbed at the fact that there were two cops sitting across from him as he ate his breakfast and sipped his black coffee. "She's just my girlfriend."

"Sounds like she's been around for a couple of years."

"None of your business how long we've been dating."

"It's nice you want to be so protective of her," I drawled, "but unfortunately, that's not going to work for us. We're here to talk about murder. No subject is off limits."

"I'm just saying you shouldn't have bothered her. It's a waste of everyone's time."

"What you're saying is you don't want her to know why we're here." Jimmy folded his hands on the table. "Isn't that right, pal?"

"You know I could've taken off already, right?" Billy washed down a bite of quiche with a swig from his diner-style mug. "I knew you guys would show up."

"I'm surprised you're not at a resort in Mexico," I said. "We expected to find an empty house."

He nodded, not seeming to believe us. "That idiot Will talked to you, didn't he."

It didn't seem like a question, so I didn't respond.

"Well?" He parted his hands. "What're you here for?"

"I think you know."

Billy grinned at me. "Do I? Will's always getting into trouble. You'll have to specify."

I felt Jimmy give an annoyed shift next to me. I could tell Billy had rubbed him the wrong way since the crack about the quiche.

"What do you know about Detective Heinrich?" I asked.

"So he's finally kicked the bucket, then."

Again, Billy didn't seem to be keen on answering questions. Instead, he made observations aloud and watched for our reactions. We had to be careful with him.

"We found Detective Heinrich dead yesterday," I admitted. "Let's start with an alibi. Where were you two nights ago?"

"I would've thought a fancy cop like yourself would've had a smaller window than that." Billy shrugged. "An entire evening? I don't remember every moment."

"Early morning," I said. "Let's say 5 to 7 a.m. on Valentine's Day. That should be easy enough to remember."

"I was home. Like most sane people."

"Anyone here to vouch?" My gaze shifted upward, hinting at Kendra.

"Kendra was here," Billy said. "But I doubt that's going to count for much, seeing as she'd cover for me even if she wasn't here. She loves me."

"You're pretty confident in that," I said. "It's funny, though, how people's loyalties can change when they're staring at murder charges."

"Sometimes yes, sometimes no."

"You don't have a good alibi," I summarized. "But you do have a motive for wanting him dead."

"Do I?"

"I hear the bowling league is a little bit..." I paused for emphasis. "Cutthroat."

"It can be."

"In fact, the way we were able to identify Detective Heinrich so quickly is because of a little knee surgery he had a few years ago. The same year he was hit by a car. The same year you happened to win the league. The only year you won, and the only year he lost. He lost because he couldn't stand without crutches."

"Ouch. I'm beginning to believe you don't think I could beat Heinrich fair and square."

"I've heard some theories about your opponent's accident. An accident that might not have been as accidental as it was first thought," I said. "Your name comes up a lot."

"I'm a popular guy." Billy set his fork down on his empty plate. "You saw the cars I have outside. If you didn't, you're not very observant detectives." He sat back in his seat, holding a coffee cup in one hand. "Would I really risk scratching the paint on a Jag just to run down an old geezer in my bowling league? The trophy's made of plastic."

"I don't think the competition is about the trophy." I folded my arms across my chest. "I think it bothers you to not be the best at something."

"I am the best, though." He shrugged as if that settled it. "That was the only year I competed in the league. Technically, Heinrich never beat me. I played once and won once. Batting a thousand, as you might say." Billy nodded at Jimmy. "You strike me as a guy who likes baseball. Watching it, at least. It's probably been a long time since you've played athletics of any sort."

Before Billy could get another rise out of Jimmy, I broke in with another question. "We heard you switched where you bowled so you didn't have to worry about competing with Heinrich."

"False. Have you been *inside* Leitner Lanes? It's a dump." Billy grimaced. "I was worried about the wheels getting stolen off my ride. The new place I go has top-shelf liquor, private lanes for exclusive clientele, and it's closer to Kendra's place."

"Why did Will text you, then?"

"Will's an idiot."

"Be a little more specific. You're the only person he reached out to after we picked him up," I said. "He gave you the heads-up the second he was released. Why? Got him on payroll?"

"I don't need to pay a guy like that. He thinks I'm a god. I've got a hot girlfriend, hot cars, and I'm the best bowler in the Cities. Will would be happy scoring one of the three. He sucks up to me, thinking it's going to rub off. The thing is, as I mentioned, he's an idiot."

"You haven't answered the question," I argued. "All you've established is that you think Will's an idiot. That still begs the question as to why he texted you."

"I told you, he thinks I'm cool." Billy looked between us. "He heard a few rumors about the car accident a few years ago. Maybe I fanned the flames just to get a rise out of the guy. I didn't run down anybody with a car, and I certainly didn't blow anybody up."

A long pause followed.

Jimmy leaned forward, a little smile on his face. "How would you know about anybody getting blown up?"

Billy leaned forward. "Because it's on the news."

Billy slid his phone out of his pocket. A slim, black model I'd never seen before. It looked expensive. He pulled up an article. According to the timestamp, it was a brand-new article.

I sat back in my chair and expelled a big sigh. The chief was supposed to go live with his press release in thirty minutes. Unfortunately, it looked like someone had broken the news early about Heinrich's body being identified. Even worse, someone had put a picture of me at the crime scene right next to the headline. I didn't need to read the byline to assume that my pal Trevor was behind it.

"Though I expected you to be better looking." Billy glanced at me. "You're looking a little worse for the wear, Detective. Is the case wearing you down already? According to what I've read, things are just getting started."

I heard Jimmy curse under his breath next to me. "Let's get out of here. He's not talking."

"I'm talking just fine." Billy slid his phone back into his pocket. "I've answered all your questions, haven't I?"

I slid out of my chair. "We'll be back with more. Don't take your pal Will's advice. Stay in town, yeah?"

Billy just smiled. "Next time you'd better bring a warrant. A heads-up phone call would be nice. I doubt I'm going to be in such a welcoming mood if you show up on my doorstep again."

Jimmy and I let ourselves out. Jimmy studied Billy's cars briefly, a thoughtful look coming over his face. Then we both climbed into my vehicle.

"A guy like that's probably got a private mechanic," he mumbled. "He could've gotten his car touched up after an 'accident' without there being a record of it."

"You're just sore he eats his quiche without crust."

"What kind of psychopath leaves out half the egg when they cook? Egg whites? Why discriminate against the yolks?" Jimmy shrugged. "I'm just saying, there's something off with the guy."

Healthy eating habits aside, I had to agree with Jimmy. I couldn't say whether Billy Burton was guilty, but he was wily. He was smart and well-connected.

A guy with his level of computer knowledge and attention to detail would be difficult to catch. The only weakness I could see was his confidence. If he got too cocky, he might make a mistake. Otherwise, I had a feeling we'd be going in circles soon enough with this guy's very expensive lawyer.

"I'm just saying, the guy could rig up a bomb," Jimmy said. "I'm pretty sure he could do it with his eyes closed, and he's going to make it next to impossible to prove it."

Chapter 10

"Let's make this quick," I said as I pulled up in front of Will Comice's girlfriend's house. "I don't think Comice is our guy. If anything, I think he's playing up his role in everything, trying to seem important."

"He doesn't have the guts to pull off premeditated murder." Jimmy climbed from the car and looked over the windshield at me. "Or the smarts to get a bomb in working order without some help."

"Let's do our due diligence here and head out. There's one more person I have to visit today."

Jimmy frowned and looked down at his watch. "I didn't hear anything about another person on the interview list for the day."

"That's because there's not."

I blinked in Jimmy's direction. He blinked back. Then he got it.

"Oh, right." He gave a fake cough. "You can drop me off at the precinct after we check in on Will. I'm overdue for lunch anyway."

I knocked on the door to Sally Monrovia's place and waited. Out of the corner of my eye, I spotted a car a block away. It obviously belonged to one of the officers tasked to keep an eye on Comice's movements. I turned back to the door in time to see a half-naked Will rubbing his eyes like he'd just rolled out of bed.

"Hey, there." Will grinned at me. "I thought you might stop by. I dressed up just for you."

Jimmy made a tiny gagging sound in his throat. Apparently Will's patriotic boxers weren't doing much for my partner.

"Why'd you text your pal Billy Burton last night?" I asked. "You do know that aiding and abetting will get you time. Or impeding a murder investigation. There are lots of ways we can go about this."

Will's smirk disappeared. "How'd you know that?" He took a step closer to me and half closed the door behind him. "You don't have permission to tap into my phone. I think that's illegal. I could call a lawyer on you."

"I could put in a call to some of my buddies too," I said. "Seems like the IRS has some interest in you. Then there's the issue of a few outstanding parking tickets." For good measure, I added one more acronym on Asha's recommendation. "I've got friends at the FBI, as well, that might be interested in hearing your name."

Will's eyes shifted between me and Jimmy. "That's a low blow, you cornering me at Sally's place. You couldn't have waited until I got home?"

"If we waited around for you, then Billy Burton would've been on the move already. Lucky for us, he was home. We had breakfast together."

Will paled. "What'd he say?"

I shrugged. "If you're buddies, you should know. Why'd you text him last night? Tipping him off to flee and hoping for some sort of kickback?"

"I was just messing around. I didn't mean anything by it." Will scratched at his chest. "He's a little bit of a lunatic. I just figured he was guilty. I didn't know if he was or not. I was just trying to help a brother out."

"You do realize you're practically admitting to a crime, right?"

"No?" He looked like he'd just realized he was standing in quicksand. "I'm just trying to be honest. I'm not looking for trouble. I didn't kill anyone, and I don't know for sure who did. I just thought..."

"Why'd you say Billy's a lunatic?"

"He's supersmart and superrich and supercompetitive. The rumors about him running down Heinrich, well, I'm pretty sure he did it. Then with Heinrich turning up dead after Burton's other comments, I guess it just all made sense in my head."

"We're going to be keeping an eye on you," I said. "If you happen to hear anything more concrete than rumors, you let me know."

"Yeah, yeah."

"Or else someone's going to come knocking on your door asking about a lot more than parking tickets."

I turned to leave. Jimmy followed me. Will called after us.

"But you're not gonna worry about the parking tickets, right?" Will said. "I mean, that's water under the bridge by now. Spilled milk and all that."

I climbed into the car without a response. Jimmy slid in next to me and glanced across the console. As I pulled away from the curb, he itched at his forehead.

"How many parking tickets does a guy rack up before he's *that* worried about having to pay them?" Jimmy asked. "It's almost impressive."

We cruised back to the precinct. I stopped in front of the doors, and Jimmy glanced over at me.

"I'd be happy to come with you on your next leg of the journey," he said. "I don't have to say a word. I can be sort of silent but deadly."

"I don't think that's a good idea," I said. "At least not the first time."

"But—"

I raised up my phone. "I'll record."

"Well then, good luck, partner."

As I turned away from Jimmy and turned my car in a very familiar direction, I hoped I didn't need luck. I sincerely hoped I didn't need anything at all. The only thing I was hoping to get out of my next interview was an airtight alibi.

***

I trudged up the front walk of my parents' house. Now that they were officially remarried, going home felt like stepping into an odd sort of time capsule. They lived in the same house I'd grown up in, the house where I remembered my parents being young and in love. Way back before Heinrich had helped to put my father behind bars.

I knew my mother wouldn't be home because I'd glimpsed her through the café windows as I'd left the precinct. I thought it best my mother wasn't home for this interview anyway. Then again, I fully expected my dad would tell her all about it, and I'd receive a terse call from her later this evening.

I knocked on the door, and it swung open quickly.

"I don't have an alibi. I'm not guilty." My father smiled at me. "And yes, I do have a good lawyer if you'd like her number."

My lips parted in surprise. "Hello to you too."

My father pulled the door open wider and gave a grand gesture for me to enter. "I've been waiting for you. Would you like a cup of tea?"

"Since when have you started drinking tea?"

"Since your mother started locking the caffeine in a safe after 10 a.m. because she says it doesn't help my anxiety."

"I'll take a tea, thanks."

My father putzed in the kitchen, scrounging for the tea kettle for so long that eventually I got up and pulled it out of the cupboard and set it on the stove myself.

"Still getting used to the layout," he said, sitting down as he waited for the water to boil. "Your mother's changed things around since I lived here last."

"Yeah, things change when you're gone for twenty years."

My father's face remained passive. "If you need my alibi for the night of the thirteenth, into the next morning, I was home with your mother."

"Dad, you know—"

"I know that doesn't amount to much, all things considered." My father spread his hands in a plea. "What do you want me to do, kid, lie to you? I was here, sleeping."

I pulled out my phone and set it on the table. "Do you mind if I record this?"

My dad's eyes hardened for a second, then he relented with a sigh. "Yeah, sure. Go ahead."

I hit the button to start things rolling. "Can you tell me where you were late Sunday night, the thirteenth, into the morning of February 14?"

"I was spending Valentine's Day morning with my Valentine." My dad gave a cheeky smile. "I was right here in bed with my wife. We watched the news the night before, fell asleep, and I woke up about seven thirty the next morning."

"Was Mom—er, was your wife still in bed with you when you woke up?"

"No. She left a little earlier for the café."

I sighed. An already weak alibi was made even weaker by my mother's early morning jaunt into her place of employment. It wasn't that I didn't believe my dad. But it would've been really nice to be able to concretely rule him out, so I didn't have to waste time investigating him.

"You sound disappointed." My dad's eyes twinkled. "Should I have been somewhere else?"

I glared at him. "You are familiar with Detective Jeff Heinrich?"

"Sure. We worked together back in the day."

"I read the transcripts from your court case. Detective Heinrich testified against you."

"He put the nail in my coffin, so to speak." My father's face didn't give a thing away. "I'm just quoting the headlines from back in the day. He scrounged up the damning evidence. He testified against my character. I didn't stand a chance afterward."

"A testimony like that might make someone angry." I found myself intensely curious about my father's response.

Even though I didn't believe he'd killed anyone, this was new territory for us. He and I had mostly glossed over the actual details of the events that had gotten him put in prison—court proceedings included. Now that I'd developed a new, tenuous but increasingly hopeful relationship with my father, I found myself wondering about the details during that wild time of his life. I'd never thought of it from his point of view before.

"It sure might make the right person upset."

"Did it make you angry?" I asked softly. "Were you upset with Heinrich?"

The tea kettle whistled. My father stood up and turned off the stove, taking some time to think.

"I'd be lying if I said I wasn't a little frustrated. You work with these guys, you think they'll have your back, and then..."

He waved a hand. "But I've had a long time to think about it."

"And?"

"The anger I felt at Heinrich was really anger for myself that had been misdirected. Jeff wasn't doing anything except his job. I was the one who made the mistake. I don't blame the guy at all. Never did, really. Not once I stopped to think about it."

"So you're saying you didn't harbor a grudge against Detective Heinrich?" I asked. "Despite the fact that he effectively put you behind bars?"

"He didn't *do* anything. I did. Why would I hold a grudge against him?" My dad winked at me. "It was my fault for being stupid enough to be caught."

"Dad."

"I'm joking, Kate. But in all seriousness, I never once held a grudge. I didn't blame anyone but myself. In retrospect, I'm even glad that I was caught and paid for my missteps. It cost me dearly, but it's provided me with a true second chance."

"What do you mean?"

"Everything is in the open now. I'm not spending my life looking over one shoulder, wondering if my past will catch up to me. I committed a crime. I served my penance. Does that make what I did right? No. But I can sleep at night knowing I don't have secrets. You know everything about me. Good and bad. And when I remarried your mother, I promised there would be no more secrets between us anymore." He waited a beat. "Except the code to the stupid safe where she locks up my coffee beans, but that's on her and not me, and it's mostly doctor ordered."

"I see."

"I wouldn't throw all this away, Kate." My dad gestured to the kitchen. "I think you know that."

I reached forward and hit stop on my phone. "I know, Dad. I have to ask. The news—"

"I saw it. I'm sorry. Look, I know it's my fault you're taking so much flak. Is there any way I can convince you to drop the case?"

"Are you joking?"

"Drop it for you—not for me. I can take anything the media will throw my way; I'm a seasoned pro. But you... You've got a good career. The reporters can be wolves. They twist things completely out of context."

"I can handle myself. I want to be on the case."

"You know they're not going to let up on you. They'll paint the picture that I had a motive to want Heinrich dead. They'll point out that my daughter's investigating the case. It's going to be a mess."

"It's already a mess."

"I do have a great lawyer. If you want, she could help slow things down," my dad said. "Sometimes a strongly worded legal letter can help encourage a reporter to back off."

"Thanks, but I've got it."

"I love you, Kate."

"I'm sorry." I hesitated, then stood up and prepared to leave. "I wish I didn't have to be here."

He just smiled and nodded. And that was it. I headed to my car, wondering if my father's past would ever be left where it belonged: in the past.

Chapter 11

I went straight from my dad's place back to the precinct. I cast a wary eye at the coffee shop next door. Very regretfully, I dragged my feet toward the café instead of the welcoming doors of the precinct.

With the press release coming out and the interview with my dad, I knew it was only a matter of time before my mother heard mumblings about Heinrich. Things would only get worse the longer I avoided her.

"What are you doing here?" I asked, pulling the door to the café open, and spying Jimmy in line.

"Late lunch," Jimmy said. "I stopped by the office to go over some paperwork. Just grabbing a sandwich. How'd things go with Angelo?"

"Better than expected."

"I'm not surprised," Jimmy said. "I'm sure your dad understands. It's not like you wanted to be there. At the same time, it's not like he can erase his past either. It's a tough spot for both of you."

"That's the long and short of it. I guess his one mistake is going to haunt all of us for a lifetime."

Jimmy took a closer look at me. "Hey, I'm sorry. It's not fair to you. None of the shade you've had to deal with because of your dad is fair."

I raised my eyebrows. "I thought there would be a *but* to your statement. What's the but?"

"No *but* this time." Jimmy gave me a lopsided smile. "I'm just saying it sucks. That's the long and short of that."

"Yeah."

We waited silently next to one another as the lined shortened before us. When there was only one woman ahead of us at the register, the door flew open behind us. Someone gasped for breath. A moment later, a hand grabbed at my arm.

I flew around, startled, drawing a hand up as if needing to defend myself. Erin "Lassie" Lassiter took a step back, flinching.

"Can't a girl just talk to her friend?" Lassie asked, relaxing as I lowered my hands. "Jeez Louise. You looked like you were going to karate chop my head off."

"It's a hazard of being friends and family with Kate Rosetti." My mom cheerfully joined the conversation from behind the counter. "It's quite an unattractive trait, I agree, but I can't quite seem to wring it out of her."

My mother winked at Lassie. Lassie gave a sympathetic nod toward my mom.

"So I've heard," Lassie said. "Poor Jane told me she just about lost her eye a few times when Kate was feeling a little trigger happy."

"And she wonders why she's single." My mother tsked. "She should have never broken up with that Jack. At least he carried a gun and could probably defend himself against her startle reflex."

"I don't know about that." Lassie raised her eyebrows, a gleam coming to her eyes. "I think there might be someone else out there who loves Kate even more."

My mother leaned an elbow on the counter. "Do tell."

"What are you talking about?" I asked. "You do realize I'm right here?"

"Take out your phone," Lassie proudly announced. "Scan the local news stories from today."

"I don't need to," I said shortly. "I saw them already, but it's irrelevant. The chief's got my back."

"Why does Chief Sturgeon need to have your back?" My mother frowned, looking down at her own phone. "I don't like the sound of this. I've been busy all morning and haven't been as tuned in as I guess I should have been."

"I'm not talking about the reporter or the big, ugly case. Not really." Lassie gave me an extra big smile. "I'm talking about the other breaking news."

"What other big news?"

"The news that's blocking your little kerfuffle with the dead cop."

My mother paled and looked up. "There was a dead cop?"

"Sure was," Lassie said, "but based on the news today, you wouldn't know it."

I started to ask what she was talking about, but Jimmy had already pulled out his phone and had gotten down to the business of finding out for himself. He handed it over for me to see.

There were headlines, all right. Headlines that had nothing to do with me. I did recognize the face next to the news articles along with the name. Apparently Alastair Gem had some big news of his own.

"So what?" I asked, quickly scanning the article. "Gem's coming out with a new company. He does that every day."

"I really don't think it's an accident that he broke his news about an hour after your news broke. But"—Lassie held a hand to her heart—"I'm not complaining. I owe you one. I got to break it first."

"So Alastair Gem's coming out with a candy company," I said, scanning the headline and remembering the box of chocolates he'd dropped off at my place. "So what? He's got a billion companies."

"Yeah, but he's pulling a Willy Wonka sort of charade to kick things off. Check it out. In five of the boxes of chocolates, there are precious stones—a ruby, a sapphire, an emerald... You get the idea, very on theme for Gem. There are other prizes too. Huge ones. All-expenses-paid vacations to Greece. New cars. Over five million dollars in cash. And the best part of all is that the only place the chocolates are being distributed is his local store. So your chances of winning are pretty high. There's already a line three blocks long."

I thought back to the box of chocolates I'd given to Pete Winkler. I was pretty sure there hadn't been any prizes in it. Though I was feeling like I could've used an all-expenses-paid vacation to Greece right about now, or a one-way ticket to Mexico, the way my mother was looking at me made me want to melt on the spot.

"You don't think it was a coincidence?" my mother asked Lassie with an excess of curiosity. "You think Mr. Gem asked you to break this story today on purpose?"

"There's a big controversial case right now with the blown-up detective," Lassie explained. "Kate's in the middle of it, and the media's all over her."

My mother waved a hand, shocking all of us with her indifference. "I'm not surprised."

"Huh?" I asked. "What do you mean you're not surprised?"

"I mean, I'm not surprised the media is trying to pick you apart."

"You're not worried?" I pressed. "You have no big lecture to give me?"

She gave a short laugh. "The media's only an issue if there's truth to their story. Nobody's a straighter shot than you, and I'm confident there's nothing to find. If they think you're going to be biased about investigating your own father, they're dead wrong. If anything, you'll go harder on him than anyone else."

"I guess I should say thank you," I said. "But I'm not sure it's a compliment?"

"It's mostly a compliment," my mother said. "The part I'm more interested in is the bit about this rich suitor who is madly in love with you."

"Hold up. Don't go throwing that word around."

"What word, rich?" My mother looked confused. "Oh, you mean love. Well, it's true. He is rich, and he does love you."

"He doesn't." I looked at my friend, then my partner. Nobody came to my defense. "Gem doesn't love me."

"Okay," Lassie said. "Well, you might want to take another Benadryl before you go thanking him, or else he just might decide he feels differently."

"Your eyes really look a bit possessed," my mother said. "I didn't want to say anything, but since Lassie started it..."

I gave an exaggerated eye roll that probably made things worse.

"And you really shouldn't do that ever again," my mother chastised. "Now, what can I get you all?"

Jimmy slid in front of me and put in his order for a crispy chicken sandwich. I asked for the same, mostly because I didn't have enough brain power to place my own request.

Lassie cornered me. "You've really got to thank Gem for me, okay? He let me break the story first. Everyone else was hot on my tail after that, but still. He didn't have to do that, and I know he only chose me because I'm your friend."

"What if it's just a coincidence?" I replied. "I'd feel like an idiot assuming he did all this for me."

"Dude." Lassie stared me down. "Dude."

"Okay, okay," I said, brushing her hand off my arm as she gripped me tighter and tighter. "I'll tell him thank you."

"Just give it, like, an hour." She scanned my eyes and grimaced. "Maybe two. Think happy hour time. And use this cream for the swelling under your eyes—please."

She shoved a little tube into my hand, then breezed out of the café in the same whirlwind in which she'd entered. My mother deposited two chicken sandwiches on an open table. Jimmy followed the smell of fried food and took a seat in front of it.

"I've packed you a doggie bag," my mother said in a flutter of eyelashes. "It's an extra meal. I thought you might want to bring it to your suitor."

"Stop calling him that. This isn't *Bridgerton*."

My mother fanned herself. "You're telling me. In that story, I do believe the two actually *stop* fighting their love and get to a happily ever after."

My mother returned to the counter. Jimmy was completely engrossed in his sandwich. I sat, then pulled out my phone camera and turned it on myself. Tentatively, I squeezed a little cream onto my finger and rubbed it on the puffy area under my eyes.

"Nope," Jimmy said. "That doesn't help anything."

"Everyone's full of compliments today."

"Who knows? Mr. Gem might even find your bleary eyes endearing." Jimmy winked at me. "Get out of here, Kate. Take him that sandwich before it gets cold."

"But—"

"I'll keep cracking on the case. I'll see you in a couple of hours."

"But—"

"Bye."

I eventually stood. Jimmy had a point. I was a little too distracted to focus on the case. Not to mention I hadn't taken a break all day. I packed my own sandwich into a to-go container, demanded Jimmy call me with any updates, and pretended not to see my mother trying to flag me down. Then I set my sights on Minnesota's newest chocolatier.

Chapter 12

For the first time ever, I handed over my keys to the valet outside of Gem Industries. My previous visits to the towering skyscraper had largely been on official police business, so I'd felt comfortable plunking my car at the curb and flashing my badge. It felt different this time.

"Oh, it's you." A familiar voice spoke from behind the reception desk. "I expected you to stop by sometime today. I hope you're happy."

I glanced up to find Ms. Karp, the receptionist, frowning at me.

"Sorry?" I said.

"You *should* be sorry." Ms. Karp sniffed and ran a hand through her gorgeous brown hair. "Don't get any ideas that he's going to do things like this for you all the time."

Ms. Karp wore a tight pencil skirt with a white button-down blouse. Her legs looked like shapely little pencils sticking out from the hemline. Her heels propped her up at least four extra inches. "He's expecting you."

"He is?"

Ms. Karp extended a keycard in response. "I trust you know how to get to the penthouse by now."

A bit bewildered, I took the card from her. I had been to the penthouse before, back when I'd been investigating Alastair Gem's then-fiancée's presumed kidnapping. Though we'd recovered Mindy, their relationship had ended shortly after.

I made my way through the lobby to the impressive atrium. The space was currently in the process of being transformed from a Valentine's Day paradise—glittering heart rubies dangling from the ceiling, spiraling silver icicles, diamonds touching every surface— into a delightful spring masterpiece. I ducked under a man carrying a live bird in a giant cage and slipped down a back hall to Gem's personal elevator.

The elevator whisked me up what felt like a zillion floors in the snap of a finger. I briefly wondered if Gem knew I'd arrived. Then I remembered he had security on every inch of his building, and it would take a lot more than a casual visit from me to surprise him.

When the doors drew open, I stood inside for a long moment. A beat too long. I stood for so long that the elevator doors began to automatically slide shut, and I was forced to stick my leg out and let the doors bounce off my calf to reopen like a real idiot.

A soft laugh sounded from inside the breathtaking penthouse, and I realized my little elevator mishap had not gone unnoticed. As I stepped onto the landing, the man behind the laugh strolled into sight, one hand shoved in the pocket of his expensive suit.

I studied him for a moment, wanting to ignore the fact that my heart hammered against my chest as I laid eyes on him. Gem's playful curls fell softly onto his forehead. He leaned against the wall, looking trim and expensive and downright magnificent as a smile tripped up his lips while he studied me back.

My breath felt short and hard to catch, like my throat was burning every time I inhaled oxygen.

Gem's gaze grew concerned at my strange breathing pattern. He studied me closer, and I could feel his stare landing on my bloodshot eyes. "Your sister mentioned you were..." He searched for the right words. "Under the weather."

"You mean she told you I looked a little like Shrek?"

"For what it's worth, I think you look great."

"I brought you lunch." I handed him the doggie bag from my mother, grateful for an excuse to change the subject. "It's not much, but my mother insisted on sending this for you when she heard I was coming by."

Gem gestured for me to follow him as he made his way into the spotless kitchen and proceeded to put a kettle on the stove to heat. There were no dirty dishes in the sink, no coffee maker sitting on the counter. There was one potted plant (possibly fake) and a few vintage-looking cutting boards next to a window. The rest was all shiny marble countertops with off-white walls and sunlight bouncing off every corner.

"So why'd you really come?" Gem asked. He held up the bag of food. "You're too busy chasing murderers to be side-tracked with a DoorDash career, I'm sure."

I shifted uncomfortably under his stare. "I came to say thank you."

"You already thanked me for last night, if that's what this is about." Gem glanced at my eyes again. "But I guess I should be the one apologizing. Were you allergic to the chocolates?"

"I think it was the roses." I winced. "It's not your fault."

"I mean, I could've done tulips. Ranunculus. Begonias." He raised a shoulder. "I guess now I know better for next time."

"There doesn't need to be a next time." I cleared my throat. "You've already filled up my living room with flowers once. I don't expect you to ever do that again."

"What'd you think of the chocolates?"

"That's actually what I'm here about." I hesitated. "Why'd you go ahead and announce your huge news today about your latest business venture? From what I gather, that wasn't in your business plan."

"Yes, well..." Gem spun on a heel and grabbed a teacup from a nearby cupboard. "Plans change."

He set his teacup down and poured the hot, steeped beverage into it. He slid it over to me.

"You're not going to have one?" I asked.

"I'm not much of a tea guy. But my tea sommelier brought this back from Japan, and it's supposed to help with inflammation."

"Gotcha." I pointed to my eyes. "Here's hoping."

I raised the cup to my lips, took a sip. I couldn't place the floral flavor, but it was delicious.

"I'm glad you like it," Gem said, observing me carefully and seeing the appreciation on my face. "Do you have plans for tonight?"

"I'm actually working a case. I can't stay long today, I just wanted to—well, I guess I wanted to talk to you."

"Can't stay long?" Gem asked, glancing at the clock. "Or won't?"

"It's complicated."

"Yes. I read about it in the news. Very dramatic, explosions and whatnot."

I swallowed a gulp of tea too big, and it scalded my throat on the way down.

"It's hot," Gem said unhelpfully.

"Yep." I hiccupped. "Got it."

Gem moved from the kitchen island and strolled over to a wall made of windows. I took my tea and followed him, coming to a stop by his side, admiring the view of the city that sprawled before us.

"It's true, then?" I wondered aloud. "You announced your chocolate business earlier than intended because you knew it'd be a splash in the papers that would help take some of the pressure off me?"

"I don't like people like Trevor Sime."

"Me neither, but I can take care of myself."

"You shouldn't always have to."

"Maybe I want to."

"I know. That's the problem." Gem cocked his head to one side. "Don't sweat it. I consider it my civic duty to—"

"Yeah, yeah," I interrupted. "Your civic duty to help out the police because you're so rich and you want to give back and yada yada."

Gem seemed mildly amused. "You know me so well, Detective. As it so happens, I know you better than you think, too, and I don't think you came here of your own accord."

"What are you talking about?"

"I'm sure Lassie encouraged you to come down to thank me properly. I find it hard to believe this was all your idea."

I ran my tongue over my lips, dismayed at his perceptiveness. "You're not wrong."

"I know."

"I'm sorry," I said. "Though technically I did come of my own accord. I could have ignored her suggestion. I have before."

"You can prove it to me."

"Prove what?"

"That you really want to be here." Gem faced me. "Come back for dinner tonight. Then I'll believe you."

"Dinner?"

"The meal that comes after lunch."

"Why?" I blurted.

"Because that's what friends do. They spend time together for no reason at all."

My phone buzzed. I looked down at the number. Russo—of course. *We always did have perfect timing.* I swiped away his name and hoped Gem hadn't noticed.

"Well, I should get going," I said, breaking the tenuous silence. "I have a case."

"You always do." Gem's smile was tight. "The person who ends up with you has to understand that, don't they?"

"Is that a comment on Jack?"

"That's a comment on you. Detective." The last word was a complete sentence. He took a breath, let it out. "Don't let me keep you."

"Thanks for the tea." I dropped the mug on the counter as I made my way to the exit. "And for everything else."

As I stepped into the elevator, the air felt heavy between us. As if the conversation that had passed between us had been only a small part of what we'd really wanted to say, while layers and layers of unspoken truths flowed by underneath.

I refused to be distracted by the nuances of my relationship with Gem, however, when I had so many more pressing issues I needed to focus on. Forcing myself to march out of the building without thinking about the awkwardness I'd left behind, I glanced at the front desk. Ms. Karp had abandoned her post for possibly the first time ever. A young blonde woman with oversized glasses sat there instead.

I left through the front doors, fishing for the valet tab in my pocket. I handed it over to the same gentleman I'd seen barely half an hour before. My car was returned to me in a jiff. As I drove away from the glittering skyscraper, I couldn't help but feel like Gem's eyes were following me. Of course there was no way to know if Alastair Gem could see me from his bird's-eye perch above the city, and even if he could, I was sure he wouldn't be wasting his time staring out the window looking for my car. He'd already be on his next business call. So why couldn't I get rid of the pit in my stomach?

"Tell me something good," I greeted Asha as I drove toward the precinct. "It's been a day."

Asha and I caught up on the case. I let her know about checking in with Will Comice and Billy Burton. I left out the part about Gem. Then I added the part about interviewing my dad.

"Speaking of your dad," Asha said when I finished my recap, "I have some good news for you. I've got concrete evidence that your dad's cell phone pinged off the phone towers around his place the night in question. We also have some traffic cam footage from around the scene of Heinrich's murder, and I've scanned the license plates for all your family cars—there's nothing."

"Jeez. You didn't waste a minute checking out my family."

"The faster we can prove your dad had nothing to do with it, the faster we can find the guy who did it."

I blew out a breath. "Sorry. And thanks."

"I know none of that is enough to convince a jury—there could be an alternative explanation for the cell phone, for example, but it *is* a helpful place to start."

"Thanks, Asha."

"While Burton is a good lead, I'm still digging into his records." Asha coughed. "As a computer programmer, he's quite talented. His security systems have slowed me down a bit."

"Don't tell me you've been outsmarted."

"Oh, please." The click of Asha's fingernails against her keyboard sounded across the phone line. "I just need another few minutes, and his files will be opening themselves for me. In the meantime, let me present to you some information on Charles Randolph."

"I'm listening."

"You probably already know most of it. Detective Heinrich put Randolph away. He escaped prison once, then was put back by Heinrich himself. Randolph then served out his sentence and was released exactly nine weeks ago on parole."

"The timeline certainly checks out."

"Sure does," she said. "He's staying at a little apartment near Lake Nokomis. Bit of a drive, especially leading into rush hour. Traffic will be a bear to get to his place. But I do have a piece of good news for you."

"What's that?"

"He's at home," she said. "I was able to take a peek into the security system on his apartment complex. He arrived at his apartment an hour ago, carrying a bag of groceries. I thought he might've skipped out after the news broke about Heinrich's death, but it doesn't seem that way. I talked to his parole officer too. So far, Randolph's been an angel—his words not mine."

"So either Randolph is playing it cool and hanging around, confident we won't catch him," I said, "or he didn't do it."

"If he were to leave the city, he'd be breaking parole. Even if he's innocent, he'd be thrown in prison."

"I mean, technically, he was supposed to stay in prison the first time, but he didn't follow those rules," I said. "So I'm thinking he's not much of a stickler for the law."

"Agreed. But he'll have a lot more freedom once his year of parole is up," Asha countered. "My bet is that he's just playing the role of a changed man. It's after his year is up that I'm going to start worrying. In my experience, guys like him don't quit."

"Thanks."

"What's your plan?"

"I'm not sure yet."

"Wait until tomorrow morning to visit this guy," Asha offered. "He's not going anywhere, or he'd be gone already. Double bonus is you'll be able to beat traffic tomorrow morning."

"Keep me posted if you find anything else, okay?"

"Is everything okay?"

"Yeah, why?"

"You seem different, a little off."

"We'll talk more later," I said, dodging her question. "I've got another call."

I hung up with Asha. I didn't have another call. But I did need to use my GPS. I pulled over, found Charles Randolph's address in the file Asha had zipped my way, and plugged it into Google Maps. Then I set off to pay a visit to our little friend with a penchant for arson.

As I drove, I ignored the thoughts curling into my mind. Asha was probably right. I should wait for tomorrow to interview Randolph. I *should* take Jimmy with me. I should, I should, I should do lots of things, and yet I wasn't going to listen to that little voice in my head because I needed to do something now. I needed to be distracted, and Charles Randolph was just the man to distract me.

Chapter 13

Charles Randolph lived in an apartment that was probably more expensive than it looked on the outside. He was in a good location in the middle of Minneapolis, a little plot of residences tucked between the snaking bodies of water that made up Lake of the Isles.

I glanced at the security camera as I opened the front door and hoped Asha wasn't peeking at me behind her computer screen. Just in case, I silenced my phone so I wouldn't hear it if she called. I very specifically did *not* want to be talked out of my plan.

I made my way up the first floor to Apartment 204, which Asha's files told me belonged to Charles Randolph. I knocked on the door, and it didn't take long for it to open. As I faced Randolph, I had a moment of doubt about my judgment. But it was too late to turn back now.

Randolph smiled at me. "I thought you'd be coming by."

I waited a beat. "You know who I am, then?"

Randolph was right around my father's age, but he looked a few years older in person. I wondered if the wrinkle lines around his eyes were due to his time in prison. Or a stressful criminal career. Or maybe it was just unlucky genetics.

The wrinkles made him look harder, worn rough around the edges. A scar cut across his chin, raised and faintly purple. I glanced at his hand, remembering that he'd actually burned off his fingerprints years ago—voluntarily.

Randolph raised a can of beer and took a swig. "It wasn't too hard to figure out you'd be swinging by. I'm not a dumbass."

"Should I consider that my invitation to come inside?"

Randolph contemplated for a moment. "A few minutes ago, I was gonna turn you away. But I've changed my mind."

I followed Charles into his apartment. Despite the scar and the general worn-rough nature of him, he wasn't an unattractive guy for his age. He was around my height, and his build was sturdy and muscled. He looked like a knock-off version of Stallone. He had dark hair, a brooding gaze, and a careful glint in his eye.

Randolph's apartment looked to be a simple one bedroom. The living room was neat, furnished appropriately for an older single man. He had a couch with an old TV perched in front of it. An armchair that looked more comfortable than it did stylish lounged on one side. A single blanket was strewn on the couch.

I couldn't see into the bedroom or the bathroom. The kitchen was open to the living room, separated by a barheight counter. Randolph nodded toward the barstools, and I slid onto one. He walked around into the kitchen, facing me across the standard black granite countertop.

"Do you want something to drink?"

I shook my head. "I'm on the clock."

Randolph gave me a shrewd smile. He spun his can around. It took me a minute, but I glanced closer at the label and saw that it was some fancy sort of non-alcoholic beer.

"No thanks," I said. "I'm still good."

"It's all about appearances." Randolph leaned against the counter. "Then again, you know that, I'm sure. Underestimate and overdeliver, ain't that right?"

"You mean, you like to let people think you're stupid, old, and drunk." I crossed my arms. "Then you turn around and blow them up?"

"That escalated quickly."

"You seem like the sort of guy who cuts right to the chase."

"I'm real glad I invited you in. I haven't had this kind of entertainment since I was behind bars."

"Happy to help," I said. "Now maybe you can do me a favor and tell me where you were two nights ago? Let's say between 3 and 7 a.m."

"That's a big window."

"Not really. Most people have an easy answer," I said dryly. "They're at home sleeping, for example."

"I'm not most people."

"So where were you?"

"Home."

"Not sleeping?"

"I don't need much sleep," he said. "I'm an early riser. I walked my dog around six in the morning."

"You don't have a dog."

"You're getting faster." He smiled. "I was here. What I was doing is none of your business. And yes, I was alone."

"I'm assuming you know why I'm paying you a visit?"

Unlike Billy Burton, Randolph didn't make me expand. He simply carried on as if the answer was obvious. "You know, Detective, there's a big question you're missing. Why would I have waited until now to kill Heinrich?"

"Detective Heinrich made it his life's work to put you behind bars. When you escaped prison, you probably thought you had it made. Then he pulled you over for speeding, and back you went."

"I've been out for over two months. Why wait until now? If I was looking for revenge, I wouldn't have waited this long."

"You like to be prepared. You'd have learned a bit about patience in jail. I imagine your little explosion in the mess hall took more than a couple of days of planning time."

"Who says I was behind that?" He shrugged. "Nothing was ever proven. I just took advantage of a messy situation."

"Uh-huh. I'm just saying, you have a link to Heinrich. You also happen to know what you're doing when it comes to explosives. There's a reason I'm here tonight, and we both know it."

"Okay."

"Heinrich put you in jail," I reiterated. Then, "Twice."

"Sure, he was a pest." Randolph gave a faint smile, looking as if he were using the term almost endearingly. "But he loved me."

"Sorry? I'm having a difficult time believing that Heinrich loved you. You were the bane of his existence from what I gather."

"Bingo. He loved to hate me." Randolph studied me carefully. "You and I aren't so different. Two sides of the same coin. Without guys like me, you're nothing."

"That's where you're wrong. I'd *love* to have my job rendered useless, but because of people like you, that'll never happen."

"That's not true, though, is it? You love what you do. You thrive on it. Why else are you here tonight?"

"Excuse me?"

"It's getting late. I know where you live." He paused to let that sink in. "It's not an easy drive to get here. I'm obviously not fleeing. I'm not even your best lead. Why not interview me tomorrow morning with your partner, once you've had a little time to prepare?"

I tried my best to keep a poker face despite the fact that Randolph had hit a nerve.

He raised his fake beer in my direction. "You use people like me to hide from the rest of your life. You're just like Heinrich. He did the same thing. He had no real life. The job *was* his life."

"I'm not like Heinrich." I thought back to files I'd studied on the former cop. It'd become quite evident that Heinrich was indeed a loner, married to the job. Most people hadn't even said he was friendly. There hadn't been a lot of personal information to uncover about him, period.

"There's nothing wrong with the way you are, Kate Rosetti. Or should I say Detective?"

"Don't pretend like you know me."

"You're the yin to my yang. I understand you better than anyone else in your personal life. Better, even, than your own father. He got out of the business. He's happily married from what I can tell. He's living his life. You and me, Kate...we live for this kind of thing. The adrenaline of it. We live life on the edge, a different edge than everyone else."

I stared at him, transfixed, frozen. I hated it, yet I couldn't stop listening to his low voice as he spoke in soothing tones.

"Everyone else is tucked cozy in their homes tonight. Eating dinner. Watching movies. Petting their dogs. You, though, you came to spend time with me." He raised his can and took another swig. "I let you in because I recognized that. You and I, we get one another. It's why people like us don't change."

"You shouldn't be telling me that you haven't transformed," I said. "I could go to your parole officer."

"You're not recording this. Even if you were, the conversation is too embarrassing for you to share with anyone." He shrugged nonchalantly. "Stop fighting it, Kate. Don't worry about other people 'not getting you.' We blow off commitments. We don't get attached. We push people away. It's what we do."

"Shut up," I said, placing my hands on the counter. "Stop talking like you know me. Don't call me Kate. You don't know anything about me."

He set his drink down and raised his hands. "Touched a nerve there. I'll back off. But I think we both know that you're only bothered by me because you know it's true. Otherwise, you'd roll your eyes and leave."

"If you killed Heinrich," I said, "I'm going to find out. And you'll be put in prison for good this time."

Randolph gave a big smile, a true grin, his eyes glinting with the challenge. "I look forward to playing with you, Detective."

"This isn't a game."

"Sure it is," he said with a wink. "Cops and robbers."

I turned and stormed to the door.

"Thanks for coming by tonight." Randolph followed as I let myself out. He called after me down the hallway. "Take care, Kate."

It wasn't until I was in my car, stuck in a mind-numbing traffic jam, that I began to decompress. Slowly, reluctantly, like a balloon with a pinhole leak. Randolph had taken advantage of my lack of preparation and rattled my cage. I'd let him toy with me.

He knew me better than I knew him. I'd rushed into the situation against my better judgment. That was a mistake I wouldn't make again. A mistake I couldn't afford to repeat.

Because of that, I'd let him push my buttons. I'd made the whole interaction a piece of cake to him, a game. No wonder he'd let me in. He was like a cat batting around a mouse, and it was embarrassing.

I wasn't sure if it was the fact that I'd effectively lost the first battle with Randolph that bothered me, or if it was the fact that he'd drilled into something—*some things*—that bothered me on a personal level. Maybe both. *Probably both*, if I were willing to admit it, but I wasn't sure I wanted to.

I was still stewing over the fact that I'd barely touched on the subject of an alibi with Randolph, let alone teased any useful information out of the botched interview, when my phone rang.

"I told you not to go tonight," Asha said. "You ignored my calls."

"Sorry. I had my phone on silent."

"Gee. How unfortunate." She waited a beat. "I called Jimmy."

I groaned. "Is he on his way?"

"No, but only because I told him not to go anywhere. I told him to wait for me to give him the green light." She made me wait for one more painstaking moment. "I already texted him to stay home and that you're fine. But he's not happy with you going to Randolph's without letting him know. Frankly, neither am I."

"I'm sorry." I glanced out at the sea of red brake lights in front of me. "I made a mistake."

"Excuse me, but is this the Kate Rosetti I know and love? The famed detective?"

"Hey, I can admit when I'm wrong."

Asha sounded more concerned when she spoke again. "What's going on with you? I'm starting to get really worried."

"It's nothing," I confirmed. "Except the fact that I have no clue what I'm doing with my life."

"Wow. Well..." Her fingernails stopped typing in the background. "Yeah, that's not nothing, honey." She paused. "It's going to take you thirty-seven minutes to get to Bellini's. I'll gather the girls."

I hung up, both dreading the impromptu therapy session with my friends and also feeling desperate for it. I was in over my head, and I wasn't sure how to get out.

For my sake, and the sake of my partner, my friends, and my family, I needed to clear my mind before it cost me dearly.

Chapter 14

I walked into Bellini's and came face to face with my cousin Angela. She took one look at me and wrinkled her nose.

"Yeah, I'll grab you that margarita," she said without preface.

I headed to the usual table I shared with the girls. I had beaten the other three women to the restaurant and was first in the booth. As I slid off my coat, Angela appeared with a drink.

"I gave got you an extra-large. Size upgrade on the house," she said. "Looks like it was that sorta day, huh?"

"That's one way to put it."

"Sorry, hon. Anything I can do?"

"Bring me a straw?"

"You got it. Drown your sorrows on me tonight."

Angela snapped her gum and plunked a straw in my drink. Then she turned tail, the frosted tips of her hair flicking back and forth as she sashayed away. I waited a suspiciously long time for the other girls to arrive. I was well and truly feeling the buzz of my margarita when Melinda showed up.

"Asha called me." Melinda's hair fell in soft curls over her shoulders. She shrugged deeper into her powder blue peacoat. Her cheeks were a picturesque rosy from the cold.

"I figured." I patted the seat next to me. "Everyone else is late."

"The other girls aren't coming." Melinda remained standing.

"But Asha said—"

"I know; she told me. She called me first, and I requested to meet with you alone."

"Should I be concerned?"

"Come with me for a drive," she proposed. "I thought we could have a conversation just the two of us for old times' sake."

I shrugged on my jacket and gave her a grateful smile. "You do know me the best."

I threw some money on the table, took one last sip of my drink, and climbed out from the booth. I followed Melinda to her newest lease, a sparkling white BMW that matched her pristine, furry, white gloves. We climbed inside. The car and seats were still warm from her drive over.

As Melinda took off, I didn't ask where we were going. She didn't seem particularly sure herself. We just cruised around with no destination in mind. It took several minutes for her to speak first.

"I know we've both been busy lately," she said finally. "I know we haven't spent as much time hanging out just the two of us as we used to."

"It's not your fault."

"I know it's not." She gave a short laugh. "You share the blame with me."

"Touché."

"But you know I care about you, Kate. I love you like a sister."

"You really don't have to do this. I'm sure Asha made it sound like I was having a midlife crisis or something, but I'm really not. I've just got a lot on my plate."

"That's fair, but it doesn't mean you can't talk to me anyway."

I didn't particularly want to have *that* sort of a conversation, but Melinda didn't seem keen on driving me to my house. She didn't seem keen on stopping the car at all, and I suspected she'd sort of commandeered my freedom by trapping me in her BMW until I spilled my secrets. I watched a few houses flash by. Keeping my gaze focused strictly out the window, I took a shaky breath.

"I don't know what makes me happy anymore."

Melinda remained silent. I heard the shift of fabric as her gloved hands tightened around the steering wheel. She took a right and drove down a side street.

"The job has always been enough for me," I continued. "It *is* enough for me."

"And yet you're having some doubts."

"It is *so* annoying to be uncertain," I said. "I don't know why I'm suddenly having doubts about my life choices. This has never happened before."

She gave a tinkling laugh. "It's not a bad thing, Kate. As humans we're meant to change. We grow, morph, transform. I don't have to give you a speech about cocoons and butterflies, do I?"

"Yeah, right. You'd probably give me a speech about the life cycle of maggots or something."

Her smile was still faint on her lips, but her tone turned serious. "What's actually on your mind?"

Since I couldn't figure a way out of this moving vehicle without offering up some sort of explanation Melinda deemed satisfactory, I decided to try my best. I told her about my perspective on the case. About Heinrich and his life, a life in which he ended up alone, died alone. How I couldn't even find much in the way of friends or family to interview.

"Stop drawing parallels where they don't exist," Melinda said. "You have friends. You've got me, Jimmy, Asha, Lassie. Your parents, your sister. And more."

She let the last word hang, as if she wasn't quite sure who else to include. The glaring options would be Gem and Russo.

"I know. It's not just that. I also visited Charles Randolph tonight, and he got in my head. About people like me. People like him."

"His job is to get in your mind," Melinda argued. "He's a career criminal. His whole life is based on toying with people's emotions. You can't let him get to you. It's a game to him; that's all it is."

"Normally I can shake off people like him," I said. "Why am I so off my game?"

"Because things are changing. Your perspective is changing," Melinda said. "And that is okay. You know what's interesting? You haven't once mentioned the fact that you've been through a breakup recently. That's a big life change. Jack was someone you really cared about. He still is."

"I guess." I briefly thought of Jack's missed phone call. "But for all I know, he's moved on already."

"Are you moving on?"

An image from Gem's penthouse flashed into my mind. The way he'd stood close to me, the way my heart had felt like it was rattling around in my chest, out of control.

"I don't know," I admitted. "I can't quite figure out what I should be doing."

"Do you want my opinion?"

Melinda accelerated as she pulled onto the highway. It was dark outside now, and soon enough we were streaking down the road beneath the glow of streetlights and the wash of a bright moon.

"I think you're going to tell me anyway," I said. "So go on."

"I wanted you to marry Jack."

I glanced at her finally, surprised. "Huh?"

"I thought he was perfect for you." She flickered a quick glance in my direction before swiveling her attention back on the road. "He understood your work schedule and the ties that bound you to your job. He's just like you."

"Okay. Is this supposed to make me feel better?"

"Better yet, he's charming in a down-to-earth way. He really loved you, Kate. And seriously, the guy is attractive." She tapped her fingers against the wheel. "The two of you were perfect together."

I swallowed.

"And yet, I was wrong. For a couple weeks after the two of you broke up, I thought he'd come back and grovel. I thought maybe you'd fly out there and visit him. I really thought it wasn't over."

My throat felt scratchy. My phone, Russo's name on my call log, felt like a brick in my pocket.

"But I'm beginning to think it might be over. Then I got to thinking it's sad, sure—endings always are—but maybe it *should* be over. Maybe that was the right choice, as much as I didn't want it to be."

"I'm sorry to disappoint you."

"Not for my sake, but for yours," she said without missing a beat. "I don't actually care who you end up with. I just care that it's the right person for you, and a few months ago, I would have bet a lot of money on the fact that the guy to do it was Jack."

"You changed your mind?"

"No. I didn't change my mind. You changed my mind."

"What do you mean?"

"I think that maybe Jack's not the one who is causing you to question everything," Melinda said. "I think he could have been a part of it. A part of realizing what you don't want. Or rather, realizing what your heart needs instead of your head."

"I think you're leaping to conclusions."

"I'm not talking about any one person," Melinda said. "I know you think I'm talking about Gem, but I'm really not. I'm talking about love in general. About your life. You've watched your parents reconcile and remarry. You've watched your sister fall in love. You lost Chloe in a sense, a friend and colleague, to the love of her life. All in a couple of months' time."

"I'm happy for them."

"Right," Melinda said. "And maybe it's giving you some ideas about what your life is missing."

Melinda pulled off the highway and drove in silence for a few moments.

"I know the only reason you *think* you're bothered is because you made a questionable decision at work tonight, and that's unlike you. I know you, and you don't like feeling a step behind, especially at work." She waited for me to acknowledge her. When I gave a reluctant nod, she continued. "But I don't think you're going to feel like yourself until you sort out some of these personal issues."

"I've always been able to separate personal from business."

"Until now." She gave a glimmer of a smile. "Like I said, things change."

Melinda nodded out her window. I followed her gaze and saw that my best friend had, in fact, been driving with a destination in mind. She was parked outside of Gem Industries.

"I don't see how talking with Gem can help anything."

"I don't know if it will help," Melinda said, "but it's worth a shot. You've got to start somewhere."

"But—"

"Get out of the car, Kate. You can find your own way back. It shouldn't be too hard."

"Melinda—"

"I'm your best friend, and I'm doing this for you. Tough love, Rosetti."

Somehow, in the next few minutes, I found myself abruptly standing outside of Gem Industries as snowflakes began to fall around me, staring after my best friend's receding taillights. I glanced down at my phone, debating who I could call for a ride, when I noted the forecast called for a winter storm warning beginning anytime.

My fingers itched to select my Uber app, to call for an easy ride home. Gem never had to know I was here. But I hesitated, and in that hesitation, I had my answer.

When I looked up, I found the man of the hour standing before me. Gem was dressed in a long, black coat—open, flapping against the wind. His signature curls dripped onto his forehead, frosted white from the snowfall. Beneath his coat, he wore a tailored suit, perfectly fitted to his tall, lean form.

"Gem," I murmured.

He stood there, his hands in his pockets, waiting for something. For me? I took a few steps forward. Tentative steps. Then my feet moved faster and faster until I reached his side. We stood together, under the light of the moon, the snow cocooning us in a flurry of winter.

"I know you weren't going to come upstairs," he said, though it was a gentle admonition, not an accusation.

I looked down at my feet. "I hadn't decided yet."

"All I know is that someday, you'll choose me." Gem spoke with intensity, his eyes dark and serious. "Someday you'll choose me without my having to ask for it."

"I wasn't... It's not what you think."

"In the meantime," he murmured, undeterred, "I'll keep choosing you until you tell me not to."

He raised a hand, cupped my cheek, and leaned toward me. I paused for a moment, my breath sharp, broken in the cold air. Then he closed the distance between us, our lips pressing together, until everything felt just right.

His other hand came up, drew me closer, and I relaxed against him. He was everything warm and thrilling, the beacon of light against the darkness that extended in every direction around us.

We melted together, his hands on my face, his lips against mine, that signature scent of him spiraling around us. He tasted just like I'd thought he might, like mint and fresh air and sweet familiarity. It was like we'd been here before, like we'd done this before. Everything was new and sparkling, but also warm, a trusty blanket of security and safety.

I pulled away, breathless. "That wasn't supposed to happen."

"I know." Gem gave a wry smile. "You were planning on sneaking home before you had to face me."

"Did Melinda put you up to this?" I glanced around, as if expecting hidden cameras somewhere.

"Melinda?" His face registered genuine confusion. "As in, Dr. Brooks? What does she have to do with any of this?"

"She kidnapped me and left me here."

"I didn't know that. I was just notified that you were standing outside the building by my security team."

"You have people watching me?"

"No, I have people watching my building. Would you like to come inside?"

I raised a hand and pressed a finger to my lip, to the place that still felt warm from Gem's touch. "I think that would be a bad idea."

"Or it might be the best idea you've had in a while. It's only dinner."

"You're sure?" I wasn't convinced. "Just dinner?"

"Just dinner."

Chapter 15

As the elevator rose through the floors toward the penthouse, I chanced a glance at Gem. He stood with his hands in his pockets and stared straight ahead. His face was unreadable. I was in the middle of questioning my decision to join him for dinner when the doors opened and released us into the uppermost level of the high rise.

"Be honest," I said as Gem led me to the kitchen. "Did you actually think I'd show up for dinner?"

"Does that matter?"

"Just curious."

He pulled out a bottle of wine and began to uncork it. "Will this do?"

"I drank a margarita with a straw earlier tonight." I slid onto the barstool and folded my hands on the counter. "I'm not picky."

Gem poured out two glasses. "How do you feel about pasta?"

"It's hard to feel anything but love for pasta," I said. "Especially if it's slathered in cheese."

"I was thinking we'd make it from scratch."

"Make what from scratch?"

Gem gave me a little smile. "The pasta."

"I didn't actually know that was possible," I said. "It's hard enough for me to boil the water it takes to make boxed pasta."

Gem gave a playful tsk. "My mom was of Italian descent. She made sure I knew how to make fresh noodles. I already have the dough made and resting in the fridge. If you're up for it, I thought we could try ravioli."

"That sounds labor intensive."

"Are you physically starving?"

"Well, no."

"Then what's the rush?"

I glanced outside, knowing I couldn't get anywhere if I wanted to with how much snow was starting to pile on us. The even more surprising part was that I didn't want to go anywhere. Gem's apartment was warm and cozy. He was promising me wine and pasta. I'd almost forgotten that we'd shared a kiss outside that had made me equal parts wildly uncomfortable and deliciously intrigued.

"Fair enough," I said. "Ravioli it is."

An hour later, we were in the homestretch of our pasta-making extravaganza. A pot of boiling salted water gurgled on the stove. Next to it, a bowl of misshapen ravioli sat ready to dive in headfirst. The kitchen was dusted in a layer of flour that was probably my fault.

"I'm a mess." I glanced down at my clothes which were powdered white. "And I'm sorry about your kitchen."

Without an explanation, Gem ducked out of the room. He left me behind with the pot of boiling water. I tapped my fingers nervously against the countertop. When he returned a minute later, he held a stack of clothes in his hands.

"I have a pair of sweats I think you might fit into," Gem said. "Care to rinse off before dinner?"

"No, Gem. I'm not taking a shower here."

"You're a mess," he insisted. "Every time you move, a cloud of flour floats behind you. It's as much for my furniture as it is for your comfort. I won't begin to comment on what your hair looks like."

A glance in a mirror mounted on the wall told me plenty. I looked like I'd gone prematurely gray.

With a huff, I grabbed the stack of sweats from his hands. He nodded down the hallway.

"First door on the right," he said. "Towels are in the cupboard."

I marched reluctantly down the hall toward Gem's bathroom. It felt like such an imposition to be taking a shower at his place, but he'd had a point about me being a threat to his surely expensive furniture. That, plus the fact that I had no car and no real way of getting home, considering the blizzardy conditions outside, was enough to convince me that I was staying put for the near future.

It didn't take long before I was convinced I'd made the right choice in agreeing to shower. Rinsing off at Gem's penthouse felt more luxurious than a trip to any spa I'd experienced. He had one of the rainfall-type showerheads where water poured from the ceiling, and a fully stocked array of spendy soaps and shampoos.

A large window to the outdoors had me feeling self-conscious at first until I realized that absolutely nobody could see into the bathroom at this elevation. But the view out was magnificent. City lights stretched into the distance, blurred with the whirling snowflakes. Much of the city was buried under a pile of white, giving off a quiet, calm, cozy ambiance—a stillness, as if everyone was tucked in for the night.

I quickly washed, taking deep inhalations of the expensive shampoo, a brand I was certain couldn't be found at my local Target. A sprig of fresh eucalyptus hung from the shower handle. The faint odor of lemon fluttered about in the air.

Forcing myself to shut the water off, I dried off with a towel made of clouds, then sifted through the pile of clothes on the counter. There were no less than three sweatshirts, two pairs of pants, a couple of shorts, socks, the works.

I selected a large T-shirt that draped with a V-neck and the smallest size shorts in the stack. I left my feet bare since Gem's penthouse was plenty warm. I found a comb in the drawer and ran it through my hair, spiraling my still damp locks into a messy bun. When I finally finished and glanced in the mirror, I was beyond relieved that my eyes seemed to be looking distinctly less bloodshot and my hair distinctly less gray.

Feeling surprisingly refreshed, I followed my nose to the scent of marinara and padded toward the kitchen. Gem was at the stove shutting off the burner when I slid onto the barstool. He turned and did a double take when he saw me, as if he hadn't heard me enter.

He studied my face for a moment, for so long I shifted with discomfort, before he seemed to snap out of his daydreams. Grabbing a colander, he drained the pasta at the sink.

"I hope you're hungry," Gem said finally.

My stomach growled in response. The stress of the day had gotten my adrenaline racing earlier, and I realized that I was famished. As Gem pulled out two plates and began to serve up our meal, my phone beeped.

"I'm so sorry," I said, glancing down and seeing Asha's name on the screen. "I have to take this."

I stepped back from the kitchen and into Gem's living room. His place was modern, an open floor plan, and there wasn't much in the way of privacy.

"Hey," I said. "What's going on?"

"Just checking on you. Your car is still at Bellini's, but Angela says you left a while ago."

"I'm fine," I said. "Are you tracking my car?"

"That's it?" she asked, ignoring my question. "That's really all I get?"

"Melinda took me for a little drive."

"Are you with someone whose last name starts with G and ends with EM?"

"That would be a Y followed by E-S."

"Very interesting. Well, lucky for you, I'm actually calling about business. I found out a little fun fact about your pal Trevor Sime."

"The reporter?"

"The one and only. Turns out he was actually fired from his job at the North Star Press, and I can't figure out why."

"How was he fired if he still works there?"

"He was quietly reinstated a few weeks later. I'm also not sure how that happened, but it does smell fishy to me."

"I concur."

"On the off chance you want to pay him a visit tomorrow morning, I've taken the liberty of peeking at his calendar. He's got some required staff meetings, so he'll be at the office."

"Thank you, Asha. I appreciate it."

"Do you need a ride home?"

I glanced at Gem, at the snow outside. I considered my options. "No, thanks. I'll find my own way back."

Asha smacked her lips on the other end of the phone as if blowing me a kiss. "Sweet dreams, chica. Let me know when you're en route to the North Star Press tomorrow."

"You got it."

I made my way back to the table set for two. The ravioli sat doused in an aromatic red sauce. My stomach growled again, like a caged tiger. Gem looked up at me, his expression pensive as I took a seat across from him.

"That was Asha," I explained. "She had an update about the case."

"Do you need to leave?"

I cleared my throat. "Not tonight. Er, not yet, I mean."

Gem poured me another glass of wine in response. I took a sip, letting the liquid warm my belly. I tucked my bare feet under me, feeling delightfully cozy and clean and hungry. I turned my attention to the view outside, where the wind whipped by, and it felt like I was cocooned in a snow globe.

"You'd shell out a lot of money for a view like this at a restaurant," I murmured. "Not to mention the handmade ravioli."

Gem took a sip of his wine. "I do shell out a lot of money for this view."

"You know what I mean. Do you like it here?"

"It's a place to stay," Gem said. "I don't live here full time. It suits my needs when I want to be downtown. Why?"

"Just curious. It's beautiful and all, but..." I shrugged. "I don't know what I'm trying to say."

"You don't think it feels like a home."

"I guess. I don't know. It's just so perfect it's hard to imagine actually living here."

"It's funny you should say that. Actually, Mindy liked this place." Gem swirled the wine in his glass. "We stayed here together quite often."

I forked a ravioli and popped it in my mouth. "Speaking of Mindy, how are you feeling after your breakup? Are you...okay?"

Gem sat back in his seat, looking carefully at my face. "I am okay. I appreciate you asking."

"Of course."

"What about you?" he asked. "How are things between you and Jack?"

"There is no 'me and Jack.'" I took my time to chew another bite. "I don't know what's next for me, to be honest. I'm trying to figure that out."

"I see."

"Gem, about earlier tonight..." A flash of the kiss we'd shared wiggled its way into my brain, and I found it hard to focus. "I don't want you to think it means more than it should."

"It doesn't have to mean anything. It's not a problem."

I opened my mouth to respond, but once again, my phone buzzed. I looked down, annoyed, ready to silence the second interruption of the evening. Then I saw a name I hadn't seen in months, and it sent a chill down my spine.

"I'm sorry," I said again, already standing and moving away from the table. "I think I need to take this."

"Hi, Kate." The female voice on the other end of the line dove right into the conversation. "I'm sure you weren't expecting to hear from me."

"No, uh, I wasn't." I sat on Gem's living room couch and played with the edge of a throw blanket. The voice on the other end of the phone belonged to Mindy Hartlett.

"I'm sure you're wondering why I'm calling," Mindy said. "I'll make this brief. Your father reached out to me today."

I groaned. "*You're* the lawyer he mentioned?"

"You sound utterly thrilled."

"It's not anything to do with you," I added. "I told my father I didn't want anyone interfering with this case. I can watch my own back."

"That's fair, and I respect that." Mindy waited a beat. "I would also urge you to consider the fact that I understand men like Trevor Sime. I know the ins and outs of the law—what folks can get away with and what they can't. I'm extending the offer to help you. Free of charge, of course. I still owe you one."

I assumed she was referencing the kidnapping case in which she'd been the kidnappee, and I'd helped secure her safe release. "You don't owe me anything. I was just doing my job."

"I won't argue with you. Just know that I have my ways of making tricky situations like yours, shall we say, disappear."

"I know this is a change of subject, but aren't you backpacking across Europe or something?"

"Look, I gave traveling my best effort. I tried to *Eat, Pray, Love* my way across Italy and find my Zen in India and what have you, but honestly, I'm more of a power suit sort of woman. I'm back in the States, currently based in Chicago, but it's a quick flight up if you'd like to utilize my services."

"I'm okay, but really, thank you."

"I'll be here if you change your mind. You have my number."

In the background, Gem answered his phone. There was a long beat of silence at the other end of the line. I crossed my fingers that she hadn't heard his voice. My wish, however, had been made in vain.

Mindy gave a polite cough. "Please tell Alastair I say hello."

"Mindy, wait—"

"Good night, Kate. Speak soon."

Before I could explain myself, she hung up the phone. I stood there for a long moment, stunned. I felt another prickle skitter across my skin, unsure exactly what to make of the phone call. Both her offer to help me free of charge and her subtle nudge that she knew exactly where I was—and *whom* I was with.

I turned around, heading back to the table, unsure of how I was going to share the news with Gem that his ex-fiancée had called me with the offer of working together.

But Gem wasn't at the table. He'd stepped into the kitchen, his back turned to me. He spoke in low murmurs. I returned to my place and sat before my ravioli, toying with the last of the dish. I took a sip of wine. I tried not to eavesdrop on Gem's phone call, but it was next to impossible not to overhear some of it.

"That is what I pay you to do," he snapped. "Schedules are meant to be flexible. Yes, well, I changed the date, so it's up to you how you'd like to handle that. I trust you'll figure it out. Good night, Eric."

Then he hung up, and I wasn't entirely sure if Eric had been ready for the conversation to end.

"Sorry," Gem said, returning to the table. He looked a bit miffed but quickly composed himself as he slid into his seat. "Business."

"You know, now that you mention it, I never hear your phone ring when you're with me," I said. "Which is pretty shocking, considering the number of people who probably want to be in contact with you."

"Of course my phone doesn't ring when I'm with you," Gem said, reaching again for his wine. "I turn it on silent."

"Oh. Right."

"Don't take that the wrong way," Gem said quickly. "I'm not insinuating you should silence your phone when you're around me. Your work is decidedly more pressing than mine."

"I didn't mean to eavesdrop, but I couldn't help but hear a little bit of your conversation," I admitted. "Is someone upset with you for moving your new business launch up?"

Gem considered his words. "Yes."

"I'm sorry. I feel like it's my fault."

"My company, my choice. Eric works for me, and he's paid handsomely to follow my lead." Gem replaced the napkin in his lap. "End of story. Shall we continue our dinner?"

"Before we do, there's one more thing I have to tell you," I said. "My phone call was from Mindy."

"Ah, speak of the devil."

"My dad reached out to her. She was offering to help me, legally, with the media situation right now."

"You should take her up on it."

"Excuse me?"

"She's one of the brightest legal minds in this part of the country. And she has experience dealing with unscrupulous types. In fact, it's her specialty. Trevor Sime is nothing compared to the sort of company Mindy used to keep."

"She knew I was here," I said. "She heard your voice in the background."

"So?"

"I wasn't sure if that would make you uncomfortable."

"It doesn't."

Gem seemed suddenly short on words. I couldn't tell which part of our conversation had upset him, so finally, I nodded and played with my fork. I wasn't exactly ravenous anymore.

Gem and I feigned interest in the ravioli we'd spent an hour making, but after a few more minutes of small talk, he suggested we break for dessert. I declined sweets but took him up on his offer of a decaf coffee.

"What do you say to a movie?" he asked, pressing the button on a Nespresso machine in his kitchen. "There won't be any Ubers out in this weather."

I glanced outside and saw that we'd accumulated at least six to eight inches of snowfall in the time I'd spent at Gem's penthouse, and the snow was coming down thicker and thicker. The roads would be slippery and dangerous.

"Let me guess," I drawled, turning my attention back to the kitchen. "Your limos aren't out and about in this weather either."

"That would be a grave safety hazard for the drivers." He gave me a playful smile. "What kind of a boss would I be to suggest my workers drive in extremely precarious conditions?"

I accepted the mug of coffee, wrapped my hands around its warmth, and followed Gem to the sofa. He handed over a plush blanket, and we curled up next to one another. Not close enough to be considered an official snuggle. Not quite far enough apart for it to be considered platonic.

The movie played on, leaving us in comfortable silence. Around the halfway point, I suddenly found it difficult to keep my eyes open. The wind brushed the outside of the building in a lulling, rhythmic way. The couch itself was as soft as cotton candy.

I felt a kiss brush against my forehead as I drifted in between consciousness and sleep.

"Stay tonight," the whisper encouraged against my ear.

I grumbled a half-hearted, "But—"

"It's too dangerous to leave. Sleep here, and I'll drive you home in the morning."

I was drowsy enough to think this murmured idea was pretty sound. "Only if I can take the couch."

"I insist on letting you take the bed, and I'll take the couch."

"Sorry, but that's my final offer."

Another kiss against my forehead as my eyes began to close. "Goodnight, Kate."

Chapter 16

The next morning, consciousness rolled over me like a gentle wave. I stirred, a prisoner beneath the plush blanket Gem had draped over me the night before. I snuggled in deeper, wishing for just five more minutes of sleep.

But, somewhere, deep in my subconscious, alarm bells were ringing. I sat bolt upright. *Alarm bells.* My alarm always went off before the sun, but today, there'd been no alarm, and yet the sun was streaming through the windows.

It took a full thirty seconds for me to place my surroundings. Eventually, the realization that I had slept over at Gem's penthouse sank in, leaving me feeling flustered, as if I were already a step behind.

"Good morning, Kate."

Gem strode from the kitchen, dressed in a sharp-looking power suit, his hair still slightly damp from a shower. He looked flat-out gorgeous. Even more gorgeous was the steaming mug of coffee perched between his hands.

He handed over the mug, smiling gently down at me. I greedily took a sip, stalling for time as I let the smooth coffee work its magic.

"How'd you sleep?" Gem asked. "I wish you would've taken the bed, but—"

"I wasn't going to kick you out of your bed."

Gem gave a mischievous smile. "We could've shared."

I tossed a throw pillow at him, carefully balancing my coffee in the other hand. "You shouldn't have let me sleep so late," I argued. "What time is it?"

"I wasn't tiptoeing around; you were dead to the world. And it's seven thirty."

I stared at him. "I'm going to be late to the office."

"I texted Jimmy."

"You text with Jimmy?" I gulped more coffee. "Since when?"

"Since I had something to tell him. We've worked together multiple times now. Do you have a problem with that?"

Reluctantly, I forced my arms to throw the furry blanket off my legs, even though every inch of my body was rebelling against the motion. I could probably have slept until lunch if I closed my eyes again.

"No," I said, standing, "but I have a problem with you interfering with my work. It's not your place to do stuff like that."

"Relax." Gem held up his hands to stop me. "I just told him you and I had a cheeky little sleepover, and I kept you up so late I thought I'd let you sleep in."

"You what?!" I picked up a second pillow and launched it at him, this time meaning it. "You did not."

"Of course I did not," Gem said with an impish grin. "I told him that I'd asked you to swing by this morning for coffee because I had an urgent matter I needed to discuss, and I apologized for keeping you from the office."

"He's still going to know something's up. He's a detective."

"Are you hiding something?"

"No, but you are making this seem more complicated than it is. We kissed. Once. That's it." I heaved a huge breath. "It's not a big deal."

Gem retrieved the two throw pillows from the floor and tossed them back to the couch. "How about this: You tell people whatever you want about us. Just let me know what you decide to share, so we can get our stories straight."

"Fine," I agreed, feeling a little guilty about how agreeable he was being about everything. "Well, I should be going, then."

Gem cleared his throat. "I think you're forgetting something."

"What now?"

He nodded at me. "Your clothes."

I cursed. "I forgot about that. I'll have to stop home first."

"I had your clothes laundered last night," Gem said, waving to the kitchen where said clothes were draped delicately over the back of a barstool. "I hope you don't mind. I found them in a little pile in the bathroom."

"You have a 24-7 laundromat here?" I said, and then I held up a hand. "I'm not going to ask."

"You're welcome to shower or use the restroom or whatever it is you need to do before you take off," Gem said. "The place is yours."

"Are you going somewhere?"

"Normally I wouldn't leave in such a rush, but I've got an urgent call."

"Ah. Let me guess. Your botched chocolate shop launch."

"I'm not sure if it's a botch job if we've completely sold out," Gem said, eyeing me. "But yes, I've got a few unhappy employees to deal with."

"Sorry."

"What else can I get you to make your stay here comfortable?"

"Nothing," I said. "I, uh, I can just go out with you."

"No need. Take your time getting ready."

"Should I leave your key card with the front desk?"

Gem grabbed a second mug and poured himself a coffee. He backed out of the kitchen and raised it in a cheers. "Why don't you hold on to it for now? Just in case."

"But—"

"Goodbye, Kate." He backed into the elevator. "Have a lovely day."

And then he was gone, and I was alone in Alastair Gem's penthouse, wearing his clothes, drinking his coffee, and having no clue how I felt about any of it.

Chapter 17

"Shut up." I greeted Jimmy as I slid into his car outside of Gem Industries. "I don't want to hear a word."

Jimmy looked positively gleeful. I'd texted him from the penthouse asking for a ride this morning. Gem Industries was already halfway to the North Star Press headquarters, so I didn't see the point of getting an Uber back to my car, which was stuck at Bellini's, only to come right back in this direction.

"So is this an official walk of shame?"

He stared straight ahead as he spoke, but I could see right through him. The man hadn't been this enthused since he'd scored free doughnuts on his birthday. I just rolled my eyes in response.

"You wore that shirt yesterday." Jimmy nodded in my direction as he cruised onto the highway. "But somehow it looks cleaner than it did yesterday."

"How many days until you retire again?"

"I'm just glad you had a good night."

"It's not what you think."

"I'll pretend I believe you."

The building in which the press offices were located was in downtown Minneapolis. It connected into the skyway system, and it'd been a nightmare to find parking with all the snow emergency alerts, especially during morning rush hour.

The offices were labeled with the local newspaper's signature star logo on the front door. We made our way to the front desk and introduced ourselves. The young man behind the desk didn't look impressed with our credentials.

"We have a PR team to handle people like you," he drawled.

I glanced at the young man's nameplate. "Thanks, Elliot, but we're not looking to talk to your PR team. We have some questions for one of your employees."

"We follow a strict no—"

"Maybe my partner's not being clear." Jimmy leaned on the front desk. "We're in the middle of a homicide investigation, and we need to talk to somebody here about it."

The man's eyes widened. "Oh, so you're not, like, here to give a quote or something?"

"On the contrary," I said. "We'd be happy to keep this little issue quiet for now with a little cooperation."

"Uh, okay, do you want my boss?"

"Where does Trevor Sime sit?" I asked. "He's a pal of mine. He's expecting me."

"He's that way. By the window. If you hit the printer you've gone too far."

Jimmy and I left the freckle-faced Elliot staring after us as we headed deeper into the newspaper headquarters. The place was buzzing with activity. It seemed everyone had a latte in hand as they flitted between desks and conversations and computer screens. The place was all open workspaces and glass-walled conference rooms.

As it turned out, Jimmy and I weren't the best at following directions. We hit the printer and backtracked a few steps. A young woman sitting behind a desk must have caught sight of our confused expressions and asked if she could help us.

"Sure," I said. "I'm looking for Trevor Sime. I was told he sat somewhere over here."

"You've found him. His desk is that one." She gestured off to one side. "Trevor's a part of my team, but he's not in yet this morning. Can I help you with something?"

"Do you work closely with him?"

She shrugged. "I guess you could say that, but it doesn't mean much. He mostly works alone. Our team is small, though, so I help him out on occasion."

"I'm Detective Rosetti, and this is my partner, Detective Jones. Do you have a few minutes so we can ask you a few questions?"

"I guess," she said. "I do have a deadline, but—"

"It won't take long," I assured her. "Is there somewhere more private we can chat?"

The woman stood and introduced herself as Meredith. She wore ripped boyfriend jeans and a pink zip-up sweatshirt with fur around the cuffs. She wore matching pink glasses that I suspected were probably not prescription strength.

Meredith sat us around a small table in a conference room and halfheartedly offered us coffee. We both declined. She eased into a chair across from us and folded her hands on the table, looking uncertain.

"I'm not sure if I should get my boss in on this, or..." She hesitated. "I'm pretty new here."

"No need to involve your boss just yet." I pulled out a notepad and set it on the table in front of me, a clean page facing up. "If it's necessary, we'll be in touch with her after this."

"What's this about?"

"We're investigating a murder," I said. "A man by the name of Jeffrey Heinrich was found dead. He used to be a detective. Ring any bells?"

"It rings a bell, but not because I knew him personally." She furrowed her eyebrows and pushed up her pink glasses before speaking again. "The story of his death made a splash in the news, didn't it? Something about corrupt cops and whatever?"

"Yes. Trevor actually wrote some of those very articles you're referencing."

"I guess I wasn't aware. Like I said, I'm pretty new here. When Trevor thinks he's got a good story, he doesn't tell anyone about it. That's why he got fired in the first place."

I looked at Jimmy, unable to believe my luck. "So you did know he got fired?"

"This is confidential, right?" Meredith looked between us, a streak of panic on her face. "I probably shouldn't have said that, but when I was hired, it wasn't a secret or anything. I only figured out that the whole debacle was a hush-hush thing after orientation."

"Why did he get fired?"

"I don't know the nitty-gritty details. I just know that I was supposed to be his replacement down the line. The team was planning to train me up so I could eventually take over his role."

"Fill in the gaps," Jimmy suggested. "How is Trevor still working for the North Star Press if he was fired?"

"I guess Trevor wanted his job back." She paused. "He's the sort of guy who will do whatever it takes to get what he wants."

"But he was fired," I said. "Why would he want to work someplace that fired him?"

"Trevor's not emotional like that. He doesn't care about people, or their feelings, or how people look at him."

"What does he care about? The fame? The prestige? The awards?"

"I don't know," Meredith said. "If I had to guess, I'd say he has an ego. He wants to be the best—whatever that means."

"Tell me about your team," I said. "Who fired him?"

"That would be Rose. Who is technically my boss, even though I work closest with the other three: Trevor, Ava, and Angie."

"Who are Ava and Angie?"

"They're the other reporters on the team under Rose."

"Are the three of them competing for a job? If Rose left, would the job go to Trevor or Ava or Angie?"

"I guess, but I wouldn't spend much time thinking about that. I don't think Rose will ever leave the company." Meredith tapped the table with her colorful fingernails. "She's been here since she was twenty-three, and she's fifty-four now. I've heard her say she plans to die at her desk, and I think she means that literally."

"Any idea why Trevor got fired, more specifically, I mean?"

"Trevor's main goal is to get ahead. He doesn't care if he breaks rules or offends people." Meredith lowered her voice to just above a whisper. "I obviously wasn't here when it happened, but I heard he got a really good lead at the last minute. He fudged Rose's signature on some paperwork for a last-minute change in copy. He replaced one of Ava's stories with one of his own without permission. That's a big no-no, in case you weren't sure."

"Understandable."

"To make matters worse, the story totally blew up overnight." Meredith's eyes widened. "Think of how Rose must have felt when she showed up with her sugar-free hazelnut latte to a C-Suite meeting and had no idea what the other executives were talking about when they started discussing Trevor's story."

"Ouch."

"It made her look really bad. Like she had no control over her team. Rumor is that she came directly back from the meeting and fired him on the spot."

"Yet he's still working here," I prompted.

"This is hearsay because I wasn't here for the dramatic part of the story. Don't quote any of this as fact."

"You got it."

"The week after Trevor was fired, they had a job posting out. I applied right away because I was working an unpaid internship before this at some blog, and it was going nowhere. North Star Press invited me for an interview the next day and offered me a job that afternoon. It was a no-brainer to take it."

"When did you start?"

"I started a week later. I didn't know much about Trevor at that time, except that he'd been fired. I did look up the story that got him fired, though. I can email it to you if you want."

"Sure," Jimmy said, handing her his card. "We'd appreciate that."

"It wasn't long before Trevor came back to the office. He just strolled in one day like he owned the place. He took his desk back—the one I'd been assigned, mind you—without bothering to introduce himself. I got moved to the desk where I'm sitting now."

"Awkward."

"Awkward and confusing," she said. "I went into Rose's office because I was afraid that I would be losing my job if Trevor was actually back. Long story short, I wasn't fired, but she shared that Trevor had been reinstated. It was weird. Nobody commented on him rejoining the team. We all just continued like nothing had ever happened."

I scratched something down on my paper, but my pen ran out of ink. Meredith smiled and rolled her pen across the table. It had a tiny diamond on the top of it that glittered under the fluorescent lighting. I picked up the pen, twirled it around, and scratched out a note on my pad to confirm Meredith's story with her boss later.

"You mentioned that Trevor would do just about anything for his job," I said. "Have you ever seen him break the rules?"

"I'm not about to rat out a colleague from my new job." Meredith looked between me and Jimmy. "You have to understand that."

"You have to understand we're investigating murder."

She sighed. "I haven't seen Trevor do anything, personally. I've just heard rumors."

"Rumors?"

"The rumors about how he got hired back. Or *why* he got hired back." She blew out a breath. "Again, I don't know if these were true, but I heard he was having an affair with someone."

"Any idea who?"

"No evidence. But use your common sense."

"Rose?" Jimmy guessed. "If he was having an affair with Rose, why would she fire him in the first place?"

"Think about it, Detective. That would have been a double betrayal to Rose," Meredith explained. "He would've betrayed her on a business level *and* a personal level. I'd totally be pissed if my boyfriend did that to me."

"Fair," Jimmy said. "But then why'd she hire him back?"

"Because she loved him?" Meredith said, clearly uncertain. "I really don't know. They both have different personalities. I don't know what makes them tick. Rose is standoffish herself. It's hard to picture her having a romantic relationship with anyone."

"Another explanation that seems pretty obvious to me here," I said, "is blackmail. Trevor seems to be exceptionally good at digging up dirt on people. Don't you think it's possible he blackmailed Rose into getting his job back instead of charming her?"

Meredith gave me a tight smile. "He's got his eyes set on you, huh?" She blinked, then did a double take. "Oh my gosh, *you're* the detective from the article. You're the one with the corrupt dad on the Heinrich story. I mean, I'm sorry, but I didn't recognize you—"

I just kept smiling until she shut herself up.

"Sorry," she repeated. "Well then, I guess you know firsthand how good he is at his job."

"Could he have been blackmailing Rose for his job back?"

Meredith met my gaze head-on. "I think you know the answer to that as well as I do."

"Where is Rose?" I asked. "Is she in the office today?"

"She left yesterday for a two-week trip to London. She won't be back until the end of the month."

"How convenient," Jimmy muttered. "I don't suppose you have her contact information?"

"I can email it to you when I send over Trevor's article." Meredith tapped Jimmy's business card with her fingertip. "You don't think she had anything to do with the murder, do you? I mean, why would she? Why would Trevor, for that matter? Do you really think this is all about some big story for them?"

"We don't have all the answers," I said. "But we're looking for them. And we'll find them."

Her eyes flicked up over my shoulder. "Speak of the devil, it looks like Trevor just got to his desk. If you don't need anything else from me, I'd prefer not to be seen speaking with you two."

Without waiting for an answer, she stood and let herself out of the room, zipping in the opposite direction from Trevor. Jimmy and I made our way out of the small office and turned to find the reporter. He found us first.

"Good morning, Detectives." Trevor smiled at us and raised a Starbucks cup in salute. "I heard rumblings about visitors waiting to ambush me this morning."

"We'd like to ask you a few questions," I said. "If you have a few minutes."

"I always have a few minutes for you, Kate." Trevor pushed open the door to the same conference room we'd just left. "I might as well have a chat with you when you're in a good mood."

"A good mood?" I asked warily, dreading the answer to his cryptic statement.

He winked. "You must have had a very interesting night, Kate Rosetti. A sleepover with a billionaire?" He paused, smiled brighter. "I'd pay to read about that. Interesting company you keep, Detective."

I felt Jimmy give me a gentle nudge as we entered the conference room. A part of me wanted to reach out and give Trevor a good shake, but I refrained. It wasn't easy to keep my cool around him, but I had to try, if for nobody else than for the chief. Sturgeon had taken a real leap of faith keeping me on this case, and I wouldn't be able to live with myself if I let him down by exploding on some nosy little reporter.

"What brings you in for a visit this morning?" Trevor slurped from his latte. "I know you didn't stop by for a coffee. We've got crap coffee here. Then again, you guys are cops. You know all about crap coffee."

"It's your lucky day," Jimmy said. "We came to see you."

"About what?"

"You know what. We're looking into the Heinrich murder, and you've got your paws all over it," Jimmy said. "I don't think we ever actually got an alibi for you the night of the murder. Where were you, night before Valentine's Day, until the wee hours of the morning?"

"None of your business."

"This is a murder investigation," Jimmy said, cutting me off before I could speak. "It is our business."

It was rare that Jimmy took the lead on interviews like this. I suspected it was due to extenuating circumstances, specifically that I intensely disliked our subject.

Trevor sat back in his seat. "Come on, guys. You can't think I'm that stupid. We're all in this business together."

"What business would that be?" Jimmy asked. "As far as I know we're the ones doing the work. You just write about us doing it."

Trevor smiled amiably. "We both work for justice. You might handcuff the bad guys, but I'm the one who exposes them to everyone else. It's important work, you know, because sometimes *you* guys are the ones who need exposing. Kate knows a thing or two about corrupt cops."

Jimmy set his hands down on the table. I could tell he was pressing hard against the tabletop, trying to keep his cool.

"You're right," I said, surprising both myself and Jimmy with the calmness in my voice. "I do know a lot about corrupt cops. A lot more than you. My problem isn't with corrupt cops. You want to write a story about my dad? Go ahead. So long as you tell the truth, I don't have any issue with it. His stint in prison is hardly a secret, and I've never tried to sweep his choices under the rug."

Trevor tapped his fingers against the table.

"What I have a problem with is you interfering with an investigation by stirring up dirt where there's none to be found," I said.

"We don't know if there's something to be found until the dirt has been kicked around a little," Trevor argued. "That is literally my job. To stir the pot and see what shakes out."

"I'm not here to argue about your job title, I'm here to—"

"What *are* you here to do, then?" Trevor pushed back his chair, grabbed his latte, and stood. "I'd like my lawyer."

"Trevor—"

"You heard me," he said. "I'd like my lawyer. You're not getting another word out of me."

"Fine." I stood. "It's not going to do you any favors to lawyer up if you're innocent, but that's your call. Maybe before you reach for your lawyer's card, you want to tell me why you got fired."

He clearly hadn't been expecting the change of subject, and he reacted with a double take. "I'm still working for the North Star Press, aren't I? How do you figure I got fired?"

"That was my next question," I said. "How'd you get your job *back*?"

Trevor's quick reflexes had caught up to him, and he'd reinstated his calm façade. "Here's what I think. I don't think you came here to interview me regarding the Heinrich case at all."

I waited for him to continue.

"I think you came here to try to intimidate me." Trevor brushed a hand through his hair, ruffling it the slightest amount. "You think I'm getting too close to the truth, and you're worried about it. I've seen this whole rigmarole before. Well, you can't intimidate me off this story. If this story has legs, I'm going to find them."

I raised my hands. "You can dig and dig, and you're not going to find anything on me. So go ahead and dig all you want into my past, but don't interfere with my current investigation."

"You shouldn't be on the investigation." Trevor sniffed. "You're hardly unbiased."

"That's the chief's call, not yours." Jimmy jumped in, standing to emphasize his point. "Detective Rosetti is the best chance we have of catching this killer. She's the best there is—period. The last thing you should be doing is trying to get her off this case. Understand?"

Trevor headed toward the door. "I understand she's got you under her little spell, Jimbo. Nice chatting. My lawyer will be looking forward to hearing from you."

The door swung closed behind him. I glanced at Jimmy, and he looked more frustrated than I'd seen him in a long time.

"Relax," I told him. "It's fine. It doesn't mean anything."

"They don't get it." Jimmy crossed his arms and shook his head.

"They don't get it?" I repeated. "Who doesn't get what?"

"Everyone," Jimmy said. "Nobody can comprehend what you've had to go through to get where you are today."

"Even I'm not seeing where you're going with this, partner."

Jimmy met my gaze. "It's not an easy job being a cop, even on the good days. You've got it harder than the rest of us. I see firsthand how frustrating it is for you to deal with your dad's past. You've never broken the rules yourself, but you're being punished as if you have. And the only reason why is because you share your dad's name. You were a kid when he went to prison, for crying out loud. It's not fair for you to carry his guilt."

"It's fine. I've gotten used to it."

"I don't know if you can ever get used to it. It just never ends, does it?"

"No, it doesn't."

"There's a shadow that follows you around, and it makes me sick." Jimmy expelled a breath. "You're the best detective on the team, and this guy's got it in for you. It takes guts to do what you do, Rosetti. I wish it weren't so hard for people to understand that."

"Hey, it's fine. You don't need to get riled up. It's just part of who I am. I'm used to it."

"It's got to bother you."

"Sometimes. But I can't change it. Neither can you." I shrugged one shoulder. "I guess a part of it makes me who I am. It makes me the cop I am. For better or for worse. Not to mention, it's my cross to bear, not yours. I became a cop knowing what I'd face because of who my dad is. That's on me."

"Sorry." Jimmy gave a little shudder. "That guy just rubs me the wrong way."

I winked at him, trying to lighten the mood. "Aw, you care about me, you little teddy bear. Admit it."

"You're gonna miss me when I retire," he scoffed. Then he straightened, put on his business face, and briskly changed the subject. "Do you want to talk to the rest of the team while we're here?"

I shook my head. "In a way, Trevor's right."

"Right about what?"

"Do we really think Trevor was involved in Heinrich's murder?"

"It'd almost be nice if he were," Jimmy said. "If we've got to arrest someone for it, it might as well be him."

"Yeah, but do we *really* think he's good for it? What's his motivation?"

"A big story," Jimmy mused. "I don't know. Maybe Trevor and Heinrich knew each other from back in the day. You know how cops and reporters love each other so much."

"We haven't seen any personal links between them. At least not yet. As for the story, I just don't see it being big enough. Trevor Sime murdering a guy just to write about a local crime? The risk versus reward doesn't really match up. It's not exactly Pulitzer material. As sad as it is, deaths like this happen all the time."

"He was the first reporter on the scene," Jimmy said. "Trevor beat everyone else there. How'd he know about it so quickly?"

"I don't have all the answers, but I do feel like we're letting him win with every second we stay here. He wants us to get swept up in the drama. He wants us to threaten him, to give him fodder for a story. The best thing we can do is ignore him and try to let it roll off our backs. If something turns up that links him to the case, we'll be back."

"You mean we'll be having conversations with his lawyer," Jimmy muttered. Then, "Yeah, I guess you're right. Let's take off."

"I haven't actually been home yet today," I said. "I'm going to stop at my house before heading to the precinct, but I'm going to need to grab my car. It's still at Bellini's. Drop me off?"

His eyes twinkled. "This walk of shame is the best part of my day."

"Shut up, or you're buying me lunch."

"Your mom's café?" Jimmy offered, obviously with no plans to shut up. "I need to hear about your visit with Charles Randolph last night anyway."

"Do we have to go to my mom's café?"

"You can't hide from her forever."

"Touché," I agreed with a sigh. My phone buzzed, and I looked down at it, ready to reject the call, when the number surprised me. I glanced up at Jimmy. "Speak of the devil."

"Hi, Kate," my mother said breathlessly on the other end of the line. "We need you to come home right now. To our house. I mean, my house, not yours. Now."

"Is everything okay?" Besides sounding out of breath, my mother sounded somewhat discombobulated. "What's going on?"

"I think it's best if you see for yourself."

Her voice took on a thin tone, a brave, emotionless one I knew well. It was the same tone she'd used back when my father had gone to prison. She'd used it to talk to the press, to his colleagues, to the family and friends that called her to ask if the news about my father was true. It was how she separated the loving, emotional part of herself from the front she needed to deal with a difficult situation.

"I'm coming," I said. "Are you safe? Is it Jane? Dad?"

"Don't dillydally," she said. "It's very important that you come straight home."

The line disconnected.

"She hung up on me," I said to Jimmy. "Something's wrong. We have to get to my parents' house. My car can wait."

Chapter 18

Jimmy parked outside of my parents' house, pausing a minute before he opened the door. He glanced my way as he removed his seat belt. "Look, Rosetti, I've got your back in there. Whatever you do, I'll follow your lead. No questions asked. Got it?"

I gave a hard swallow and nodded.

"Do you want to call this in?" he asked. "Or are we waiting?"

I considered, but I shook my head. "For all I know, Jane could've canceled her wedding and my mom's in a fit. Let's see what is going on before we phone it in."

Jimmy nodded, though we both knew my theory was wishful thinking. My heart was racing, and the first order of business was to make sure my family was safe. Everything else would follow.

I didn't have to wait long. As Jimmy and I started up the driveway, the garage door began opening. Jimmy took the lead as we moved toward my parents' vehicles.

"Hi, Kate." My mother stood in the garage next to my father. The garage door creaked to its final resting place above us. Aside from the stiff smile on her face, she looked perfectly fine.

"Mom?" I said cautiously. "Are you okay?"

"I'm fine."

I crept forward and gave her a hug. It took her a second to return the hug which was also weird. My mother was first and foremost a hugger. She loved hugs. Kisses on the cheek.

Affection. I stepped back, watching my mother stiffly turn to face my father.

"What's going on?" I asked, looking between my mother and my father.

My dad stood in his garage dressed in jeans and an I LOVE NYC sweatshirt that I was pretty sure Jane had bought him as a souvenir. He looked for all the world like a normal dad standing in his garage, surrounded by some rusty old tools, a bunch of improperly labeled cardboard boxes, and bikes that hadn't seen the light of day in years.

My father cleared his throat. "Your mother asked me to pick up a few things from the store this morning. I went to the trunk before leaving to make sure it was empty because I needed to grab salt for the water softener, and those bags are huge. I once went to the store to pick up salt and had a bunch of tools in the back, and I couldn't get the salt bags to fit in there. I learned my lesson."

I resisted the urge to hurry my dad on in his pointless story about water softener salt. I recognized it as a stalling technique.

"So anyway," he continued, "I went to make sure the trunk was clear before heading to the store, and when I popped it open, I found this."

My dad opened the trunk to his vehicle and stepped back, gesturing for me to look inside. Jimmy and I took baby steps forward until we could see the contents. I wasn't a member of the bomb squad by a long shot, but even I could tell that the items spread in the trunk looked pretty darn incriminating.

My dad watched me carefully before speaking. "I don't need my detective badge to let you know this is probably a match for the stuff that was used on Heinrich. The incendiary device, I mean."

"Dad." I swallowed hard. "Where did these supplies come from?"

"Didn't you hear him?" my mother snapped. "He just told you. He opened his trunk, and it was there. He didn't put it there, and I'm ashamed you would even insinuate such a thing."

My father raised his hands gently in the direction of my mother. "Thank you, sweetie, but you don't need to defend me. To answer your question, Kate, I don't know how it got there. I just know it *is* there."

The unspoken message in my father's eyes was the pleading phrase, *You have to believe me.*

"Your father's the one who told me to call you." My mother spoke sharply. "I told him he should just get rid of it. Toss it in a ditch somewhere."

"Mom," I said. "Don't tell me that. I'm a cop."

"I'm telling you the truth. That's what you want, isn't it?"

My dad moved to stand by my mother. He put an arm around her shoulders, and she leaned against him. The pair were newly married, for the second time, and the reason they'd been separated in the first place was because of a huge betrayal on my father's part. He'd operated outside of the law, and he'd been punished for it. My mother had stood by him then as long as she'd been able. It seemed she'd made the choice to stand by him again.

I glanced down at my feet feeling a pinch of envy at the bond they had. The love they shared. A love so steadfast it would survive not one terrible storm but several. It was clear from my mother's stare that she believed my father to his core. She'd been willing to help him dispose of evidence in a murder investigation—that was how much she believed in him. I wondered if I'd ever find that kind of love. My mind flashed to Gem, to Jack, and I felt the pit growing larger in my stomach.

"Say something, Kate," my mother said. "You can't possibly think your father had anything to do with this. It's crazy."

"Honey," my father said softly. "It's okay. Give Kate a minute to process."

"No, it's fine." It took effort, but eventually I focused all my attention on the matter at hand. "I'm just thinking about how to handle this."

"Your father is obviously innocent. It doesn't take a rocket scientist to figure it out. If he was guilty, why would he have left this stuff in his trunk and allowed me to call the police?" My mother's voice went shrill. "Angelo isn't an idiot."

"When's the last time you checked your trunk?" I faced my dad. "Do you know how this could have happened? Or when somebody else could have planted this stuff there?"

He shook his head. "Honestly, I probably haven't checked it for two weeks. Your mother usually does the shopping. Like I said, it was just because of the salt bags that I even looked at all. I've used the car a few times in the last week. I got gas, met the guys at the restaurant last Tuesday." He stopped, considered. "I left it parked outside in the driveway one night. It had started to snow a couple of days ago, and I just didn't feel like moving it, so I let it sit there until the next morning."

"So someone had ample opportunity to access your vehicle," I said. "Do you keep it locked?"

My dad shrugged. "It's not a fancy car. If I remember to hit the beeper, I lock it. I'd say there's about a fifty percent chance I remember to hit the beeper. I honestly couldn't even tell you if I locked it or not."

"That's okay," I said. "It's fine. That means it would have been easy for someone to get into your trunk and frame you."

"Finally you're talking some sense," my mother said, relief evident in her voice. "Your father told me you'd believe him, but I just couldn't be sure with your track record."

I glanced at my mother. My father just gave a small shake of his head and patted my mother's shoulder, trying to smooth things over.

"Your mother is just worried," my dad explained to me. "The second I saw this, I called Annie at the bakery and had her come straight home."

"You called Mom before you called me?" I asked.

"It's not a ticking bomb," my dad said. "Yes, I called your mother. She's my wife. I wanted her to know first. I wanted her by my side when I made my next move. I wanted her advice, and I wanted to give her the option to... Well, to sit this one out if she needed. I've put her through enough."

"It's a good thing you didn't end up taking Mom's advice." I shot my mother a little glare. "I'm going to pretend I never heard you mention anything about evidence disposal."

My mother fanned her face. "Your father's not guilty. You know that; I know that; we all know that. Hasn't our family been through this before? When are we going to catch a break?"

"If Dad's innocent, there's nothing to worry about," I said.

"If?" My mother pressed. "It's not a question, Kate."

"It's a figure of speech," my dad said. "Come on, the last thing I want is to have this come between us. I'll go to prison again before I let this break up my family."

"Your going to prison is what broke up our family the last time," my mother argued. Then she turned and stalked into the house, leaving the door to the house to slam shut behind her.

"I'm sorry, Dad," I said. "I didn't mean to offend her."

"Just give her some time." My father looked saddened by his wife's departure. "I'm asking a lot for her to trust me again. After everything. Now this."

"But you didn't do it, Dad." I looked him dead in the eyes. "Did you? Because now's the time to tell me if there's anything else I should know."

My dad met my gaze head-on. "I had nothing to do with this, Kate. I don't know anything about it at all—rumors, nothing. Honest."

It looked like there was more he wanted to say, but at the last second, he bit his tongue. Instead, he let the silence stretch before us, the eye contact between us speaking volumes. Finally, I cleared my throat.

"I know," I said. "I believe you."

"I told your mother you would. I told her the only real choice was to call you and let the chips fall where they may. I think she knew that, too, deep in her heart. I think, in a way, she was relieved to hear me say it."

"By you coming forward," Jimmy added encouragingly, "it shows your willingness to work with us. Like your wife said, you're not an idiot. It'd be pretty idiotic to drive around town with this stuff in your trunk, then call us one day just for the hell of it."

My dad broke into a real smile and thumbed at Jimmy while speaking to me. "I always knew I liked this guy."

"Careful, don't let him hear it," I said. "He's already got a big head."

Jimmy laughed, but the smile faded quickly, the fleeting moment of reprieve slipping away as my dad's gaze slid back to the trunk.

"I've got a few more questions to ask you, as I'm sure you already know," I said, "but I also think you realize that I have to call this in."

"I'll call it in myself if you'd like," my dad said. "The option is yours. If you want, you and Jimmy here can take off, and I'll dial the precinct directly. Nobody needs to know you were here at all if you don't want to be involved."

"I'm not going anywhere, Dad. We've got nothing to hide. But I do think it needs to go straight to Sturgeon."

A concerned expression crossed my dad's face, but he nodded. "I'm going to go find your mother. I'll be inside when you need me."

I waited until my dad had rejoined my mom in the house. Then I glanced at Jimmy.

"I believe him," Jimmy offered, "if that's what you're asking. I'm behind you on this every step of the way. That hasn't changed."

"Thank you."

"Don't mention it. Are you going to do the honors, or do you want me to get ahold of the chief?"

I raised my phone. "It needs to be me."

Jimmy took a step back, hands shoved in his pockets, as I dialed. Chief Sturgeon picked up on the third ring.

"It's Detective Rosetti," I said. "What's your schedule this afternoon? There's something I think you need to see. In person."

He blew out a slow breath on the other end of the line. "Any chance you want to be more specific?"

"Yeah," I said, and then I rattled off my parents' address. "I'll be waiting out front for you to get here."

***

"Who's going to tell me what I'm doing here?"

Chief Sturgeon strode up the driveway to the garage. He was dressed in a suit, and I had the sinking feeling that I'd dragged him out of some bureaucratic-type meetings. The sort of meetings that always put him in a bad mood, which didn't bode well for me.

"I got a call from my parents just before I reached out to you," I said. "They explained there was something I needed to see here. I came over, took a peek, and immediately dialed you."

He cursed under his breath, then made his way toward the trunk of my dad's car, which was propped open. He added a couple more choice expletives as he looked inside.

"What's the story?" The chief's eyes were hard as he looked at me.

"Not much of a story," I said. "My dad was going to buy salt from the grocery store, like the kind for the water soften-er..." I quickly realized I was doing the same thing as my dad. Dragging out the story in an effort to stall. "Basically, my dad checked the trunk this afternoon before heading out and found this inside. He has no clue how any of it got there."

"Could someone have feasibly gotten into his car to plant it?"

"Easily," I said, and then quickly caught him up on the information I'd gathered from my dad.

He stared at his feet for a long moment. "What do you think, Rosetti?"

"About what, sir?"

He looked up, squinted at me. "The situation."

"I think it's like my dad said. I think someone's trying to frame him for Heinrich's murder."

"And you believe your dad?"

"I do, sir."

"You know, I should take you off the case." The chief scrubbed at his brow. "I'm not going to, but I should."

"I appreciate that," I said. "I won't let you down. For some reason, it seems like someone's out to get me or my family with this one. Someone is making this case personal, and I have no idea why."

The chief looked thoughtful for a moment. "You know, that's a great point."

"Sorry?"

"Maybe this isn't about Angelo at all."

"Sorry?" I repeated.

"Maybe this is about you," Sturgeon continued. "By throwing shade on your father, by using his tenuous connection with Heinrich to link him to the case, the only thing it does is force my hand to take you off the case."

"I hadn't considered that."

"Me neither." He retreated to his thoughtful musings as he stared into the trunk. After a few minutes, he gave a decisive nod. "I'm keeping you on the case, if for no other reason than I think the killer's just given us a sign. He *wants* you off the case, which is why I'm going to do the exact opposite and keep you front and center. As long as you're okay with it."

"Fine by me," I said.

"I agree," Jimmy cut in. "By making this move and trying to force Kate off the case, the killer is showing their hand, signaling they're getting worried. If they weren't worried, there'd be no reason to plant evidence in Angelo's car and rock the boat. It's a distraction."

My mind was churning a thousand miles an hour. I had conflicting feelings about this new revelation, especially since it wasn't something I'd considered—primarily that I might be the target and not my father. Guilt was at the top of the list because if I *was* the real target, that would mean my family was suffering because of me. Again.

"It's not your fault," Jimmy muttered out of the chief's earshot, as if reading my mind. "Don't beat yourself up. We don't even know if any of this is true. It's all just a theory at this point."

"A solid theory," I remarked. "Even you thought so."

"True. It still doesn't mean it's your fault."

After another moment of silence, I cleared my throat.

"I've got something of a radical idea," I said. "But I'd like to lay it out with my dad in the room. We need to interview him anyway."

"I don't like radical plans," Sturgeon said. "I like logical plans."

"I don't know if my dad will go along with it anyway. But it might be our best shot."

"I'll listen," Sturgeon said. "That's my best offer."

It was better than I'd expected, so I took the opportunity to shut the trunk of the car and close the garage door. Then I led Jimmy and Sturgeon inside. I called out for my parents, and my mother replied from the kitchen. I could already smell the coffee and cookies. My mother baked when she was stressed. She must've hightailed it straight to the chocolate chips.

I sat my parents and colleagues down around the table and did quick reintroductions. My mother greeted the gang by forcing mugs of coffee and plates of cookies on everyone. Once we were all situated with our cookies and caffeine, all eyes turned to me.

"Chief Sturgeon brought up an interesting point," I started. "He suggested that Dad might be collateral damage in this situation, and I'm the real target here."

"Well, that's a relief," my mother said. "Someone's always after Kate. I just wish they'd leave your father out of it."

"Thanks, Mom," I said. "If that theory is true, I think we need to go with it. We should make it look like we believe the evidence."

"You mean, you want to arrest your father as if he'd actually blow somebody up?" My mother was already shaking her head. "No. I won't stand for it. He's already done his time. He's not doing time for something he didn't do. Where's your lawyer, Angelo? Can't you call that Mindy woman? Surely she'd tell you not to talk to anyone."

"No lawyers needed." My father rested his hand again on my mother's arm. "Tell me what I need to do, Kate."

"We would have to make it look real to convince anyone. We'd bring you down to the station for questioning. Maybe let it leak to a reporter that we're holding you as our primary suspect. All that jazz."

"What will any of that accomplish?" my mother asked.

"It will allow the murderer to relax a little," I said. "That's when he or she might make a mistake. It could give us the time we need to catch up."

"I don't like it," my mother said. "I don't like any part of it. My vote is a hard pass."

"Dad?" I turned to my father, hoping he could help steer this conversation in a different direction. "What do you think?"

"I'll do what you need me to do." He raised a finger. "With one caveat."

"What is it?" Sturgeon asked.

"My wife has to agree to it." My dad gave a sideways glance at my mother. "Annie's the one who stood by me when nobody else would give me the time of day. I owe it to her to respect her wishes. If she says no, the answer is no."

"Mom, just consider it," I said. "Please."

She shook her head. "I *have* considered it. The department didn't do Angelo any favors when he was in trouble the first time. Why should he help you out now? No offense, Chief."

"That's because Dad was in the wrong," I said, exasperated. "What did you want them to do, look the other way?"

"I'm not talking about courtroom proceedings." My mother stared at her hands. "I'm talking about the fallout after. Your father worked with others at the department for years. He had friends there."

Silence filtered into the room.

"I understand your father made a mistake, and he paid his price. He held his head high and didn't argue about it. But he is still a human being, and he has always been a good person. His friends should have known that." Her gaze didn't move from her hands. "Did any of his friends reach out to him, even to ask if he was okay? What about me? What about you kids? You girls didn't do anything wrong. We hosted weekly dinners for your father's friends before things soured. Once he was accused, his friends vanished into the woodwork."

"Honey," my father said softly, "what could they do? It was my fault."

"A friend is a friend through good times and bad," my mother said firmly. "I'm not saying they should've supported you or testified to your good character in court. But what about a phone call? A letter? A birthday card for the girls? Our daughters were completely innocent."

"Mom," I said, "I understand you're upset, but you've got to let it go. That was a different time. The department has practically changed over completely. Technically, Jimmy and I are from a totally new team that didn't even exist when Dad was around."

"Let it go?" my mother said shrilly. "Just let it go?"

"Mrs. Rosetti is right," Sturgeon said. "Your family doesn't owe us anything, Detective Rosetti. We'll proceed as we would in any other case. Thank you for your time, Mr. and Mrs. Rosetti. Angelo, if we could ask you a few questions before we take off, I'd appreciate it. You understand it's protocol."

Sturgeon waited a beat. When no one objected, he took that as an affirmative. When the chief pulled out a recorder and set it on the table, asking permission to turn it on, my mother left the room. There was a group pause as if we were all waiting to see if she'd return, but she never did. Sturgeon spoke into the recorder, giving the date, time, and location of the interview.

My father and Sturgeon went back and forth easily on the record, replaying my father's story in an official capacity. I'd already heard it, though I listened intently all over again, striving to tease out any tiny detail I might've missed the first time.

As the interview progressed, I was impressed with Sturgeon's attention to detail. The guy might've been in political-type meetings all day, but he'd earned his title by climbing the ranks as a regular cop first and then a detective second. He was good at his job, and his skills hadn't slipped after all these years behind a desk.

"We're almost through," Sturgeon said, "but I want to discuss Detective Heinrich for a moment. You're aware of his death, Mr. Rosetti. Could you talk a little bit about the connection between the two of you?"

"Former colleagues," my dad said shortly.

"Is that all?"

"He testified at my trial," my dad said, exhaling loudly. "I'm pretty sure that was the answer you were looking for."

"I'm not looking for specific answers," Chief Sturgeon clarified. "We're following the facts. How do you feel about Heinrich?"

"Sorry for him."

"Sorry for him?"

"He's dead," my dad said. "I'm not dead. Seems like a sensible way to feel."

"What about before he died?"

"You mean, did I have any motivation to kill him?" My dad hesitated, chewed on his lower lip. When he spoke again, there was a slight falter to his voice.

I looked up, surprised to see tears in his eyes.

"Look around you, Sturgeon." My father gestured wide with his hands, but his eyes were focused on me. "Look at everything I have. My life is precious. I lost this all once. I would rather die before losing it again."

Sturgeon reached forward and shut the recorder off. "I'm sorry, Angelo. I know it's got to be hard to talk about the past."

"Don't be sorry. All anyone's doing here is their job."

Sturgeon nodded. "The lab will be running tests on the supplies found in your trunk. I've already called the team to come collect it. They'll be arriving outside any minute."

"Take the whole car if that's easier," my dad said. "I don't need it."

Sturgeon gave a wry smile. "You're not thinking of fleeing?"

"It's gonna take handcuffs to pry me out of this house. I'm a lucky man, Chief. I'm not going anywhere without a good fight."

Sturgeon faced my dad, and the two men eyed one another carefully. There seemed to be a hefty weight between them. I was surprised once again when Sturgeon stuck his hand out and shook my father's gruffly.

"I'm sorry, Angelo," Sturgeon said. "About everything."

Then the two men parted ways. The chief disappeared outside, presumably to meet the tech teams who'd be arriving to commandeer my father's car. The air in the kitchen felt thick.

"I'm sorry, Kate." My dad turned to me. "But I just can't go against your mother. After all we've been through, it's the least I can do. I hate choosing between my daughter and my wife, but when push comes to shove, she's my everything."

"I understand, Dad. I respect it."

"It's nothing against you."

"I know. Don't worry, the idea was stupid anyway. I shouldn't have tried to involve you more than you're already involved. It's not fair to you."

"It wasn't a stupid idea. You were thinking outside of the box. It's what makes you a great detective."

"You do realize if they find a match with the lab results, they'll have enough to bring you in and hold you." I raised and lowered my shoulders reluctantly. "We won't have an option."

"Oh, I know. I also expect there will be a match, and when that time comes..." He winked. "You know where to find me."

Jimmy cleared his throat. "I'm going to head out. Nice seeing you, Mr. Rosetti."

I waited until Jimmy left the room. I knew I should join him, but I needed to speak to my father first. In private.

"Dad, I'm sorry," I said. "Hearing what Mom had to say about your friends abandoning you after everything that happened... It made me realize that I wasn't any better. Except I was your daughter."

"Exactly. You're my daughter. It's different."

"I don't know. You and Jane seemed to carry on a relationship," I said. "It was my fault for not giving you a chance sooner. I guess, even after all these years, I never thought about it from your point of view once. I never even tried."

"I made a bad decision that affected your life greatly. You didn't owe me a relationship after that. I'm just glad you've come around."

"I wish I'd done it sooner."

The ground beneath my feet felt shaky. I'd never once in my life considered the fact that I might have been in the wrong, even a little bit, when it came to the shredded relationship I'd shared with my dad. In my brain, I saw rules in black and white. I found it unsettling that there was a gray area at all. But my inability to empathize with my father had cost us years of working to repair the tenuous bond between us.

"You were five, Kate. You couldn't fully comprehend everything that was happening, and neither could Jane. Frankly, it was a blur even for your mother. I was the one who blindsided you all. The last thing I ever want is for you to feel responsible for my mistakes."

"I know I'm not responsible for your mistakes. I really hated what it did to our family. I just wish..." I took a deep breath. "I wish I'd been able to understand you a little better despite it all. Especially once I was old enough to learn what you did and why you did it."

"I shouldn't have taken dirty money," my father said. "Even if it was for my family. I've never tried to argue that."

"I know. And actually, I'm really proud of you." My throat felt a little dry. "Looking back, you handled everything with more dignity than most people would have in your shoes. I'm not ashamed to be your daughter, even if I've made you feel that way."

My dad smiled, and a tear streaked down his cheek. "I appreciate that, Kate. More than you'll ever know."

"I love you, Dad."

He pulled me in for a hug. "I love you too."

We parted, and there was a moment of awkward silence. Neither my dad nor I were big on mushy emotions, and we'd shared more than either of us cared to admit in the last five minutes.

"I hear them working on the car," my dad said. "It'll probably be faster if I just give them the keys. I'll meet you outside in a minute?"

"Sure thing."

I returned to the garage and found the chief barking orders to the forensic crew. Jimmy stood near the vehicle, watching everything happening in great detail.

"Rosetti," Sturgeon called over to me. "I think it's best if you take off now. We've got this under control."

I understood when I'd overstayed my welcome. "You'll call me when you get the results?"

"I will."

Jimmy sauntered over. "You ready to head back to the precinct, then?"

I dropped my voice so only Jimmy could hear. "Actually, I was hoping to take an hour or two to myself. Could you give me a ride to get my car from Bellini's?"

"I sure can, but—"

"It's personal," I said, before he could ask. "There's someone I need to see."

Jimmy studied me for a long minute before relenting. "You keep me on my toes, Rosetti. Hop in the car."

Chapter 19

Once again, after a brief detour to pick up my car, I found myself standing in the lobby of Gem Industries, mostly confused as to why I was there. Even I couldn't say for certain what had drawn me back to this place after the morning I had, but for once, I was following my gut when it came to personal matters.

I felt a bit like a dog with my tail between my legs as I approached Ms. Karp at the front desk. "Hello," I said warily. "I was hoping to see Gem. He's not expecting me."

"You have a keycard." The faintest smile appeared on Ms. Karp's lips. "That means he welcomes you to come and go as you please."

"Thanks."

"He's in his office. Your keycard will get you there. Just use the main elevator banks and select the penthouse floor."

I nodded my thanks, feeling Ms. Karp's gaze following me as I made my way through the building, past the newly spring-ish atrium. Instead of swinging a left to go down the private corridor to Gem's personal elevator, I hooked a right to go to the banks on the other side that led to the many, many floors of offices above.

When the elevator doors opened, I made my way to Gem's assistant's desk. I recognized her from my last visit, though I couldn't place her name. Apparently she recognized me, too, because she beamed in my direction.

"Detective Rosetti, it's lovely to see you again." She rose from behind her desk. "Please follow me."

"Oh, but Gem's not expecting me."

"He said earlier this week that I was to bring you straight up if you arrived here asking for him. So, I suppose in a way he is expecting you."

My heart gave a small thump at the idea that Gem had taken the initiative to think of me, even when I'd given him no reason to do so. The man had persistence, I'd give him that.

The woman led the way up the winding staircase to Gem's office. "His calendar says he's free now, so you can go right in." She gave two polite taps on the door, then gestured for me to head inside.

I was still in shock at how quickly everything had gone, from the moment I'd decided to drive myself downtown to now—the moment I was standing before Gem. Before I could thank Gem's assistant, she'd backed out of the room and closed the door behind her, leaving me alone before the billionaire.

Gem sat behind his desk, a smile fixed on his face as he stared at me in surprise. "Kate?"

"I'm sorry." I took a deep breath, then quickly continued before he could interrupt, and before I got cold feet with what I wanted to say. "I just want you to know that I'm sorry for the way I've acted around you."

"Really, Kate, now's not the time—"

"Please, I want to speak first," I insisted. "I just had to come here to let you know that I'm trying."

"Trying?" he said mildly.

"I'm trying to be better. All I've done is push you away. I've done nothing to deserve the way you treat me. Then last night when we kissed—"

The sound of someone clearing their throat stopped me in my tracks. I hadn't cleared my throat. Gem hadn't cleared his either.

My blood chilled. With a racing pulse, I slowly turned to look opposite of Gem. I hadn't had eyes for anything—or anyone—except for Gem since the moment I'd entered his office. It hadn't even crossed my mind that someone else would be there. His assistant had assured me his calendar said he was free.

Unfortunately, it wasn't *someone* else in the room with Gem.

It was *a lot of* someone-elses.

On the opposite side of the room was a screen that covered the length of the wall. Projected onto the screen were hundreds of tiny little boxes. Boxes that had individual faces in them. Faces that moved. Faces that looked to be paying avid attention.

"Oh, crap," I said.

"Ladies and gentlemen, we'll circle back on this next week," Gem said, a small smile curving his lips upward. "That'll be all for today."

Then Gem clicked a button on his computer. Simultaneously, the video feed shut down, and the projector screen began retracting into the ceiling. My hands were beyond clammy.

"I'm going to die," I informed Gem. "Just arrange my funeral right now."

"I think you're overreacting a bit."

"Were you here, in the same room as me?" I threw an arm in the direction of the screen. "Because I'm pretty sure everyone heard me."

Gem inclined his head to one side, acknowledging my point.

"What was that, an entire company call? An earnings meeting with your board members?" I placed a hand dramatically over my face. "Don't tell me, actually. I don't want to know. Your assistant promised me you were free."

"I was free until a few minutes ago. We had an impromptu call regarding..." He gave a soft laugh. "It doesn't matter. It's really not a big deal."

"You could have warned me."

"To be fair, I tried, but you seemed pretty intent on speaking first."

"Still. You could've, I don't know, shut the camera off or something."

"I was a little surprised. I'm sorry. I wasn't thinking."

"No, *I'm* sorry," I said, wincing. "I feel like I made you look unprofessional. All you ever do is help me, and all I ever do is mess things up for you. I knew I shouldn't have come here."

"Kate, hush."

"Gem, I just—"

Gem shocked me by whipping up from his desk and crossing the distance between us in two short steps. His hands were on my face, and his lips were on mine within seconds. A heat blistered between us as I found myself desperate to cling to him just a half a beat longer. Because as long as I was in his arms, I could forget everything else in the universe. It was a real shame when he stepped back.

"I wasn't planning on doing that, but it was the only way to get a word in edgewise." Gem gave me a sheepish smile. "I'm sorry. This whole thing caught me off guard."

I nodded, unable to find the words to follow that up just yet. This whole visit had been a whirlwind.

"Forget about the meeting already, okay?" Gem insisted. "They're just colleagues. People who will float in and out of my life on a business level, end of story. I don't care what they saw or heard. I'm just pleased you're here, and that outweighs anything else."

"I don't believe you, but I appreciate you trying to make me feel better."

Gem stood close to me, dressed in his power suit and smelling like pine and mint. His eyes were dark, clouded with an intensity I couldn't quite read as he studied me at arm's length.

"Why are you really here today, Kate?"

I licked my lips, stalling. "To be honest, I'm not sure. I came here on a whim after my dad found explosives in the trunk of his car."

Gem gave a confused smile in my direction. "I have to say, despite the fact that I think I can read people quite well, I can never predict what's going to come out of your mouth. Is he all right?"

"He's fine. It wasn't a bomb, just the supplies to make one." I waited a beat, thinking about how I could explain what I was feeling when I could hardly make sense of it myself. "My dad's being framed for something he didn't do."

"There's no doubt in my mind you'll get to the bottom of it. If there's anyone who can prove his innocence, it's you, Detective."

"The thing that stuck out to me, above all, was my mom." I glanced down at my hands and twisted them together. "She never once questioned him. She never doubted him. For Pete's sake, she offered to dispose of evidence in a murder investigation to help my dad."

"And you have a problem with that?"

"No. Well, yes. I mean, yes. I told her it was a stupid idea to dispose of the evidence," I corrected. "But I didn't think it was stupid that she wanted to help my dad. I thought it was pretty admirable she'd stand by his side despite everything they've been through."

"I, too, applaud her."

"It went the other way as well. My dad wouldn't do anything that my mother disagreed with, despite his own convictions." I blew out a breath. "It just hit a nerve for me."

Gem murmured a note of agreement, but I could tell he wasn't sure where I was going with this.

"My point is that I'm starting to understand what you've understood your whole life," I blurted. "Unfortunately, with your mom being gone so young, and your time with her so fleeting and precious, I think you probably learned early what's really important in life. Money, a career, all of that is nice. But the people we love are only here for a short amount of time, and we never know how long that's going to be."

Gem's face was impossible to decipher.

"It's taken me a while, but I think I'm finally starting to get it," I said. "Up until this point, I've only ever cared about my career. I always thought it would be enough. I like knowing I'm helping people in my own way. But some days, I wonder..."

"Wonder if there's something more out there?"

"Yeah." I waited, silent, for a long minute. "I think I'm finally realizing that being in a relationship, even a friendship, is a two-way street."

"Of course it is."

"With you, our friendship has been mostly one way. You'd drop everything for me, Gem. I know that. You've let us use planes, cars, and access to your contacts at the drop of a hat."

"I don't do that because I expect anything in return."

"That's exactly my point." I waited for it to sink in. "All I've ever done in return is push you away."

"That's not entirely true."

"It's mostly true."

"I don't mind."

"I guess the reason I'm here is to say thank you. I really mean it, Gem. I'm not here for any reason except to say I recognize all you've been doing for me, and I appreciate your patience." My words felt heavy, weighted. "I wanted to tell you that before you lost hope. Before you started thinking that I didn't care about you at all. Don't give up on me yet."

I took a step back, trying to make my leave. I'd come. I'd said my piece. I didn't want Gem to feel obligated to say anything back to me. Also, I was more than ready to turn tail and stick my head in the sand for the next three weeks. I figured if I could hightail it out of his office before conversation resumed, it'd helped me maintain some sense of normalcy in my day.

But Gem wasn't letting me go that easily. He reached out, grabbed my wrist, and curled me into him even as I was still moving toward the exit.

"Kate." Gem stroked his thumb down my cheek once I'd stilled against him. "Take all the time you need."

I looked up at him, realizing I really, truly hoped he meant it. But my throat was too dry to say any of it. As if he could read my mind, Gem smiled tenderly down at me, brushed a kiss on my forehead.

"I promise you, Kate," he murmured. "I'm not going anywhere."

***

"Are you ready to hear from me?"

Jimmy's voice boomed on the other end of my phone as I left Gem Industries. My encounter with Gem had left me feeling a bit shaky and vulnerable, which were two feelings I didn't love. I was more than ready to get back to the precinct and focus on what I knew best: murder.

"Yes, hit me," I told Jimmy. "I'm just leaving the downtown area. Tell me you've got a lead."

"Meet me at Billy Burton's," Jimmy said in response. "We've got a warrant."

"For Burton? How?"

"I had Winkler pull some old case files regarding the car accident that put Heinrich in the hospital. When he was looking through them, Winkler discovered some evidence that hadn't been followed up on thoroughly. Paint samples from the car that hit him, more specifically."

"And?"

"At the time, the team identified the type of paint used on the car, but for some reason never were able to find a match," Jimmy said. "However, they didn't have Asha working the case. We do. She just so happens to have intel that one of the cars registered to Burton might be a match for the paint. Judge signed off real quick on the warrant on account of Heinrich's case being so high profile."

"Excellent. I'll meet you at his place."

Twenty minutes later, I pulled up outside of Billy Burton's Sunfish Lake estate. I found Jimmy waiting beside his car. He waved me over the second I parked.

"Where are we with everything?" I joined Jimmy and one other officer, a forensic guy I hadn't met before. "Has the warrant been served?"

"Ten minutes ago." Jimmy nodded at the house. "Burton wasn't happy about it."

"Is his girlfriend here?"

"Kendra? Yeah, she's inside now. She was pretty shocked. She wanted to take off, but I had the guys ask her to wait around."

"Good thinking. What'd Burton have to say?"

"Just that our entire theory was ridiculous and unfounded, that too much time had passed, that we would've arrested him earlier if he was actually guilty of anything. Then unfortunately he got smart and called his lawyer."

"For a smart guy, that sounds like a pretty nervous reaction to me."

"He has every right to be nervous," the other officer said. "There are only one hundred and twenty-five cars that have the specific color of paint found at the scene of the accident. That's in the entire world. It's a rare shade."

Jimmy nodded. "Asha narrowed it down further. From her preliminary research, only three of the vehicles with this type of paint are registered in Minnesota. It's a high-end custom paint that's special order from one shop. The other two cars with this paint in Minnesota have been located. The owners have nothing to do with Heinrich. One lives three hours away, and the other is a famous NFL player who has a very public alibi for the time of the accident."

I sucked in a breath. "That puts Burton in a pretty tight spot. Even so, that doesn't link anything to Heinrich's actual murder. The best we can do is link Burton to the scene of an accident that's four years old."

"Agreed. But if we can get him for the hit-and-run, it'll be a start. We might be able to cut a deal. Asha's already asking for a warrant to get her hands on Burton's computers. That could help us make some real progress if Burton is actually behind the murder."

"Looks like we got lucky," I said. "But I won't complain."

"It's also pretty stupid," Jimmy added. "If he'd gotten rid of the car, it would've made things a lot trickier for us."

"If it weren't for ego, our jobs would be a lot harder."

Another officer approached us from the front door of Burton's mansion. He handed over his notes. "Everything's in order," he informed us. "The girlfriend and Mr. Burton are inside waiting when you're ready to speak to them."

Jimmy and I thanked the two officers and left them behind as we headed to the front door. Billy Burton and Kendra were sitting at the center island where we'd sat the last time we'd spoken to him. This time, we weren't offered coffee or egg white quiche. We weren't even offered a smile. Kendra looked like she'd been crying, and Burton looked pissed.

"It's me again," I said with a smile, and then I nodded at Jimmy. "You'll recognize my partner too."

"I swear I don't know anything about this mess," Kendra said, sounding a mixture of weepy and whiny. "I told Bill, if he actually did this, we're done."

"Makes a lot of sense," I said, "seeing as he'll probably be headed to prison. And a nice young woman like you can do a lot better than that."

Burton rolled his eyes. "I'm not saying anything. My lawyer's on his way over."

"Great," I said. "You'd better make yourself one last cup of coffee to enjoy in the comfort of your own home. A good cup of joe doesn't exist behind bars."

"I'm not going to prison," Burton said. "My lawyer's too good for that."

"I notice you're not actually claiming innocence," I informed him. "That's going to be interesting for the jury to hear. If I were you, I'd start thinking about how you're going to come clean on Heinrich's murder sooner rather than later so you can at least try to cut a deal."

"I didn't kill him."

"Maybe, maybe not," I said. "But you probably ran him over with your car, and that doesn't bode well for the story we'll tell the jury when this all comes to trial."

"Detectives," a voice called from the entryway. "We've got something."

Kendra put her head on the table. She didn't cry. She just seemed defeated. Burton sat back in his seat, looking angrier by the second. He tapped his fingers on the table. That was how we left them, with a couple of officers standing by, as we made our way out to the garage.

One of the crime scene techs waved us over. He gestured for us to squat beside him as he flicked his flashlight at the front bumper of a very expensive, very bright blue vehicle. The paint shade definitely was unique.

"I think we've got it here," the tech informed us. "According to the evidence files, and Heinrich described this location as the spot that would have struck him. Turns out he was right."

"You found something?"

"A very, very good repair job," the tech admitted. "But it was definitely repaired. No way around it. I think we have enough to bring this car into the lab to get it tested, but if you want my opinion, it'll be a match for y'all. You'll have enough to hold Burton on until we get the results, at the very least."

"Wonderful," I said. "Thanks."

The garage was airy and bright. The doors were all glass, and there were windows everywhere. It really had been Burton's ego that trapped him. If Jimmy hadn't noticed the cars, if Asha hadn't been able to track the registration to him, we'd still be empty handed.

"Kinda funny, isn't it," Jimmy muttered. "Heinrich was married to the job up until the day he died. He's still helping us from beyond the grave. If it weren't for his notes, we wouldn't be here. The man is solving his own damn murder."

"It always seems that people are saying he was very dedicated to the job," I said, feeling a twinge of uneasiness. "Do you think I'm like that?"

"Huh?"

I nodded toward the doors, and Jimmy and I went outside. "I need your opinion. Not as a cop but as a friend."

"Sure."

We stood under a tall cluster of evergreens, the snow thick beneath our feet.

"I'm worried my life has been following the same path as Heinrich's."

"Let me tell you something, Rosetti." Jimmy crossed his arms and looked off into the distance. "I'm a good detective. Good. That's about it. I'm not going to leave any legacies behind. I'm not a pretty face the chief's gonna show off in the paper. I don't do flashy work. I like my job, I work hard at it, and then I go home to my wife."

"Well, you're not a good cop, you're a great cop, but I'll concede your point."

"My point is that when I die, sure, it'd be nice if people remember me as an honest, loyal cop who did a pretty fine job." He scratched at his head. "But on my tombstone, I want it to say that I was an honest, loyal husband who loved his family a helluva lot more than he loved his job, for starters."

"Let's not talk tombstones just yet."

He laughed. "You get my point. You're already the gold standard of a detective. You've got that one on lockdown."

"It just feels like I'll be letting people down, maybe even myself, if I take my eye off the ball and focus on something that's not work."

"Falling in love, looking for love, anything to do with love isn't taking your eye off the ball. If anything, it'll enrich your life. It will give you a new perspective. And if it makes you happy, that's how you know you're doing the right thing."

"Thanks, Jimmy."

"Hey, I'm happy for you."

"I'm not getting married or anything. I'm just, you know, considering my options."

He winked. "And having sleepovers."

"Okay, time to go."

"He's a good guy, Rosetti. You know, I'd always hoped we'd have this conversation someday. I really did."

"You're just saying that."

"I'm not. My job here is done. I can happily retire now."

I rolled my eyes. "By the way, do not mention this to my mother."

Chapter 20

Jimmy and I headed back to the precinct. The officers at the scene would be responsible for bringing in Billy Burton once they'd wrapped up at his house, and I'd have ample opportunity to question him when we received results back from the lab. I wanted to wait until I had some more ammunition in my back pocket before I sat down again with the programmer.

I headed to my desk to check in on my emails. I'd barely flicked on the power when Asha appeared behind my monitor.

"Hey, hot stuff," she said. "How was your sleepover?"

I groaned.

"Word travels fast," she quipped. "You're lucky I don't have time for you to buy me a coffee while I pick your brain."

I peeked sideways at her. "You found something?"

"Don't I always?"

I pushed an extra rolling chair toward Asha, the one Chloe Marks had occupied in her short time at the precinct. My friend plopped in the seat and wheeled toward me with a sheaf of papers in her hand.

"I've been poking around in this Burton guy's profile," she said. "He's an interesting character."

"You always do like a challenge, and he's a challenge because he's got good computer security."

Asha fanned herself. "You say that like he's actually competition. C'mon, sister, he's got nothin' on me. Anyway, I dug this up."

I studied the paper she placed in front of me. "A marriage license?"

"Turns out the girlfriend is actually the wife."

The name on the certificate matched the name of the woman I'd interviewed in the kitchen. I had to admit the finding was peculiar. "I wonder why Kendra and Billy are keeping their marriage a secret."

Asha shrugged. "I couldn't figure that out from my online stalking. It just looks to me like they up and went to the courthouse one day. I guess you'll have to ask them."

"That is really odd. I can't figure out why they'd be hiding something like that without some specific reason. She wasn't wearing a ring. Neither was he."

Asha looked at me.

"I always check people's hands," I said. "Habit after all these years on the job. People lie."

"What about you?" she asked. "Are you considering a ring anytime soon?"

"Subtle," I said. "So subtle."

"Asha?" Another voice joined our conversation. "Since when is Asha subtle?"

I glanced up as Melinda approached us with a smile.

"What'd I miss?" Melinda asked.

"Nothing," I said.

"Just wondering when we can expect wedding invitations from this one." Asha nodded toward me. "You know, what with her sleepovers and everything."

"It's not like that," I hissed. "I got snowed in. And I wouldn't have even been stranded there if not for you." I glared at Melinda.

The doctor preened. "You're welcome."

"Poor baby," Asha muttered with sarcasm in my direction. "Trapped inside the penthouse of a gorgeous billionaire. Cry me a river."

"Speaking of diamonds, I've got some news," Melinda said. "While I hate to interrupt this compelling banter, I think we might have found a lead in the case."

"Do tell," I said.

"Our team just got done combing through Heinrich's car, his clothing, everything that was incinerated in the blast."

"And?" I asked.

"And we found a diamond," she said. "A small diamond. I don't know what it means, but it's a real diamond. The lab is running additional tests on it. It was wedged into the passenger's seat. It was probably blown there during the blast."

"What do you think it means?" I asked. "Do you think the killer left it behind without realizing it?"

"I don't know. It's impossible to say right now. We might be able to narrow things down, but I wouldn't hold your breath. It will be difficult to trace the origins of a loose diamond."

"I don't see Heinrich as the sort of guy who wore jewelry," I said. "From everything I've read about him, I don't see any reason why there'd be a stray diamond in his car."

"There's a possibility it could have been left behind by the killer inadvertently," Melinda acknowledged. "But that won't mean much until we can match it to something."

A sudden flood of memories tumbled into my head. I thought of my visit earlier in the day at the North Star Press headquarters. Of the moment in the conference room when Meredith's pen had flashed at me as she'd handed it over, and I'd noticed the diamond studded into the side.

"There's a woman who works at the North Star Press who had a diamond on her pen," I said. "Maybe it wasn't the only one of its type. You know, maybe pens like it were handed out as holiday swag for the company. I wonder if Trevor has a similar pen that's missing a diamond? I know it's a long shot, but at least it's a shot."

Melinda gave me an encouraging nod. "I'll take anything, even if it's a shot in the dark. Any chance you can get me that pen? It won't take long for me to tell you if it's even in the realm of possibility."

"It's worth the drive downtown," I agreed. "I'll have Jimmy get a warrant. He's got the judge on speed dial for this one."

The door to the large office opened then, and in walked the chief. He didn't look happy. He walked over to us and threw down an article on my desk. It sat askew on the marriage license.

"Tell me how this happened," the chief said.

I glanced at the headline. I didn't need to read much into the article to understand that it was about my father and the equipment that'd been found in his trunk. Even at a glance, it looked pretty damning against my father.

"It's not the article I'm concerned about," the chief said, "although it is a pain in my ass. I'm looking at the time-stamp."

I sucked in a breath. "But, sir, this article came out *while* we were at my parents' house."

"Exactly," Sturgeon said. "I checked the log on my phone. The timestamp on the article shows it came out online before the tech teams even showed up at the scene. That means the only people who knew about the bomb equipment at that time was me, you, Jones, and your parents. Nobody else could have known except the person who planted the evidence."

"We didn't leak this to the press. We were all together, and no one used their phone except when I called you. That would mean..." I stared at Trevor's name.

Sturgeon nodded in agreement. "I think that gives you enough to bring in this clown. I want Trevor Sime here, at the precinct, ASAP. Either he put this crap in your dad's trunk, or he knows who did."

Sturgeon stormed out, the article glaring up at me from my desk. Asha and Melinda sat wordlessly next to me. Jimmy was behind his desk, his hands linked across his belly, listening intently to every word.

"I already gave the judge a heads-up about the warrant for Meredith's pen," Jimmy cut in. "We'll have that shortly. Let's head to the North Star Press, and we can collect the pen and Burton in one go."

"I'll get the car," I said. "Thanks, everyone."

Jimmy joined me in my vehicle a few minutes later. He confirmed the warrant was in the process of being signed. I pulled away from the curb and slapped a siren on top as we raced downtown. Jimmy had sent ahead a team of officers who were in the area to make sure Trevor and Meredith stayed put.

This time, I parked illegally in front of the building. We took the stairs two at a time to get to the offices.

"The guy, Trevor, was already gone when we got here," one of the local cops said as he reached our side. "The other one, the woman, is waiting for you in a conference room."

"Did you ask around about Trevor?" I asked. "Did anyone see him leave? He was here this morning."

"According to the front desk receptionist, Trevor took off shortly after you left this morning."

"Huh," I said. "So he was already gone by the time he published his article."

Jimmy gave me a funny look. "People have these things called laptops these days. He could've published it from anywhere."

"I know, but if he was innocent, don't you think he'd have stuck around here to finish up his work before jetting off?"

"Maybe, or maybe he just went out to lunch and worked from a coffee shop," Jimmy said. "We won't know until we find him. He can't have gone far."

The cop led us back toward the office area we'd visited that morning. A hush had fallen over the modern, streamlined space that housed the usually busy press. The sun beamed through the windows and glinted off the shiny white surfaces, but it seemed the urgency and excitement had been flushed out of the room to be replaced with an air of trepidation. Eyes followed me and Jimmy as we came to the conference room where Meredith was seated.

"We'll take it from here," I assured the cop waiting with Meredith. Then I waited for him to leave the room before I turned back to her. "Long time, no see, Meredith."

She raised a hand, bit her nails, and glanced across the desk. "I don't really know why you're back. Trevor's not here."

"I'm well aware. I was actually hoping to talk to you again."

"Why?"

"Where were you the night before Valentine's Day? Let's say February 14 between three and six in the morning?"

"I was home," she said. "I had dinner with my boyfriend. He didn't stay over, though, because he had an early morning. He's a lawyer. What's this about?"

"Same thing we were here about this morning."

"I don't know what you're talking about. I'm new here. If you're still investigating that murder, I don't understand why you're talking to me. I didn't even know the detective who died. Why would I have killed him? I don't have anything to gain from it."

"Tell me about your pen," I said. "The one you lent me earlier this morning. The one with the diamond in it."

Meredith looked confused, then she nodded. "Uh, okay. It's over at my desk. I didn't bring a notebook in here—didn't think I'd need one."

"Where did you get it? Is the diamond real?"

"It is," she said. "They handed out the pens as swag at some event. I didn't even go to the party, but Ava snagged a couple of extras. She gave me one the week I started."

"How many other people in the company have pens like yours?"

She shrugged. "A solid handful. Whoever attended."

"Did Trevor attend?"

"I'm not sure," she said. "But I know our entire team was invited. So he could have gone. Or he could've picked up a pen later. I've seen them circulate around."

My phone rang. I looked down at the number. "Excuse me," I said. "This is the lab. I need to take it."

I left Meredith staring wide-eyed at Jimmy. I hit answer the second I stepped outside.

"Hey, Melinda," I said. "What's up?"

"You don't have to bother bringing that woman's pen in."

"What do you mean?"

"Asha already figured out where the pen in question came from. I'll give you one guess who was handing out pens with gems embedded in the side at their event."

I groaned. "If you say it's—"

"Correct, it was Alastair Gem's event," Melinda confirmed. "Technically. He wasn't there, but it was for his company. I gave him a call and had a nice chat with him. He had someone from his team send over specs of the pen. The size of the diamond isn't right."

"Are you sure?"

"I'm positive," she said. "It's not a match. I've sent an image of the pen to your phone—check it against her pen. If it's a match, then you can forget about it. All the pens handed out at that event had a much smaller diamond than the one we found."

"So we're back to square zero."

"I'm sorry, Kate. We knew it was a long shot anyway."

"Thanks anyway," I said. "We'll finish up here and be back soon. Trevor's already gone, so this trip was a bust. Let me know if anything else comes up."

I replaced the phone in my pocket, then took a few minutes to gather my thoughts. I was halfway through an interview with Meredith, and even though I had no reason to suspect she had killed Heinrich, I decided to press on her a little harder for another few minutes. Just in case she knew something that she wasn't letting on—it was a Hail Mary, through and through.

"That was the lab," I said, reentering the room. I took a giant leap. "They confirmed that the diamond was a match from the pens handed out at that event." I paused for a long moment. "Which means that there's likely a murderer running around the North Star Press, and they might not be happy seeing you chatting with cops—twice now. Are you sure there's absolutely nothing else you want to tell us?"

Meredith glanced between us. "Is now the time to get a lawyer?"

"You're welcome to a lawyer," I told her. "But I don't think you've done anything wrong."

She nodded and took a deep breath. "Okay."

"Okay?" I glanced at Jimmy. "What does that mean?"

"I'm not going to get in trouble?"

"Trouble for what?" I asked.

"Look, she came to me. I didn't ask for it," Meredith blurted. "I was the new girl and didn't know what to make of it."

"Who came to you?"

"I don't know. Someone emailed me under a throwaway email address, giving me information about the Heinrich murder."

"You went to Trevor with this information?"

"Yes," she admitted. "I knew he didn't like me. I over-heard him talking to Rose before her trip about me, saying that they didn't need me, that I should be fired, whatever. I really wanted to keep this job, so I thought that maybe if I could show Trevor that I wasn't a threat to him—that I could even be an *asset*—then maybe he'd back off."

"So you fed Trevor the information about Heinrich's murder from your anonymous source," I said as a click of understanding dawned on me. "*You're* the one who got the tip that explosives would be found in my dad's trunk. That's how Trevor was able to publish the article before we'd even found the paraphernalia."

"I'm sorry." Meredith looked miserable. "The email came in early this morning about evidence in someone's trunk. I didn't even see it for a few hours because I didn't check my email before I got to the office. When I saw it, I showed it to Trevor."

"Did you keep records of your correspondence with this source?"

"Of course. I have all of it," she said. "It started the day of the murder. I got an email that morning saying that the police would be called to an address."

"Heinrich's address?"

"Yes. I didn't know it at the time, obviously, but it was correct. I decided to show it to Trevor. He took a chance and followed up on the information, and it paid off, I guess."

"That's how he was there first thing in the morning," I said. "He didn't have a police scanner. He had the inside source. You realize the person you're communicating with is likely the murderer."

She looked even more miserable. "What was I supposed to do about it?"

"Let the police know," I said shortly. "We're going to need to confiscate your computer so our team can sort through the messages you received."

"Yes, of course. I-I'm sorry. I didn't know better. It's my first job. I have no clue why I was chosen."

"Did you ever respond to the emails?"

"Yes. I asked who it was. I asked if we could meet. I never got a response. I just got details as they were sent to me. It was completely one-sided."

"What did Trevor say about it?"

"At first he poo-pooed me. I didn't think he was going to go to the address the morning I first told him about the email, but I guess he chanced it. He didn't tell me he was going; I actually didn't know he'd taken me seriously at all until I saw his article about it."

"Where is he now?"

"I don't know," she said. "And I haven't heard from the source after this morning's email about your dad's trunk. I didn't know it was your dad at the time. I just passed the email along to Trevor. I didn't want to be a part of it anymore."

"Why didn't you come to the police if you didn't want to be a part of it anymore?"

Meredith looked uneasy. Jimmy blew out a breath.

"Trevor told you not to," Jimmy said. "He wanted the story, so he pressured you to keep quiet so the emails would keep coming."

"He said he'd get me fired or worse if I cut off ties with the source. I believed him."

"I see. You didn't gather any identifying information about the source from the emails by chance, did you?"

"I think my source is a woman," Meredith said. "But that's just a gut feeling."

"Why?" Jimmy and I asked at the same time.

"No concrete reason," she reiterated. "It's just from the tone of how she writes. I mean, I could be wrong. She never signed a name or anything, and her email address is just a bunch of letters and numbers that appear to be random. I just always thought of the person on the other end of my emails as a woman."

"We'll see what our analysts have to say about it," I said. "In the meantime, I'd like you to accompany us down to the station. We'll need to take your computer and a few other items once our warrant comes through."

Meredith sighed. "Sure, fine, whatever you need. It's not like I'm going to keep my job here anyway."

Jimmy and I stepped out of the office. We arranged for the local cops to stick around with Meredith until the next team arrived with a warrant. Then they'd bring her down to the precinct to take her official statement.

Chapter 21

Jimmy and I returned to my car and headed back to the precinct. An air of frustration sizzled between us as I unloaded the truth of Melinda's call, that the diamond hadn't been a match. That I'd simply bluffed on a hunch. A hunch that had paid off.

"I've got a BOLO out on Trevor," Jimmy said. "We'll get him. He can't have gotten far. I doubt he had time to hop on a flight."

"I just don't know," I said. "Do we really think he murdered Heinrich? We've got no evidence tying him to the scene of the crime. Would he really risk all this for a story?"

"We'll keep picking away. It's one theory, and right now we don't have a lot of them."

My phone buzzed again, and I answered on speaker, announcing Jimmy's presence beside me.

"It's me again," Melinda said. "I've got more news, Kate."

I could tell from Melinda's tone it wasn't good news.

"I'm sorry, but the materials in your father's trunk were a match to the incendiary device that killed Heinrich," Melinda shared. "In my opinion it's enough for an arrest warrant."

"My dad didn't do it."

"We all know that," Melinda said. "But I thought you should have this information first. I haven't told the chief yet. I'm going to step out of my office and use the restroom. Maybe grab a coffee. Then I'll have to file the official report."

I knew exactly what she was saying without actually saying it. She was giving me the opportunity to contact my dad personally before officers showed up at his door.

"I appreciate that," I told her. "Really, thanks."

I hung up with Melinda and felt Jimmy's gaze on me.

"I'm fine," I told him preemptively. "You don't have to look at me like that. We knew it would be a match."

"If you want to talk to your dad in private, why don't you pull over at that Dunkin' Donuts up ahead and let me out?" Jimmy nodded toward the approaching sign. "I'll grab us some grub."

"No time," I said, and then punched my dad's name on my phone.

The line started to ring as we flew past the Dunkin' Donuts sign. Jimmy stared forlornly out the window.

"Hey, Dad," I said when he answered. "Just so you know, I'm calling from the car and Jimmy's here with me."

"Hey, guys," my dad said. "How goes it?"

"I, well, I wanted to be the one to call and let you know the lab results," I said. "I wish it were better news, but—"

"It's okay, Kate. I know. You don't have to say anything else."

I cleared my throat. "I guess you're going to be having some visitors from the precinct at your door. I just didn't want you to be surprised."

"I appreciate it."

"I'm sorry," I echoed.

"No need to be sorry," my dad said. "The cops ain't gonna find me at home."

"Where are you?" My stomach plummeted. If my dad told me he was halfway to Mexico right now, I'd find him and slap the cuffs on him myself.

"Relax. I'm at the precinct."

It took a moment for me to process what he meant. "Why?"

"C'mon, I wouldn't have answered the phone if was in the wind." My dad paused for a beat. "I'm about to turn myself in."

"I thought Mom didn't want you to do anything of the sort."

"I had a talk with her after you left. We have an understanding, and we've agreed this is for the best."

"You didn't do anything wrong. You're being framed. You shouldn't have to turn yourself in."

"We all know that, but I'm not worried. I trust you."

I suddenly wished Jimmy weren't on the call with me. He was politely staring out the window and pretending not to hear a word, but it still made me uncomfortable.

"I trust you, too, Detective Jones," my dad said. "You keep watching my daughter's back. I don't think there's anyone better suited for the job."

"I appreciate that, sir," Jimmy said.

"We're headed back to the precinct now," I said. "I'll stop by when I get there to see if you need anything."

"Don't worry about me. Keep doing what you're doing. You'll get him; I know you will. You're close; I can feel it."

I hung up the call with my dad and turned to Jimmy. He once again politely pretended the previous conversation didn't happen. Old Kate would have been eternally grateful for the quashing of emotions. But New Kate felt a tug to say something. I cleared my throat, gathered up every last ounce of my courage.

"I agree with my dad," I told him.

"That we're getting close?" Jimmy asked. "Yeah, me too. I can feel it in my bones, and I'm a big-boned individual."

"That's not what I meant. I meant the part about you watching my back. I appreciate you. I don't think I tell you that enough."

Jimmy gave me a gentle smile. "You tell me just fine, Rosetti."

Without further discussion, we made it back to the precinct and went straight to Asha's desk. She clapped her hands together the moment she laid eyes on us.

"I'm itching to get my hands on a couple of computers," Asha said, like it was Christmas morning. "First I get access to Burton's drive, and now I get to dig into Meredith's computer to chase down an internet ghost with a sketchy email address. To what do I owe the pleasure?"

"The officers should be here any minute with Meredith's computer. Do me a favor and let me know how it all adds up, will you?" I requested. "My dad's in police custody. We've got to keep moving on this."

"I heard that, hon. I'm so sorry."

"It's fine," I said. "Let's just finish this."

"You got it, babe." Asha cracked her knuckles and returned to her desk.

Jimmy and I checked in with the team. We were directed to the interview room where Burton was waiting for us. Jimmy offered to let me have first crack at the guy alone.

When I entered the room, Burton glanced up at me. The preppy programmer who moonlighted as a weirdly competitive bowler looked annoyed. He didn't seem used to being inconvenienced. And being held at a police station without access to his computer and cushy home was a very large inconvenience.

"Howdy," I said, sitting across from him. "How's the wife dealing with your arrest?"

"She's annoyed, just like I am." As soon as the words were out, he froze. His eyes were like saucers as he looked at me. There was a fleeting moment where it seemed he was prepared to lie, and then he visibly deflated before me. "How'd you find out?"

"You're not the only one who knows your way around a computer. And pretty soon the best of the best is gonna be helping herself to each and every one of your files. If you think there's a chance any of your private things will stay hidden, you should lose hope right now. I recommend you start talking if you want me to put in any sort of good word for you with the jury. We've got you for running down Heinrich, and if there's more, we'll find that too."

"It was just a little accident," he said. "That's it. I didn't kill the guy."

"A little accident?" I studied him and sensed zero remorse. "You ran a guy over and put him in the hospital, needing an extensive surgery. His leg was probably never the same after you hit him. Why'd you do it anyway, a bowling feud?"

He looked sullen but still remorseless. "The guy was a dick."

"Okay." I nodded as if that made complete sense. I wasn't sure if Burton caught my sarcasm. "And that gives you permission to run him over and leave the scene of the crime?"

"I'm sorry," he said, spreading his hands wide. "Maybe I overreacted. But I did not kill him. You have no right to go through my computer or anything else."

"In fact, we do. We followed the correct procedures—I'm sure your lawyer has been following along—and secured all the proper warrants. You're our best suspect in a murder investigation right now. Do you realize that?"

I decided to leave out the part about my own father sitting a few rooms over.

"Talk to me," I said. "It's your best chance at looking good down the line."

"I didn't kill him. My lawyer's not here yet. I'm not supposed to talk."

"Understood. We'll wait for your lawyer, then."

"How do I prove I didn't kill him?" Burton hedged, as I stood to leave. "What can I tell you? I haven't even seen the guy recently. You know my alibi is Kendra. That's the truth. It's all I can give you."

"Let's start by talking about your relationship with Kendra," I said. "Why didn't you introduce her as your wife when we showed up at your house?"

"We're not telling anyone we got married. We got hitched a couple of months ago, but we haven't told our families or anyone else. It was none of your business."

"Why the secret wedding?"

He shifted uncomfortably. "She asked me to do it. I love her, so I said okay."

"You're lying," I shot back. "And if you think we're not going to call Kendra down to the station and grill her, too, you're wrong. I guess it just depends on how much you trust Kendra to line up her story with yours. Or, now that you're being investigated for murder, will she spill the beans on everything to save herself?"

Apparently Burton didn't have a lot of faith in his new wife's story because he noticeably paled.

"Kendra found out I was having an affair," Burton said, his face shutting down to reveal zero emotion. "I have a problem. I've been in therapy for sex addiction. It's not my fault; I can't help it."

"Uh-huh," I said. "Who was the other woman?"

"Her name is Brittany. She's someone I work with remotely. She lives in San Francisco. We'd meet up when I traveled out of town."

"How'd Kendra find out?"

"Brittany was in town for a visit, and I met her at a hotel. I guess Kendra had suspected me of stepping out on her for a while and followed me there."

Burton and his big ego had let his guard down again, I thought.

"It's not my fault," he insisted, taking one look at my expression of disbelief. "I have a problem. Kendra even knew about my problem. I told her up front."

This guy was a major narcissist, I noted. Nothing was ever his fault. He'd even made it sound like running over Heinrich had been Heinrich's fault because the man was a jerk. It was easy enough to see that Burton had the means to kill Heinrich, but I still couldn't figure out the motive.

"I'm guessing you also told Kendra you changed your ways," I said. "Am I right?"

"I tried to change. I did therapy for a while. I made a mistake. It happens."

"It sounds like you made a series of mistakes with Brittany."

"I apologized," he said. "I told Kendra it would never happen again, and I meant it. I told her I'd go back to therapy. She wasn't happy with that."

"This isn't adding up to how you got a ring on her finger."

"It was her ultimatum. Kendra was going to leave me unless I convinced her I was serious. She told me I had to propose or she was out of there."

"So you proposed?"

"I didn't want to lose her. I love her." Burton spoke slowly as if I were having difficulty comprehending. "Yes, I gave her a ring."

"And that was it?"

He shifted again in his seat. It was becoming obvious that it was a tell. I waited for him to lie to my face. He didn't let me down.

"Yes."

"Try again," I prompted. "Let me remind you we've got some fast fingers combing through your computer right now. Help us get there faster."

"Kendra said she wanted to get married the next week and that she wouldn't sign a prenup. Those were her terms."

There it was. Suddenly everything made a little more sense.

"She was after your money," I said.

"No," he said defensively. "She told me that she just wanted to enter into the next step of our relationship with complete trust. She said that if I knew I could lose half of everything I owned, I'd be less likely to cheat."

"And?"

"And what? I obviously agreed."

"Why the secrecy, then? Why not let people know?"

"That was her decision. You'll have to ask Kendra."

"If you had to venture a guess, what would your guess be?"

"For starters, her parents hated me," he said. "Her friends hated me. Nobody in her life supported our relationship. I suppose that could be why."

"Do you know why they hated you, aside from the obvious?"

"No," he said. "Who wouldn't want to be with me? I'm attractive. I make a boatload of money."

"You cheat on people repeatedly."

"I apologized and bought her a ring."

I could see that we were just never going to be on the same page, so I let it drop. I was beginning to have a clearer picture of what had been happening here. Unfortunately, while it set up the picture of a dysfunctional relationship between Kendra and Billy Burton, it didn't solve the little issue of motive for Heinrich's murder.

In fact, it seemed like Burton had his hands full with his private life, so why would he have offed Heinrich out of the blue for no apparent reason at all? Burton was egotistical and cocky. He was also a narcissist and sloppy and completely tone deaf. I had the distinct feeling that if he'd been responsible for Heinrich's death, we'd know it by now. Somehow, someway.

Someone knocked on the door. Melinda entered the room a beat later, and I was taken aback to see her interrupting the interview.

"I've got some information for you," Melinda said. "They've matched the paint from Mr. Burton's vehicle to the sample in evidence. It was his car that ran down Heinrich, for sure."

Burton sank lower in his seat.

"But what's really going to interest you is on the next page," Melinda continued. "They found a little treat in the trunk."

Melinda left me with the sheaf of papers and disappeared from the room. I glanced down at the page and couldn't believe my eyes. I read the report twice. My delay in speaking inadvertently put Burton on edge. He edged higher in his seat to peek across the table.

"You kept explosives in your trunk?" I asked. "The exact same stuff you used to blow up Heinrich?"

"Explosives in the trunk of my car?" Burton looked completely mystified. "Of course not. That'd be stupid. Do you know how much that car is worth? It's going for over a quarter million dollars, easy. If a bomb blew up that car, I'd be out a crap load of money. Do I look stupid to you?"

I wasn't sure about stupid, but I was positive he was egotistical, and I did believe both his surprise and his explanation. Shockingly, his ego might have actually saved him on this one. It didn't help that I had a bad feeling in my stomach about this. Especially since the contents found in Burton's trunk were an exact match to the ones that had been found in my dad's trunk. It was too coincidental to ignore.

"I didn't do it," he said. "Someone's framing me."

I hated to agree, but silently, I did. I didn't let my agreement show on my face.

"One more question for you, Burton," I said, as a striking realization hit me. "You said you bought your wife a ring. Why doesn't she wear it?"

"She did until she lost it," he said. "Of course, she'd only wear it at home. She'd take it off if she had friends coming over because she wanted to keep our marriage quiet."

"She lost it? How?"

"She said she doesn't know, and then she said if she did know where it was, then it wouldn't be lost." Burton rolled his eyes. "I put a new one on order a few weeks ago just to shut her up about it."

I left the conference room and marched straight down the hall until I caught Melinda outside of the chief's office.

"The diamond," I said. "Could it have come from an engagement ring? Maybe one of the smaller stones on the side?"

"It sure could have," Melinda said. "And if we had the ring, we could definitely match it."

"I think I know who that diamond belongs to. And I think I know who killed Heinrich. Have Asha look in Burton's computer for the purchase of an engagement ring. I think you'll find the diamond from the car matches a diamond on that ring."

Chapter 22

I held a quick meeting with a small group of people to explain my theory about Kendra. Melinda, Jimmy, Asha, and I stood in a half circle around the chief's desk. Chief Sturgeon rubbed his head when I finished.

"Where's Kendra now?" Sturgeon asked.

"She was gathering things up to leave Burton's place when we were there earlier this afternoon," Jimmy said. "At the time, I thought she'd be going to her place."

"That's a negative, Jones." Asha raised a finger. "In the short time I've been digging into Kendra, I've turned up a lot of lies. She doesn't have a job, for starters."

"She told me she was a nurse," I said. "That's why she said she'd stay at her place some nights, to be closer to the hospital."

"Right. She quit a couple months ago. Right around the time of her wedding to Burton," Asha said. "That got me looking into her apartment. Her lease goes through May, but I went a step further and reached out to the landlord."

"And?"

"And he said she's been moved out for a couple of months now. It wasn't financially worth it to her to break the lease because she'd have had to pay a steep penalty. But he saw her moving a bunch of stuff out a while ago. From what he can tell, she just stops by now and again to pick up her mail."

"I'm guessing she didn't go back to an empty apartment where she knows we can find her," I said. "She'll have taken off."

"I'll get a BOLO out on her," Asha said. "I'll start tracking her credit cards and cell to see if I can pick up anything. But if she's at all intelligent, she'll have ditched that stuff the second you arrested Burton."

"My thinking exactly." I turned to the chief. "Jimmy and I can swing by Burton's house to make sure she's not still there."

"I'll call ahead to her landlord," Jimmy said, "and I'll let him know to watch out for her in case she swings by to pick anything up. We'll have a team swing by to check things out."

The chief nodded. "What do you need from me?"

"Until we get a read on her location," I said, "not a whole lot. I've got my fingers crossed Asha can find something before Kendra realizes she's being tracked. It's not likely, but Asha's good."

"Keep me posted," the chief growled. "And Dr. Brooks, I'd like your team to try and match that diamond from the ring as soon as possible. The jeweler should be able to help with that."

The group split up. Jimmy made the phone call to the apartment complex while Melinda returned to the lab downstairs. Asha was busy typing away by the time Jimmy and I left the building.

"Kendra's not gonna be at Burton's," Jimmy said as he climbed into the passenger's seat of my car. "She's not gonna show at the apartment either. The landlord said he hadn't seen her in weeks. At my request, he popped into her place while I was on the line and said nothing's there except a few larger pieces of furniture. A couch, a stripped-down bed, that sort of thing. He's going to watch the front doors for us until we can get there, but he doesn't think we should hold our breath."

"Me neither," I said. "But we need to do something, and I don't have any better ideas."

"Can't argue with that."

We drove in silence to the Burton mansion. We climbed out of the vehicle and checked the garage. We headed up the front path and knocked on the door. The car Kendra was supposedly driving wasn't anywhere to be found. The house appeared abandoned. Aside from Burton's show cars, the garage was empty. We were headed back to my vehicle when my phone rang.

"What's up?" I greeted Asha.

"State troopers found Kendra's car. It was just across the border in Wisconsin. She pulled into a rest stop and left it there. It appears to have been abandoned," she said. "I'm looking around to see if we can get any footage of how she might've left from the rest stop—if she's working with some-one, or if she had a second car. I'll keep you updated."

I thanked her and signed off. "She's on the run," I said to Jimmy. "I can't shake this feeling that we're too late. It almost feels like she stuck around as long as she did just to watch everything fall apart, almost like it was a game to her. The on-ly sticking point for me is Heinrich himself. Why kill *him*? What was their connection?"

"With Heinrich dead, there might only be one person left who has that answer," Jimmy said grimly. "And I don't think she's hankering to share."

"Maybe they were secret lovers?" I wondered. "Or maybe Kendra wanted revenge on Heinrich because she loved Burton so much, and she knew they were enemies?"

Jimmy shrugged. "I wish I had an answer for you."

As I started my car, the phone rang. It was an unknown number, and I glanced at Jimmy before answering it. He nodded and remained silent as I accepted the call.

"Leaving so soon?" Kendra's voice tinkled over the line. "Yes, we have cameras on the property. Don't worry, I'm not there in person. Or am I? I guess you don't really know, do you?"

"Kendra, it's not too late for us to help you. If you turn yourself in before we hunt you down, we can work something out. I know a great lawyer who has gotten people off for a lot worse."

"That's a kind offer, but frankly I have a lot more money than you do, and I can afford my own lawyers. Then again, I know you're cozied up to that sexy billionaire, so maybe I'm wrong."

"You've been doing your research."

"Nah, I've just been playing the part of interested, supportive wife. Billy was obsessed with checking you out. I just glanced over his shoulder."

"What do you want? Why are you calling me?"

"Actually, there is a little issue. While I have way more money than you, my idiot husband double-crossed me."

"Sorry?"

"I'm sure by now you figured out that Bill and I are married, no prenup, so what's mine is his and all that jazz," she said. "The problem is, he obviously didn't trust me."

"Why are you telling me all this?"

"Because I'm flat-out broke, and I need cash. Billy locked me out of all his accounts. Every last dime is frozen solid, and I'm left up a creek without a paddle. Bring me twenty grand in cash, or your mother's going to die."

"Excuse me?"

"That's right, I forgot to tell you. I have your sweet mama here with me, and she's going to meet the same fate as Heinrich if I don't have twenty grand of cold, hard cash in my hand in one hour."

"That's impossible! There is literally no way for me to get that much money on such short notice." My heart pounded; my mind raced. "I don't think I have that in all my bank accounts combined. And first, I want to talk to my mom."

Kendra sighed. "Mama Rosetti, give a little holler so Kate can rest easy."

"Don't listen to her, Kate!" My mom's voice rang over the line. "I love you, honey. I'll be fine!"

Jimmy tensed beside me. I could barely think. I closed my eyes for a long second, trying my best to turn off any emotional part of my brain so that I could focus on logic. I needed to act strategically, to use my head and not the whims of the family ties tugging at my heart.

"One hour," she said. "Now write down these directions to follow for when you get the money."

As I scrounged for a pen, I tried to stall her. "What about Meredith at the North Star Press? Why did you send her the emails about what you were doing?"

"Guys are jerks. I liked the new girl better. I thought I'd share my story—she'll get the rest of it when I'm ready. Now listen carefully because I won't be repeating myself."

Jimmy and I both held our pens at the ready and scribbled as she rattled off a series of directions. I didn't recognize the end location, and judging by Jimmy's expression, neither did he.

"Now toss your phones into the bushes. Yes, both of you. I can see you," she reminded us. "Then you'll do the same thing with your firearms."

"If you want any hope of me getting ahold of this much money in one hour, I'm going to need to make a phone call," I told her. "One phone call."

There was a wait on the other end of the line as Kendra seemed to be considering my request.

"One phone call," she said. "And do it now—use your partner's phone and keep me on the line so I can hear you. But if I suspect you of phoning the police or alerting any of your law enforcement pals—including your ex-boyfriend—your mom goes *boom*. Got it?"

"Understood."

I gestured for Jimmy to hand me his phone. He already had it extended in his palm. I quickly dialed Gem's number from Jimmy's contacts and waited for it to ring, praying he would answer. It wouldn't be my name showing up on the other end, so I was well aware there was a good chance he would ignore it. It was in the middle of a workday for crying out loud.

"Detective Jones?" Gem answered on the last ring, a note of concern to his voice. "Is everything okay?"

"It's me," I said quickly. "I'm so sorry, but I need a huge favor. I can't explain it yet. I just need you to trust me."

"Anything."

"I need twenty thousand dollars in cash," I said. "And you can't ask me any questions. I'll pay you back when I can."

"Of course."

"The thing is I need it now. Like, right now."

His voice was low and growly. "Where should I deliver it?"

I hesitated a beat. Then, from my phone, I heard Kendra's voice.

"Have him bring it to the estate," she commanded. "I want to see him hand it to you."

"There's not enough time," I said. "Even if he leaves now and drives straight here, there won't be enough time."

"It takes approximately fourteen minutes to make the drive from Gem Industries to Sunfish Lake," Kendra said. "I'll add on an additional ten minutes for him to secure the funds."

"How did you know who I was talking to?"

"There was only ever one option," Kendra said. "How do you think I knew you'd be able to get me the money? I was just waiting for you to figure it out."

I turned back to my phone conversation with Gem and gave him the address of Burton's place. "Is there any way you can be here within twenty minutes?"

"I'm already walking out to my car," Gem said. "I can make it."

"You need to bring the money with you," I clarified. "In cash. And Gem, you can't tell anyone. Swear it to me."

"I already have the money on me," he said. "I'm on my way, and I'll take it to my grave."

***

Kendra kept us on the phone for the excruciatingly long twenty minutes that it took for Gem to arrive. I saw his car before I heard the crunch of tires on gravel and snow. Gem stepped out of the driver's seat, glanced around, and took a few steps toward me. I held up a hand for him to stop. Then I held out my phone with Kendra on speaker.

"Nice to see you, handsome," Kendra said. "Put down the cash right where you are. Then toss your phone into the bushes, Alastair."

Gem wore a long peacoat. He pulled a thick manilla envelope from somewhere on his person. He laid it gently on the ground.

"Take the money out," Kendra said.

"It'll blow away," Gem argued. "It's cold and windy."

"Put a rock on it," she snapped. "Do it now."

Gem followed her directions. A lot of cash sat on the ground.

"Good," Kendra coached. "Now be a dear and toss your phone into the bushes."

"Kendra, this is not necessary," I said. "He's not going to tell anyone."

But Gem had already chucked his phone into the tree line encircling the estate.

"Good," Kendra repeated. "Now, here's the plan. Kate, leave your phone on the ground. I want to be able to talk to Mr. Handsome once you leave."

I did as I was told and set my phone on the ground. As I stood, I felt Gem's gaze on me. We made eye contact. I looked away first, feeling guilty beyond all measure that we were here again. My begging Gem for his help. Me unable to explain anything. And Gem, as always, having my back without question.

"Your final instructions," Kendra said, "are as follows. Mr. Gem, you will stand as you are—away from your car and where I can see you—for one hour. I have cameras everywhere. I will know if you move a muscle, and if you do, Kate's mom will die. No question about it."

I felt the full force of Gem's gaze on me. I couldn't look up. My eyes were fixed on the phone.

"I understand," Gem said. "You have my word."

"I knew you'd cooperate. You love our little detective so much you'd do anything for her," Kendra said, her voice dripping with fake sweetness. "Now, Kate, you and your partner need to set your firearms on the ground. Do not approach Gem. Do not even speak to him. Detective Jones, I'll need you to toss your phone. Then grab the money and drive away."

Jimmy let his phone fly. We both set our guns down. Gem watched us, unblinking, his expression unreadable as I grabbed the money and tucked it into my jacket.

Kendra gave a dainty laugh. "I'll see you soon, Detectives. The clock is ticking."

Jimmy and I made our way to the car. I looked at Gem, unable to utter a word. His eyes followed me until I was in the car. My foot slammed to the floor, and we squealed away from the estate.

"It's going to be okay, Kate," Jimmy murmured in a hushed voice. "The department knows we were going to Burton's. When they can't reach us, they'll start looking for us quickly. They'll probably arrive before Gem's hour is up, and he can tell them everything."

"True," I said, hoping they'd start looking sooner rather than later.

In addition, I'd left them a breadcrumb clue behind at the estate with Gem. Before I'd set my gun down, I'd tucked my version of the directions into the barrel leaving the tip poking out ever so slightly, just noticeable enough that whoever picked it up would see it. Jimmy had his own set of directions, and in leaving mine behind, I hoped to give our team a slight advantage.

We raced through the directions Kendra had detailed for us and made it to the destination in exactly the amount of time she'd predicted. She had led us to a deserted parking lot at a hiking trail just outside of the city. Even the parking lot was tucked away from the main road, and at this time of year, there would be no hikers on the trail.

Jimmy and I climbed out of the car. There was no evidence of my mother or her vehicle anywhere. Then Jimmy cleared his throat and nodded to the far side of the parking lot. There, in the packed-down snow, were a couple of tire tracks leading into a cluster of trees. It was an easy bet to make that we'd find my mother and Kendra at the end of those tire tracks.

Jimmy and I made our way toward the edge of the forest where the tire tracks disappeared.

"Kendra?" I called out. "It's us. We're unarmed. We're alone. Where's my mother?"

Kendra stepped out from behind a tree. She held a gun pointed in our direction.

"Glad you could make it," she said, giving us a thin smile. "You—Jimmy—you'll find a pair of handcuffs at that oak tree ahead of you. Pick them up and put them on your partner. Tight, or I shoot you, shoot Kate, and her mother dies."

"Go on," I said to Jimmy.

Jimmy retrieved the handcuffs. He breathed heavily as he fastened them around my wrists. I could see the disdain in his eyes for what he was being forced to do, but there was no other choice.

"Tighten them," Kendra barked. "More."

The metal was starting to cut into my wrists, and again, I gave Jimmy a flicker of a smile to encourage him.

"It's okay," I breathed. Then I looked over my handcuffs to Kendra. "Let Jimmy go. He doesn't need to be here."

"Well, I have other plans," Kendra retorted. "Now, if you'd like to see your mother, toss me the money. But keep your distance or I shoot."

Jimmy glanced at me, and I nodded. Reluctantly, he pulled the envelope of cash out of my jacket and tossed it toward Kendra's feet. "There's your money. Let Mrs. Rosetti go."

Kendra bent, retrieved the envelope, and quickly glanced inside—the gun pointed at us the whole while. She awkwardly fingered the money with her other hand. "Can't count it now. I don't trust either of you, but I do trust the billionaire. He wouldn't do anything to hurt you," she said with a little smile in my direction. "Now follow me. No sudden moves, or one of the Rosetti ladies is dead." We stayed a safe distance behind Kendra until we reached a clearing inside a ring of thick evergreens dusted with snow. It was warmer here in the woods than it was in the open fields. We were nestled into a cocoon of complete quiet, the trees serving as steadfast breakers to the wind.

I caught a glimpse of my mother's car parked out of sight from the road. Sitting in the driver's seat was a familiar face.

"Mom," I shouted. "*Mom*."

My mother glanced toward me, and her eyes widened. She said something, but it was too muffled behind the window for me to make out her words.

"Let her go," I said to Kendra. "I'm here. We've followed your instructions."

"In due time. We've got a few minutes before she's in any danger."

"A few minutes?" I croaked. "Until what?"

Kendra looked at me, bored, as if this were her average trip to the bank on a Wednesday, and I was a very annoying teller. "There's a bomb, same as the one that killed Heinrich, in the car with Mama Rosetti. It's got a few minutes left on it, and if you don't cooperate, I let it go off."

"Now, that's not very smart," Jimmy said. "If you ask me, a better plan is for you to take off with the cash and Kate's car, and we'll give you a nice head start to disappear."

"Aw." Kendra clucked. "How thoughtful of you to consider my best interests."

"I'm just saying, if you murder Kate or her mother," Jimmy warned, "you'll be looking over your shoulder until the day you die. And seeing as Kate's father is Angelo Rosetti, and he won't be happy if you kill his wife or daughter, I don't think that day would be all that far off."

"That sounds like a *me* problem, not a *you* problem." Kendra cocked her head and stared at Jimmy. "Do you really think I haven't thought that far ahead? How long has it taken an entire *team* of cops to come this close to finding me? Please. You're only here because I wanted you to be here."

"What's your plan, then?" I asked. "If it's so great and all."

Kendra's eyes squinted as she looked at me. "That'll be all, Chatty Cathy. Not another word, or—"

"One more thing," I interrupted. "Why Heinrich?"

"Huh?"

"Heinrich," I repeated. "If I'm going to die because I was looking into his case, I deserve to at least know why you did it."

"It's simple, really. I met him at the bowling alley." Kendra tucked the money she'd been holding in her hand into her own jacket. "When I found out Billy was cheating on me with some hooker from the bowling lanes, I decided to do the same thing to get back at him."

"And who better to use against Burton than his biggest rival."

"Exactly. Except good old Jeff Heinrich actually fell in love with me. If it wasn't so unnecessary, I'd say it was almost cute. But he wasn't my type. He was old and poor and not all that handsome."

I detected an unexplained note of hesitation in Kendra's voice. "You fell for him back," I surmised, understanding sinking in. "You loved him."

"He did grow on me. Unlike Bill, Jeff really appreciated me. He was kind, and he was fantastic in the sack, surprisingly. He actually cared about me. Oh, and he wasn't a liar and a cheater. So, yes, I probably liked Jeff more than I'd initially intended."

"But eventually you had to break things off with Heinrich," I guessed, "because you cared more about Burton's money than you cared about a life with Heinrich."

"That's where you're wrong. I was going to have it all." Kendra gave a satisfied smirk. "The plan was simple: marry Bill without a prenup. Then I'd sit around, biding my time until I caught him knocking boots with some other woman for the zillionth time. I'd pout and throw a fit and cry my eyes out, and then I'd divorce him, take half his money, and live on the beach with Jeff."

"That would really piss Billy Burton off, you living off his money and dating a guy he hated."

"Ah, so you are a decent detective." Kendra winked. "I'm glad you're keeping up. Unfortunately, Jeff didn't like my plan."

"I can't imagine why not," I said dryly.

Kendra missed my sarcasm. "All Jeff had to do was sit around for a couple of months until I could get a divorce, but no. He didn't want any part of the plan. The idiot dumped me."

"Go figure."

"It wasn't fair. After all I'd done for him, all I'd sacrificed. It was ungrateful of him."

"So you killed him," I said. "How'd you manage to handcuff him to his steering wheel?"

"I told him I wanted to talk after he broke up with me. I put on my best weepy face and groveled, telling him I wanted to get back together. Then, when he leaned in to kiss me, I just snapped them on. He didn't expect it." She shrugged. "I dropped the backpack on the seat and locked the car. That's about it."

"Your engagement ring?"

"Fell out of my pocket in the car. I didn't realize that until later." She wrinkled her nose. "I took it off when I got in his car because I figured it would annoy him if I had it on—you know, a reminder of Bill. Usually I left it at home, but I'd forgotten that night."

"What about the explosive materials you planted in my dad's trunk?"

"I planted some in a bunch of people's cars. Bill's too. I thought I'd just sort of scatter evidence around to keep things interesting. I intended to take the stuff out of Bill's fancy car after I heard they found your father's stash, but I didn't get to it in time."

"I'm glad we're all getting along so nicely right now," Jimmy said, "but how do we get Mrs. Rosetti out of that car?"

"Here's what we're going to do," Kendra instructed, unlocking the car door via my mother's remote. "Jimmy, you open the door. I'll toss you the keys for the handcuffs, and you can escort Mrs. Rosetti out of the car."

Jimmy's jaw was set hard, but he continued to follow instructions. He caught the keys Kendra tossed over, then pulled open the door to my mom's car and began fumbling with the handcuffs. My mother let out a guttural sob as she yanked hard at the steering wheel while Jimmy wrestled her from the car.

"Kate," she said, lunging at me, held back only by Jimmy's big arms clasping her to his chest. "I'm so sorry. The message said they had you, that I should drive to this location if I ever wanted to see you again. I feel so stupid. It's all my fault I believed her. I'm so sorry."

"Mom, it's not your fault," I promised. "None of this is your fault."

My mother lunged in my direction again, and Jimmy only tightened his bear hug on her much smaller figure, suppressing her movements. Kendra raised her gun at me.

"You, Kate, get in the car. If anyone makes a funny move, she's dead before the bomb can kill her."

My mother stopped, breathing heavily, watching me. "Don't you get in that car, Kate."

"Mom, I—"

"Even if your father has been driving that car around lately, it's mine. It's the car I bought with my own money when your father left me all those years ago." My mother was breathing heavily. "Not to mention, I keep those Polaroids in the glove compartment from when you girls were kids. If the car gets blown to bits, I'll never have those pictures back."

I had the fleeting thought that my mother was delirious. My mom had never cared one way or another about vehicles. She couldn't even name the make and the model of her own car. Also, she'd only bought this car two years ago. Not ages ago like she'd been claiming. And she'd never owned a Polaroid camera in her life, so I had no idea what in the world she was going on about pictures in the glove box.

Then she looked at me, and I saw in her gaze that she was lying. Purposefully. I quickly backtracked through the words she'd uttered and dissected the information. Then I understood that she'd been trying to tell me something. A clue, a nugget that she somehow thought might help get us out of this mess. A nugget that probably was sitting in the glove compartment of the vehicle.

Jimmy reached up and wiped a bead of sweat off his forehead. "Why don't y'all let me hop in that vehicle?"

"Don't be silly." My mother and I spoke at the same time.

"Kate, get in the car," Kendra said. "Clock's ticking."

I took quick steps directly toward the car. Without waiting for further instructions, I yanked the door open, both hands still cuffed before me.

"Wait a second—"

I pretended not to hear Kendra's warning, taking the chance that she would be too distracted watching my every move to pull the trigger. I also trusted that Jimmy would take care of my mom.

Instead of halting, I kept right on barreling into the car, hoping I could capitalize on my mother's hint. If my mother was wrong, or if I'd misinterpreted her nonsensical ramblings, there was a good chance none of us would make it out alive.

"C'mon, Mom," I murmured to myself. "Please tell me you haven't gone nuts."

If there was ever a time for a mother and daughter to have a special connection, this was it. She had to be right; I *had* to have interpreted her speech correctly, that there was something in the glove compartment that might save our lives. The alternative was too unbearable to consider.

I yanked said glove compartment open, shielding my moves from Kendra by pretending to fumble as I got into the seat. It was easy to pretend I was just being clumsy seeing as my hands were cuffed before me. It really was quite awkward.

Then, finally, I spied what my mother had been talking about, and for the first time, I felt a pinch of hope.

"Sit down!" Kendra shouted. "What are you doing?"

"I'm trying," I shouted back. "My hands are cuffed."

"Sit down, right now," she said. "Close the door behind you."

"I'm going. Relax. There's no way I'm going to survive being this close to a bomb whether I'm seated or not."

Seeming a bit appeased with my answer, Kendra moved so that she had the gun now pointed directly at me through the driver's side window of the car. My mother and Jimmy were too far away to make a break for her. I knew Jimmy wouldn't risk my mother's life by disobeying Kendra's instructions anyway.

"Put your hands up on the steering wheel where I can see them," Kendra said. "I'm going to have Jimmy cuff you to the wheel, and then—"

"Run!" I shouted to Jimmy as I raised my hands with the gun I'd retrieved from the glove compartment, between my hands.

Without waiting, I squeezed off a shot through the glass. It wasn't a perfect shot, but the bullet made contact with Kendra's shoulder, sending her spiraling away in pain. The gun in her hand dropped to the forest floor, and it took Jimmy all of three seconds to retrieve it.

I was already halfway out of the car, glass tumbling off me in every direction, when I made eye contact with Jimmy. Kendra writhed in pain next to him. Jimmy had her gun and the keys to the handcuffs. He quickly relieved me of the cuffs, urgency still present in his eyes.

"Run," I barked. "Take my mom and *run!*"

Jimmy didn't miss a beat. He grabbed my mother and all but threw her over his shoulder as he moved in the opposite direction of the explosives. I hadn't seen Jimmy haul ass with such urgency since his last physical with the department, but I didn't have time to admire his form. The clock had less than a minute on the timer.

I raced to Kendra, grabbed her around the waist, and tackled her away from the car. Kendra fought me tooth and nail the entire way until finally, I pinned her down against the ground, my breath coming in jagged, painful bursts.

"I'm trying to save your life," I spit out.

Kendra relaxed, ever so slightly, and I hauled her back to her feet. I threw her over the top of the biggest snowbank I could find within sprinting distance, then I followed her with a hard barrel roll. I'd barely ducked my head into my hands when the car behind us exploded into bits.

I blacked out for a moment when something I'd later learn was the steering wheel ricocheted off my head. A few seconds later, I came to, my hearing still out of commission and my vision more than a little wobbly. I could barely make out the bleeding figure of Kendra kneeling over me. Then she pulled her fist back and punched me straight in the nose.

"Are you freaking kidding me?" I hauled myself to my feet, tasting my own blood. "You're a nut," I said, pushing her up against the tree and dragging her arms behind her. "And, by the way, you're under arrest."

Chapter 23

The cops arrived at the scene minutes after the explosion. Sirens surrounded us, and I gratefully handed Kendra off to Officer Winkler, who took one look at us and made the sign of the cross.

"I didn't take you for a religious man, Winkler," I grumbled, running a sleeve over my bloodied face.

"I wasn't until a couple of minutes ago," he said. "You don't look too good, Rosetti."

"That's what you said the last time you saw me," I said, referring to the night he'd seen me after my allergic reaction. "I'm beginning to think you've got something against my face."

He cleared his throat and hauled Kendra away to get medical attention. As the police officers descended on the scene, the bomb squad guys swarming the car, I swiftly went on the hunt to find my mother and Jimmy. It didn't take long, seeing as I could hear my mother screaming from a mile away.

"Kate!" my mother shouted, throwing herself into my arms. "What happened to your face?"

"I'm glad you're alive too." I waited a long beat, suddenly feeling bone tired, and then I cracked a smile and took a step back. "I think I owe you a thank-you."

"Me?" Tears dampened my mother's cheeks, but she was clearly still on the anxiety riddled high of surviving a near-death experience. "A thank-you?"

"Who knew you've been driving all this time packing heat in your glove compartment?"

She blushed. "Your father insisted on taking me to the range and teaching me how to use a weapon when we got back together. It was sort of a honeymoon thing. In case you're wondering, I obtained the gun legally."

"I wasn't wondering," Jimmy said lightly. "But it's good to have that in my back pocket for the red tape."

I turned to Jimmy. "Thank you," I murmured softly. "I know how difficult it was to do what you did."

"It has been a while since I've gone for a run." He gave me a mischievous wink. "I'm a little out of shape."

"You know that's not what I'm talking about."

"I feel like I let you down, Rosetti."

My mother slipped away from us, giving me a gentle pat on the shoulder. Jimmy and I stood alone, a few steps away from the hubbub, in our own little bubble.

"Let me down?" I repeated. "Jimmy, you're a big part of the reason we're all still alive."

"I don't know. I couldn't do much. It felt like my hands were tied. Me having to cuff you, me not being able to take Kendra. All I could do was sit around and wait."

"You made the right decision," I said emphatically. "You knew that above all, I wanted my mother's life saved, and I'll never be able to repay you for making that happen."

Jimmy coughed, kicked up some snow with his boots. "I'm going to miss working with you, kid."

"I don't want to hear anything about you retiring. In fact, I think you just passed your physical for another five years. I'll vouch for you."

"There's the dream team." Asha arrived with a flourish at the perfect time to prevent Jimmy and I from having to find a suitable change of subject. "Nice work at the estate. Your plan was executed perfectly, Kate, leaving us those directions. By the way, Gem's fine. He's at the precinct giving his statement. We did pull his cash off Kendra's person, but it's going to have to remain in evidence until we sort through everything."

"I'm sure he won't mind the delay in getting his funds back," I said. "It's for a good cause, and he's got more where that came from."

Asha blitzed on. "We figured out things were off when you didn't answer your phone. I tracked you to Burton's, and we found Gem waiting there. He wanted to see you, but..."

"I'll take care of it," I said. "Thanks."

"I believe these belong to you." Asha returned our phones and firearms. "Nice job, gang. By the way, the team found a second car a quarter of a mile down the road that was reported stolen earlier this morning. It was tucked into some brush, not clearly visible from the road."

"Let me guess who stole it," I muttered.

Asha gave me a pleased smile. "In it we found Kendra's go-bag. A couple of passports with fake identities, one firearm with the registration number shaved off, and enough clothes and food to get her a few states away. She's spilling her guts to the team as we speak. Her plan was pretty gnarly."

"I mean, she's a murderer. Are we surprised?"

Asha winced. "She was going to handcuff you in the car with the bomb, then hightail it to her hidden vehicle while Jimmy and your mother tried to get you out of the car before you blew up. If they tried to follow her, she was just going to shoot them instead and let you die anyway."

"I'm glad things didn't go according to plan," I said. "That would have definitely added a sour note to my day."

Chief Sturgeon himself joined us as Asha wrapped up her summary of Kendra's escape-plan-gone-belly-up. "Good work, you two."

"Really, Kate's mom saved the day," Jimmy said. "She was the one who gave us the coded message about the weapon in the car."

"The very legal weapon," my mother added, overhearing her name and hustling back to join the conversation. "Very, very legal weapon. Hello, Chief Sturgeon."

"Mrs. Rosetti." Sturgeon's eyes actually looked amused. "I understand congratulations are in order. As well as a thank-you." There was a long moment of silence. "And also an apology."

My mother dipped her head. "Accepted. And forgiven. I owe you a thank-you too."

The chief looked bewildered. I was just as confused as he looked. Last time my mother and Sturgeon had been in the same room together, they hadn't agreed on much of anything.

"I know you stuck your neck on the line to keep my daughter on this case," my mother said. "It shows you had faith in her. I hate knowing that Kate faces murderers on a daily basis. But I can rest a little easier at night knowing the sort of people who've got her back."

She eyed the chief, then Jimmy, then Asha.

Her voice broke as she continued. "Thank you, all of you. I just love that you take care of my little girl. Now, please come over for dinner sometime, maybe this Friday, and I will make you a meatloaf." She sniffed. "A very, very big meat-loaf."

"Right, thanks, Mom," I said as an uncomfortable-look-ing Sturgeon backed away from the conversation. "Very kind of you."

"I shouldn't have added that part about the meatloaf, huh?" My mother wiped at her eyes as Asha left too. "Not very professional of me."

"Hey, you're the hero of the day," I said. "Thanks, Mom. For everything you said. It means a lot to me too. You were pretty good out there. Just wait until Dad hears about it."

"Oh, your father." My mother looked concerned. "Yes, he won't like this at all."

"That's okay," I said. "Your cooking will soften him up."

"Everyone loves meatloaf, don't they?" my mother said thoughtfully. "I mean, what kind of psychopath doesn't like meatloaf?"

Epilogue

My mother's house spilled warmth from it as the dinner hour approached. As promised, my mother was currently bent over the stove trying to pull out the world's largest meatloaf.

Candles sat flickering on every available surface. The lights were dimmed, the wine was flowing, and bouquets of flowers decorated the countertops. Low music hummed in the background.

The house was already stuffed full of guests. Asha and Melinda were camped out near where the kitchen counter had been turned into a bar. The chief chatted quietly in the corner with my father. Lassie leaned an elbow against some shelving and was currently using her phone as a recorder as my mother regaled her with second-by-second details of the faceoff with Kendra for an in-depth exposé that the two seemed equally excited about.

My sister and Wes had been given marching orders by my mother to set the table, and they were bickering lovingly over which side of the plate hosted the forks. Jimmy had shown up with his wife, and the latter was already helping to serve drinks. Jimmy himself was seated silently at the table with a napkin tucked into his shirt in anticipation of the meat course.

The heat from the kitchen, the smells of gravy and sauces, the aroma of freshly baked garlic bread had my mouth watering. I was currently on drinks duty with Jimmy's wife, and I was currently in the process of refilling the ice bucket with sparkling waters from the basement. I was just about to head downstairs for another load when the doorbell rang.

"Are we expecting someone else?" My mother glanced around. "I thought this was it."

"I invited one more person," I told her. "Sorry it's a little last minute."

My mother shot daggers at me. "You're lucky I made enough food."

"Mom. You cooked seventy-nine pounds of meatloaf. I could've invited the entire department, and there would be leftovers."

"I might have run out of plates," she said haughtily, turning back to the stove. "Well, go answer the door, then."

I could tell she was itching to know who had arrived. I scurried to the front door and felt a smile on my face before I laid eyes on the man waiting on my parents' front stoop.

"Mr. Gem," I said with a dramatic flourish. "I hope you are prepared to see the biggest meatloaf of your life."

Gem looked notably surprised. "Not the greeting I was expecting, but I'll take it."

After the confrontation with Kendra, I'd seen Gem in person, but our time together had been limited and not very private. Not only had I been swamped with the casework wrap-up after Burton's and Kendra's arrests, but there'd also been the little issue of medical attention after the conk on my head from the explosion.

Then my mother had insisted on my spending the night at her place so she could watch over me "in case I had a concussion". In short, I had not yet been able to get the quality time I needed with Gem to properly thank him for his part in saving my mother's life.

"I'm glad you came," I admitted. "I'm sorry I haven't had more time in the last few days to really sit down and talk with you."

Gem waved a hand. "We talked. You thanked me. End of story."

"I mean it," I said. "Between the paperwork at the office and my mom treating me like I was a porcelain doll, I've barely had a second to myself."

Gem's eyes flickered up to the bruise on my forehead. I'd traded my bloodshot eyes from earlier in the week for a garish purple tint to my skin. Gem licked his lips in frustration, and a flash of anger sizzled across his expression.

"Truly, I understand, Detective." He raised a hand, touched his thumb to my aching bruise. "I don't blame your mother for wanting to keep you close after everything that happened. I'd have done the same thing."

"Maybe we can—"

Before I could suggest that we continue this conversation somewhere more private, the sound of utensils clinking on glass interrupted me. The chief's voice rose above the background din, calling us into the kitchen. I gave Gem an apologetic shrug, then tilted my head, indicating he should follow me.

Gem and I snuck into the kitchen as the chief began his speech. Gem had brought a bottle of wine, a box of chocolate, and a bouquet of Gerbera daisies. He deftly slid them onto the counter as we tried to melt into the background. We didn't escape undetected. My mother's eyes followed Gem like a hawk, watching his every move, a hint of approval in her eyes.

"As I was saying..." The chief raised a glass. "A quick toast to the woman of the hour, Mrs. Rosetti, for making the TC Task Force look good. Without you, Kendra might be halfway to Barbados right now—or worse."

We all raised our glasses and made sounds of agreement.

"An update on the case," he continued. "Bill Burton is currently in jail awaiting sentencing for the accident that took out Mr. Heinrich's leg. We've got a full confession, and he's hoping for a plea deal. As for Kendra, she's facing a long sentence behind bars. I have no doubt the jury will convict her swiftly, considering the mountain of evidence against her. Thanks, everyone, for another job well done."

"I'd like to also take a moment to recognize Heinrich," my dad added. "Detective Heinrich was a lot of things, but one thing no one can argue with is that he was a great cop. If it weren't for his evidence, even all these years later, y'all might not have closed the case."

We clinked glasses and took a moment of silence. The group sipped in unison, and then chatter broke into pleasantries. My mother ushered us to our seats, and the garlic bread and marinara sauces started flowing. When we reached the point of dinner where my mother could no longer pawn off any more meatloaf on her guests—including my partner with his black hole of a stomach—she announced that it was time to take a short break while she prepared the dessert course.

Despite the fact that I felt all sorts of eyes on me, some of them more curious than others at Gem's appearance, I nabbed the billionaire by the elbow and steered him through the crowded kitchen and directly out the back door until we were alone in the fenced yard.

My breath hitched in the cold evening air. The ground was covered with crunchy snow, and starlight twinkled above us. The windows were aglow with flickering warm light. From the outside looking in, it looked like one big, happy family snuggled in a safe, cozy house. I felt a sense of overwhelming gratitude that it was *my* family.

"Thank you," Gem said, his breath blowing little puffs visible in the chilled air. "Thank you for including me."

"You're thanking me?"

"For including me tonight." Gem nodded toward the windows. "It means a lot that you invited me here to spend time with your family again. I don't take it for granted. I know how much they mean to you."

"Gem." I shook my head in disbelief. "You're the reason we're here with all our limbs attached. I have been wanting to thank you in person. I couldn't do it over the phone, or over a text, and I didn't want to rush it in the short times we've been together since the incident."

"Hey..." His voice came out gentle. He nudged my chin up so I looked him in the eyes. "You don't have to thank me."

"No, I do. I really, really do. I promised myself over and over that I wouldn't involve you in my cases, and here we are. Again. I just didn't know what to do, and I had to make a snap decision. You were the only person I knew who would help me without asking questions."

Gem gave a wry smile. "And quite possibly the only person who had twenty grand in an easy-to-access location."

"There is that. But I hope you know I wasn't trying to use you for your money. I mean, I was, sort of, but it wasn't for me—it was for my mom. Long story short, I don't know how I'll ever thank you."

"Consider us even. Maybe Kendra only used you because she knew you had access to me." Gem's eyes darkened. "In that case, I believe it was *me* putting *your* life in danger."

"Don't be ridiculous. This case had nothing to do with you. She capitalized on my friendship with you."

Gem looked a little uneasy, but he blinked, and the look disappeared. He took my hands in his. "You should know by now that I'd do just about anything for you, especially to keep you and your family safe. I wish you'd stop doubting that."

I felt my lip quiver a little as it hit me, truly hit me for the first time how much Gem had done for me. My adrenaline had been firing on high ever since the face-off with Kendra, and now, finally, I was starting to relax. As I let my guard down, the suffocating realization of how selfless Gem had truly acted rolled over me like a tidal wave.

"After how I've treated you, how I've pushed you away," I argued, "I don't deserve the way you treat me. I've given you no reason to stick around, and yet here you are."

Gem leaned forward, touched a kiss against my bruised head. "And here I'll stay."

From outside the house, I heard the doorbell ring again. This time, I wasn't the one expecting surprise guests. I waited for my mother to answer as I remained still, my hands still clasped in Gem's, wishing for a few more moments of privacy.

Then my mother called out, "Kate, it's for you."

"I'm sorry," I told Gem, giving his hands a light squeeze. "I'm not expecting anyone. If you'll excuse me for a moment?"

We separated, both of us returning inside while a feeling simmered between us, a feeling that told me things between us weren't completely settled just yet. I directed Gem to the kitchen to get a cup of coffee and a plate of dessert while I went to the front door. My mother didn't make eye contact as she slipped past me down the hallway.

I opened the front door and felt all the breath *whoosh* out of my body.

"Jack?" I murmured, unable to believe it was Agent Jack Russo, in the flesh, standing on my mother's front stoop. A part of me wanted to reach out and touch him to make sure it wasn't a mirage. "What are you doing here?"

"I'm sorry," Jack said. "I tried to call. Many times."

"Right, right. I was on a case, and I kept forgetting to call you back. I'm so sorry. I wasn't avoiding you. Really."

"I figured as much. I wasn't worried about it." He cleared his throat. "Okay, I was a tiny bit worried when I read online about the explosion, but it was pretty easy to see you'd made it out alive, so..." He shrugged, seeming unsure where to go with his story.

I was equally unsure as to what he wanted. I was also acutely aware that I hadn't invited him in. I mostly wanted to pretend that my entire family wasn't having a party behind me, especially considering it'd be hard to explain why Alastair Gem was in attendance.

"So," I prompted, "what brings you to town?"

"Right, yeah," he said, flustered. "I have some news. I'm actually going to be here for a little while."

"Where?"

"Here. Minnesota." Jack looked at my face, and it was obvious he could see that I wasn't quite comprehending. "The Twin Cities, actually."

"Why?" I blurted. I couldn't help it. I was in shock. I couldn't feel anything but numbness.

"I got transferred," he said, trying to play it off as a simple announcement. "Heading up a new division."

But this wasn't a simple announcement. It was an earth-shattering one.

"The last case we worked together with The Mathematician garnered a lot of attention, both in the media and internally at the bureau." Russo cleared his throat again. "Denise—er, Agent Price, had recommended that the bureau look into setting up a more permanent collaboration between the two of us because we were so successful." He quickly clarified. "I mean, between our departments. Because the teamwork was so successful."

"Right. Of course."

"The bureau agreed and set this up as a pilot program," Jack continued. "They're considering the Twin Cities a test market, especially since the TC Task Force is already a fairly unique collaboration between two cities to begin with. If it goes well, they might look into setting up similar collaborations in other large metropolitan areas." Jack shrugged. "My boss told me I was going to be the one heading up the program. So, here I am."

"That's so..." I gulped. "So very interesting."

"It is, isn't it? Poor timing, though." Jack must have noticed the stricken look on my face as he raised his hands. "To be clear, I didn't mean anything by that. I'm not moving here expecting anything. Anything personal, I mean. We'll probably have to work together in a professional capacity."

"Right. Sure. We can do that."

"Totally," Jack agreed. "We've already done it before."

"We sure have."

There was a long stretch of silence between us.

"I feel the need to tell you something, Jack," I finally said. "I have to get it off my chest."

"Anything."

"I would feel incredibly uncomfortable if you agreed to the transfer because of me," I said in a rush. "I care about you a lot. I have in the past and still do, but I want to be very clear that you shouldn't have any expectations about us, you know, getting back together just because we'll be physically close in location."

"Roger that." Jack gave a small smile. "I hear you loud and clear."

I felt bad being so upfront and blunt with Jack, but already I knew that the only way this situation could ever work would be with honesty. Honesty with Jack, honesty with Gem, and quite frankly, honesty with myself.

"I just wanted to come here and talk to you before things were made official," Jack assured me. "The formal announcement isn't coming until next week. I figured I'd give you a heads-up in person so you weren't caught off guard, and so you had some time to process."

"I appreciate that."

"Of course." He gave me a tight smile. "Well, it's good to see you. You seem happy."

I considered my response carefully, not wanting to hurt him, but also not wanting to give him false hope. "I am. I really am. It's a work in progress, but I'm getting there."

More silence.

"And you?" I prompted. "How are you?"

"I'm good. Thanks for asking."

Longer and longer silence.

"Well, I should probably be going," he said. "I didn't mean to interrupt anything, I just—"

"There you are. I grabbed you a slice before the vultures descended on it." Gem swung to my side, holding a plate of the tiramisu my mother had crafted for dessert. "Jimmy was looking like he was gonna give up a kidney for the last piece of—" He stopped abruptly, his eyes widening as if he'd seen a ghost. "Agent Russo?"

"The one and only," Jack said, recovering from his shock faster than Gem. "I was, uh, just leaving."

"Should I give the two of you some time?" Gem asked, gesturing between us. "Or maybe I should take off..."

"No," I said firmly. "Jack just stopped by to let me know he's been transferred to Minnesota. It's not official until next week, but he wanted to let me know ahead of time."

"Transferred for what?" Gem asked. "Why?"

"For work," Jack said blandly. "That's the what *and* the why."

"Permanently?" Gem continued.

I grabbed the dessert plate before the tiramisu could slide onto the floor. We were in grave danger of losing the mascarpone with the way Gem was gesticulating.

"I'm not sure for exactly how long. It's sort of an open-ended assignment," Jack said, spreading his hands wide. "I guess it depends on how things go."

"How things go," Gem murmured. "I see."

We all stood around for a moment. I hoped my body would begin to melt like an ice sculpture so I could silently escape this conversation. No luck.

Finally, Gem broke the silence. "Welcome back to the tundra, then, Agent Russo."

THE END

Made in United States
North Haven, CT
03 May 2023

36204749R00178